SO FLOCKED

SARAH ESTEP

So
Flocked

I know it feels like you have to have it all figured out. That you have to know what you want to be when you grow up. That you have to have a plan.

You don't.

You are worthy of love, even in the midst of discovery and change.

ONE

JORDY TAYLOR WAS A FUCKING DISASTER.

If pressed to pick a moment when it all started going downhill, he would have picked blowing out the candles on his last birthday cake. The enormity of the transition from mid-thirties to late thirties hit him like a late rush from an overly enthusiastic corner: he'd seen it coming, couldn't avoid it, and it hurt like hell.

Thirty-seven.

He was a dinosaur by professional football standards. Most quarterbacks peaked at twenty-nine, which was in fact the age he had been the last time he had played in a national championship. Every year since, the Los Angeles Phantoms had fallen short of the ultimate goal. The past season had been a damn tragedy. They had clawed their way through the season with a receiving core that had been gutted by the front office, won the wild card game to make it to the playoffs, and had run into a woodchipper in the next round.

That scoreboard haunted his dreams.

Losses always stung. That one had been particularly painful because making it to the conference championship—even if they hadn't won—would have secured his place with his team for another season. Instead he had been painfully reliving every single decision he had made in that game for months while he waited to hear if the team was picking up his contract.

With the draft around the corner and no movement on his deal, Jordy's agent had suggested he get out of town for a little bit. Jordy had initially disagreed. He wanted to be at the training facility, visibly committed to the team. And that was when Priya had let some of the optimistic agent facade slip.

"Jordy, I don't know if you should be at the facility in case this doesn't go the way we want it to go."

It had been the first time Jordy had really felt the cold grip of anxiety that he might not play for the Phantoms anymore. And that had been immediately compounded by the realization that he might not play for *any* team.

Jordy had been in his backyard, throwing footballs at a target trying to prove to himself that he was still in his prime, when Graham had called him back. Friendships came easy to Jordy; he was a likable guy, easy going and always ready for a good time. The vast majority of his friendships were surface level, though. They wouldn't know when his birthday was unless they were invited to the party. But he had three friends that were more like family: Graham, Sam, and Peter. He had called Graham because Peter would have tried too hard to cheer him up, and Sam would have been brutally honest about the situation. Graham was Baby Bear's bowl of porridge to his Goldilocks: just right.

"So, you're kind of freaking out?" Graham asked.

Jordy squeezed the football in his hand. "Yeah. A little."

"Why don't you come up here?" Graham suggested. "It's quiet. You could stay at the lighthouse if you want. No one will bother you there. You were coming in a few weeks for the wedding anyway."

"I've got some interviews I'm supposed to be doing…"

"Can you do them remotely?"

"I guess." Jordy kicked at a weed that had sprouted since the lawn service had last been there.

"I'll set you up in a conference room at the hotel. No problem. I installed high-speed Wi-Fi."

A year and a half ago Graham had sold his tech company to go live in a small Oregon town with shitty cell phone service. Not that Jordy blamed him. Graham's fiancée, Eloise, was kind, smart, and beautiful. Together they owned a historic—and probably haunted—hotel. The place gave Jordy the creeps. He had taken the ghost tour offered by their assistant manager, Kiki, and after that he couldn't sleep there anymore. No one could convince him the cold spot he had felt in one of the rooms had been the ancient heating system and not a ghost.

Graham and Eloise had recently purchased the town's decommissioned lighthouse from the parks department to convert into something Eloise had described as an "experience stay." The only experience Jordy wanted from it was peace and quiet.

So he agreed. Three weeks in Crane Cove. A little vacation from his problems. A chance to spend a little time with Graham before he got married. He bought a plane ticket the second he hung up the phone.

Jordy turned down the music in his rental car. Had he missed his turn? The map app on his phone didn't work near the blackhole that was Crane Cove. Why hadn't he downloaded the directions before he left the Portland airport? He could have found it during the day. It was hard to miss a fucking lighthouse. But in the dark and in the rain? He was asking to end up in a bad horror movie.

His headlights caught something off the side of the road, and he slowed down, leaning closer to the steering wheel to get a better look. A mailbox with a post made to look like a lighthouse. Bingo.

Jordy turned down the driveway and parked next to the small house attached to the column of the lighthouse. Graham had said the key would be under the mat, and he was relieved that it actually was. With three weeks until the wedding, Jordy wouldn't have blamed Graham for forgetting.

The house was small and cold. Jordy used his cellphone as a flashlight to find the light switch. The battery was almost dead.

Graham had said they were still getting it ready for guests when he offered it, but he didn't think Jordy would mind sparse decoration. He hadn't been kidding.

The walls were white and bare. There weren't curtains up on the windows yet. A small kitchenette, with a skinny fridge, a two-burner stove, and a small table, was off to the right of the door. A couch, driftwood coffee table, and TV made up the "living room" off to the left. There was a bedroom on either side, with a bathroom next to the smaller bedroom.

Jordy went to the bedroom on the right. It was the bigger one and had a queen bed. He remembered that much from Graham's instructions. He could go to the grocery store in the morning. All he wanted at the moment was a hot shower to wash the feel of recycled air off his skin.

He laid his suitcase on the floor and rifled through it to find his toiletries. The box of condoms he had left over from a different trip felt overly ambitious for this trip. Crane Cove was too small for him to comfortably sleep with anyone. And Graham was so embedded in the community that Jordy didn't want to make anything awkward for him.

And then there was Annie.

Jordy knew all about off-limits women. Sisters. Moms. Aunts. He thought he'd known the rules. But then he had met

Dr. Annie Price and had discovered an entirely new category of off-limits: friend's fiancée's cousin.

He stripped off his clothes, dropping them into a pile next to his suitcase, and then walked across the small house naked. The cold air did absolutely nothing to stop, or even slow, the blood steadily pumping into his dick. Apparently telling himself "No" was the quickest way to get his dick to say "Yes!"

Even thinking about Annie was dangerous. Because not only was she off-limits, she was out of his league anyway.

The first time he had met Annie was at Graham and Eloise's engagement party in December. Peter, Graham's best man no matter how many times Graham insisted that all three of them shared the title, had planned it for a week when his, Peter's, and Sam's schedules lined up. Peter had ended up missing the party because his flight from London had been delayed so long there was no way he'd make it. And because Peter was missing, Jordy was picking up the slack as life of the party, in addition to being Sam's emotional support person. His best friend was never more than a few feet from his side, a shadow in black slacks and a red velvet blazer. Jordy had massively underestimated the dress code and was wearing a short-sleeve, button-down tropical print bird shirt.

The whispering touch of fingertips on his back made him shiver. It tickled, and he turned his head over his shoulder, expecting it to be Sam touching him. But instead he looked down into big, hazel eyes, blue mixed with green and flecks of gold, rosy cheeks, and a playful smile on full, red lips.

"*Agapornis fischeri, Myiopsitta monachus, Ara macao.*" She touched a different part of his shirt with every word, her fingers coming to rest on his right pec, just over the red parrot taking flight.

"What?" he'd asked, working very hard to keep eye contact and not take a nosedive into her mouthwatering cleavage held up by two thin straps. She was wrapped in green velvet that hugged every curve, and the only word his brain could muster was "soft."

"The birds on your shirt." Her cheeks flushed more. "Fischer's lovebird, monk parakeet, and red macaw. Very romantic."

His dick hadn't left his brain enough blood to function, so instead of asking her to go on, he'd stared at her. Luckily she'd barely noticed.

"Ninety-percent of birds are monogamous," she'd explained, and for the first time Jordy had understood what it meant when someone talked about eyes glittering with excitement. "Their young are fragile and require a lot of resources…"

Jordy got lost in her explanation, only understanding her enthusiasm. Whatever the hell she was talking about, she knew a lot about it. He was pretty sure they were still on birds.

"Annie," Graham's familiar voice cut through the haze, and Jordy startled, narrowly avoiding splashing champagne on the woman's tits. He hadn't even noticed Graham join the group. "I think you broke him."

Annie. It was sweet, and matched the sound of her nervous laughter.

Annie blushed. "Sorry. I get carried away. All of that was to say that your shirt caught my eye because all of those birds mate in long-term monogamous pairs."

"Uhh…" Nothing. There was nothing in his brain. Nothing but hazel eyes, red lips, and velvet-wrapped boobs. He'd never been particularly eloquent, but he had never once had a hard time talking to girls. Why didn't his brain work when he needed it to?

Jordy rested his head against the cool tiles of the shower as hot water slid down his back. That should have been the end of it. He'd never managed to join the conversation that happened around him. And when Annie finally walked off to take away a rum punch from her grandmother, Graham had told him in no uncertain terms that Annie was off-limits. She was fresh out of a long-term relationship, and Jordy's reputation with women was less than stellar. If that hadn't been enough warning, Eloise's best friend, Sybil, had caught him watching Annie from across the room and told him if he tried anything that she would cut off his nuts with dull, rusty garden shears.

He believed her.

Jordy could have behaved himself—he really thought he could have—if Annie hadn't surprised him by pulling him into a dark alcove on his way back from the bathroom. She'd pointed to the mistletoe hanging from the ceiling, and Jordy forgot all about rusty gardening shears. Nothing wrong with an innocent little kiss, right?

There was nothing innocent about the way Annie kissed. She tasted like spiced rum and apple cider, and he wanted to get drunk off her mouth. Sometimes he could still feel that green velvet under his palms.

He soaped himself up, avoiding his groin because he had to stop touching himself to that memory. Nothing had even happened. They'd kissed, groping like desperate teenagers, and when she'd asked him if he wanted to go up to her room, the words were slightly slurred. That sobered him up enough to make the responsible decision to send her to bed alone.

So, if nothing had happened, why couldn't he let his mind wander without tasting spiced rum and feeling phantom velvet?

There was no change in his erection after he rinsed the conditioner out of his hair. The damn thing wouldn't go down. Frustrated, he gave it a rough squeeze. This was necessary. He didn't have to enjoy it. He wasn't going to indulge himself in one of the fantasies he'd spun out of what could have been if she hadn't been drunk or he didn't have a conscience.

He really was a fucking disaster.

Jordy stroked himself, trying to keep it quick and businesslike. He had a highlight reel that could go on for over a week and never repeat, so he didn't need to think about his friend's fiancée's very off-limits cousin he had kissed one time. But, fuck, he wanted to know what might have happened if he'd taken her into the closest unlocked room and—

The shower curtain ripped open. Jordy saw a large knife raised and ready to strike. One thought flashed through his mind:

I'm going to die with my dick in my hand.

TWO

Annie Price looked up from the trashy tabloid magazine she was skimming to find the young cashier eyeing her grocery cart with interest. A couple bottles of wine, whipped cream, various fruits, cookie dough, and deodorant.

"You could say that."

Five months after her breakup with her boyfriend of nine years, Annie was finally going to give the relationship the send-off it deserved: she was going to get drunk off sangria, scream-sing Celine Dion, shake her ass to Jenna Fox, and eat cookies. Or cookie dough, if the lighthouse didn't have a cookie sheet. Then she was going to watch a few '90s rom-coms, and the exorcism of Jake from her life would be complete.

Maybe she would throw some salt over her shoulder for good measure.

"Party or breakup?" the cashier—Billie, according to their name tag—asked, scanning her items leisurely. It was close to closing at Hudson's Grocery, and Annie was possibly the only person in the store.

"Both?" Annie turned to a photo spread of "Celebrities

work out just like you!" which had a picture of two familiar faces in the spread. Sam Shoop and Jordy Taylor, two of her cousin's fiancé's best friends, were waiting at a crosswalk, probably mid-run. Sam was wearing a long-sleeve shirt, probably to protect his many tattoos from the fading effects of the sun, his arms crossed over his chest as he glared at the photographer. Next to him, Jordy was leaning against the pole, one ankle crossed over the other, like he was posing for a catalog, grinning at his friend. His longish blond hair was held back by an elastic headband, and his shirt was off, tucked into the waistband of his shorts. And even though he had rejected her back in December at Eloise and Graham's engagement party, she still wanted to lick a trail from his collarbone down his perfectly sculpted body.

"Are you getting that?" Billie asked, and Annie handed it over. That picture might come in handy later. Billie scanned it, announced her total, and managed to shove everything into her reusable tote as Annie paid.

Annie dug through her purse for her car keys as she stepped through the automatic doors. The weather had taken a turn for the worse. The wind had picked up, and the rain was no longer its usual lazy drizzle. Fat, cold drops smacked against Annie's face as she jogged to her car. The lighthouse was fifteen minutes away, and she hoped she could get there before this turned into a full-blown storm.

Staying at the lighthouse had been her cousin Eloise's suggestion, phrased to sound like Annie was doing her a big favor. Her wedding was coming up and she could use an extra set of hands in the run-up, the lighthouse needed a guest test run, someone had to be there to pass her an abundance of wine when her family got to town. Annie hadn't needed even half of the convincing. She needed a break from living with Jake.

When they had first broken up, she and Jake had agreed

that finishing their lease term was a good idea. They were adults. The breakup had been mostly mutual. They could certainly handle living together for a few more months. Except all the little things Annie had written off when they were in a relationship grated on her nerves once they weren't sharing a bed anymore. He left the toilet seat up and dishes in the sink. His socks never made it in the hamper, and she found them all over the apartment, usually on the couch. Nothing like accidentally cozying up to a sweaty gym sock when she was trying to watch *Derry Girls*.

There were only nine weeks left on her lease, and for the first time in her life, Annie didn't have a plan. Her job in the lab at the university had concluded in February when the project she had been working on finished, and instead of joining another project, she had opted for some time off, hoping it would give her some much-needed clarity. It hadn't. She had applied to teaching positions, some research fellowships, and a travel company looking for an ornithologist to lead birding vacations in Papua New Guinea over the summer. The last one wasn't a long-term career solution, but it sounded like fun. Annie felt like she was standing in front of an open fridge filled with amazing food, and none of it sounded good.

So what to do in nine weeks? Did she move back in with her parents? Renew her lease, find a new roommate, and get a job in Seattle? Or did she stay in the lighthouse forever and spend her days walking along the edge of the cliff, screaming out into the ocean about all of her wasted potential?

Horrible. All of it.

Annie rolled her shoulders to ease the gathering tension. She didn't need to think about any of that right now. The job applications were out in the ether. Jake and the Cold War apartment were six hours north. All she needed to do for the next three weeks was relax.

The only problem with relaxing was that when her brain wasn't busy with something exciting, it liked to replay her most embarrassing moments on loop. Its favorite clip for the last few months had been her spectacular failure at seducing Jordy Taylor.

Graham and Eloise's engagement party should have been her riotous return to the single scene. When Eloise had offered her favorite green velvet dress, it had felt like the universe was giving its seal of approval to her plan to find someone new to touch her for the first time in ten years. The dress was amazing. It hugged her in just the right places, and a swipe of red lipstick made her feel like an Old Hollywood bombshell.

And then the entire plan had gone to shit before it could even get off the ground.

"How do you hit on guys?" she'd asked Mallory as the petite blonde made her another rum punch. The bartender shrugged.

"Strong right hook?" Mallory joked. Annie's heart sank. Of course Mallory didn't need help with guys. They probably threw themselves at her feet. Her face must have fallen, because Mallory revised her statement. "If I want a guy's attention, I try to say something funny and a little disarming. I'll tease him about his shirt, his haircut. One of those two things usually gives me an excuse to touch him. Lightly only. And quick."

"As an example..." Annie looked across the ballroom. "If you were going to hit on Sam or Jordy?"

Mallory put her fresh drink on the bar, and barely looked at Graham's friends. "I'd ask Sam when his *Jersey Boys* performance is, and something about Jimmy Buffet for Jordy."

"Jimmy Buffet. Right."

Neither Sam nor Jordy had been part of her original plan to shake Jake from her system. Peter had been the plan. Peter was sweet and gentle and had sent her a fucking sword as a gift for defending her dissertation. Apparently it was a Finnish tradition. They'd become friends at the *Claymore Abbey* ball and, despite him being a movie star, had stayed in contact. And until she had been crossing the ballroom, it had seemed reasonable to proposition him for one simple rebound fuck. But Peter wasn't a one-night kind of guy; he was grand gestures and an unshakable belief in the power of true love. He'd sent her a draft of his toast for the party, and she had cried. Jordy and Sam? They were one-night guys. It was public knowledge.

Jordy's damn shirt had ruined it. The surest way to distract her was to dangle birds in front of her. Instead of being funny and charming, she'd been awkward, an entire mini-lecture tumbling out of her mouth while he had stared at her blankly. But Annie wasn't a quitter. She'd noticed a sprig of mistletoe hanging above an alcove on the way to the bathroom earlier. A little less talking might be Jordy's speed.

So, she had waited for him to leave the room, followed him, and then pulled him into the small, dark space. All she had to do was point to the mistletoe, and her hypothesis was proven: less talk, more action. Jordy kissed her like he was afraid she was the last good thing he'd ever taste, equal parts savoring and greedy desperation. Which made what happened next even more confusing. When she had pulled back, breathless and dizzy, his strong thigh wedged between hers—she'd been rather shamelessly riding it—and asked if he wanted to go upstairs, she thought him telling her to go on up meant he would follow. Split up to make things less suspicious. After an hour of nervous anticipation, she'd realized he wasn't coming.

It wasn't all bad. After the sting of embarrassment had dulled to a throb, she let herself be proud of the fact that a professional athlete had grabbed her ass and moaned when she'd sucked on his tongue.

Her headlights caught the lighthouse mailbox, and she turned down the driveway. The rain was coming down in sheets, her windshield wipers up as high as they would go and still barely able to keep up. The little house attached to the lighthouse looked cozy and inviting with the warm glow of the lights in the windows.

A chill ran down Annie's spine. Why were the lights on?

Eloise had said that Kiki was going to run some supplies up to the lighthouse and leave the key under the mat for her. The simple black sedan parked next to the house had to belong to the precious goth that worked for her cousin. It would be good to see Kiki. Maybe she would want to stay for cookies and sangria.

Annie grabbed her groceries and her suitcase, running inside. She had more stuff, but it would have to wait until the heavy rain passed.

The house was small but cute. And cold. Annie hoped Kiki had brought the space heater. She did a slow semi-circle, taking in her surroundings. With some curtains, some art, and a few area rugs, it would be perfect.

It was on the tip of her tongue to call for Kiki, surprised she hadn't seen her instantly, when the sound of water she had initially written off as rain finally registered as the shower. Annie's stomach pitched.

Why would Kiki be taking a shower?

And with the next frantic beat of her heart, Annie remembered that she didn't know what kind of car Kiki drove.

Who the hell was in the shower?

There was a knife block on the counter, and Annie grabbed one of the larger knives, gripping it tightly as she edged toward the bathroom. She had the element of surprise on her side. Whoever had broken in didn't know she was there, and they were definitely unarmed. They were so confident they wouldn't be caught they hadn't even bothered to shut the bathroom door.

She raised the knife as she gathered a fistful of shower curtain and yanked it open.

Annie noticed several things at once. The first was that the intruder in the shower was not an intruder at all. Broad shoulders, a strong, athletic body, and nearly shoulder-length blond hair made darker by the water. Jordy. The second thing that registered with her brain was that he was very naked. And the third was that she had surprised him with his cock in his hand, midstroke.

They both screamed.

The knife flew out of her hand as she scrambled to cover her eyes. It clattered somewhere behind her.

"Oh my god oh my god oh my god..." Blindly, Annie groped for the shower curtain.

"No, I got it—"

As Annie tried to pull the curtain forward, Jordy tried to pull it back out of her hand. Her shoes, wet from the rain outside, lost their grip on the floor, and she fell forward, her throat colliding with his hard shoulder. Combined with his backwards momentum, it was enough force to send Jordy, Annie, and the shower curtain tumbling into the tub.

They scrambled, twisted, and Annie landed on top of him. Jordy wheezed and tried to curl up into a ball beneath her, his face twisted in agony.

"Nuts," he gasped, unable to catch a full breath. During the fall, her knee had collided with his groin. Annie wanted to die from embarrassment. This was all of her worst anxiety dreams rolled into one and injected with steroids.

"I'm so sorry," she said, trying to carefully extricate herself but only getting more tangled in the vinyl shower curtain. The hot water soaked her leggings. "I didn't see anything, I swear... okay, that's a lie. I saw some stuff—but not everything!.... Okay, so I saw everything. But it's fine. No biggie. Not that it's not big! I mean, scientifically speaking—"

Jordy groaned. "Please stop talking and get off of me."

"Right." Annie's face burned. As carefully as she could, she tried to push herself off Jordy, but the shower curtain had tangled around them. The more she struggled, the more stuck she became. "I...I can't."

"Of course you can't," he grumbled, and wiggled himself up onto his elbows to take stock of the mess they were in. His forehead creased into a frown. "Can you get on your knees?"

Between them, Jordy's deflated erection throbbed with new life. Annie swallowed hard. "Umm..."

"*Not* like that." Jordy shook his head and looked up at the ceiling. "Jesus Christ, not like that."

Right. Of course not.

Annie wiggled her hips down to try and free them from the confines of the shower curtain, then drew her knees up so they were even with Jordy's hips. This was the worst game of Twister she'd ever played.

"Now what?" she asked, her ear pressed against his diaphragm.

"Just hold still," he said, and her head rose as he took a deep breath in. Big hands—a rush of warmth that was not from the shower flooded her underwear when she realized *how* big—slid down the backs of her thighs, getting a solid grip just above her knee. His body tensed beneath hers, and in the next moment they were sitting upright, her ass flush with his groin. The amount of core strength required to do what he'd done made her lightheaded.

"You know, I've never been in this position before," Annie joked, trying to cut through the tension that grew thicker between them with every passing second. Or maybe she was just imagining the tension, because Jordy was breathing like he was in labor.

"Don't." He released her legs. "Will this get looser if you get closer?"

Something was going to get looser if she got closer. "I think so."

"Be careful. I want kids someday." Jordy took hold of her hips and drew her closer. Mindful of his battered testicles, Annie rose up on her knees, which put his nose in the valley between her breasts. She was going to pull back so her cleavage wouldn't suffocate him, but then she saw the edge of the shower curtain.

"I think I can fix this," Annie told him, leaning further forward to grab the tail end.

Jordy's voice was muffled in her chest. "No, no, take your time."

Once during undergrad, Annie had attended a toga party with her roommate. It had been a last-minute decision, so instead of making a short, sexy toga like her roommate, Annie had grabbed the top sheet off her bed, turned on a YouTube tutorial, and wrapped herself like an origami burrito. Trying to figure out exactly how to get out of the shower curtain reminded her of that night. Except instead of being able to give up and try again in the morning, Annie was racing against the depth of the hot water tank.

"Almost got it," she reassured Jordy. "Actually, if you could lift your butt..."

A few more tugs and she was able to unwrap them. She held her hands up triumphantly at the end.

"Ta-da! Magic. Just like Houdini."

Jordy was not amused. "Off."

Carefully, Annie climbed out of the tub and stood on the mat, dripping. Behind her, the water turned off.

"Towel?"

Of course. A towel. There were two fluffy, white towels hanging from hooks on the wall, and Annie plucked one off and began to scrunch the water out of her hair. Jordy snorted.

"So, now that you've seen it all, you're comfortable hanging out with me naked?"

Annie froze. He'd been asking for a towel, not suggesting she use one. Face burning and eyes squeezed shut, she blindly passed the other towel to him.

"Sorry. I'm all..." Her hands tried to conjure up the word she was looking for.

"Hot and bothered?"

"No." *Yes.* "Flustered." She took a breath. "That was a disaster start to finish, and I'm not looking forward to telling Graham and Eloise how we destroyed their shower curtain."

"Maybe we just replace it and never tell them." Annie heard Jordy's wet feet on the tiles behind her as he got out of the shower. "I think the only thing Graham will hear is that you saw me naked, and my nuts have been abused enough for the month."

"I *am* sorry about that. It was an accident."

"Leftie thinks your aim was a little too good for that to be true."

He stepped around her, the towel wrapped low around his waist, and Annie watched a bead of water slide down his well-defined back. She licked her lips.

"I was going to, um, make some sangria," Annie offered. "Would that make Leftie feel better?"

Jordy put his hands on his hips and bowed his head for what felt like an eternity. Then he sighed. "Yeah, that would make Leftie feel better."

THREE

WOULD *that make Leftie feel better?*

There was some force in the universe somewhere that was laughing at him.

Jordy's nuts were tender from being assaulted and his interrupted orgasm. Normally, he would have finished the job as soon as he closed the bedroom door, but with the way the night was going, he was afraid to touch himself. The entire disaster in the shower had been karma. He had been thinking about Annie, and then she'd appeared *with a knife* and kneed him in the balls. A guy could take a hint.

The light in his room flickered as he stepped into his sweatpants. Outside, the wind howled, and rain smacked against the window. They could be in for a rough night if the storm didn't pass soon. Oregon was beautiful, but there were a lot of fucking trees by power lines.

He could do this, he thought as he dug out a Phantoms T-shirt from the bottom of his bag. He could be normal around Annie. He could act like there hadn't been a moment when his face was buried in her boobs that he hadn't hoped they'd be stuck like that for a while. It was just a drink or two. He could keep his head on straight.

Jordy took a deep breath, opened his bedroom door, and almost shut it again immediately. The small kitchen was across the room, and Annie was at the counter, slicing fruit, her hips moving slightly to whatever music she was listening to on her headphones. She'd changed out of her wet clothes into a baggy purple sweatshirt and a pair of plaid flannel shorts that looked soft as hell. He wanted to feel them under his palms. The cherry on top of the visual sundae were the thick wool socks that stopped a few inches below her knee. They shouldn't have been as fucking sexy as they were, but his horny brain had him writing, producing, and starring in a short but effective fantasy where those sock-clad legs were wrapped tightly around his waist while he drilled her into the couch.

Maybe he couldn't do this.

But then Annie looked over her shoulder and gave him a shy smile, and he might as well have been standing on a moving sidewalk for all the control he had over his feet.

"What are you listening to?" he asked, leaning over her shoulder, pretending to inspect her work.

"Hmm?" Annie took out one of her earbuds and tilted her face back to look at him. A blush warmed her cheeks.

"I asked what you were listening to," Jordy repeated, putting his hands in his pockets so he wouldn't brush her damp hair off her neck and nibble along that inviting curve.

"Oh." Annie offered him the earbud she had taken out. Jordy put it in his ear and smiled. One of his earliest memories was of his mom dancing around the kitchen with this song blaring on the radio, singing along into her spatula.

"Whitney Houston. Excellent choice. A little before your time, though."

"What can I say?" Annie smiled at him. "I like the classics."

Jordy couldn't tell if she was teasing him about his age or flirting with him. It could be both. It could be neither. There had never been a time in his life where he'd been at a loss for words around a woman. Flirting came as naturally to him as breathing. With Annie he felt entirely out of his depth. What the hell did he say to someone with a PhD? It was going to take her two minutes to figure out that he had limped through his entire school career, coasting through on the backs of his tutors and the rock-bottom expectations of his teachers.

"Do you want to dance with somebody?" It was a terrible line. Jordy should have been embarrassed. But Annie's smile widened, her eyes crinkling at the corners.

Fuck, she was pretty.

"Depends. Do I get to feel the heat of somebody?"

She could have all of his heat.

He must have been staring again, because she added, "Because it's freezing in here."

Blank. Again.

He needed cue cards to talk to her.

"At least you're used to this weather," he tried. "I've been living in Southern California for almost twenty years. I feel like a Jordy-sicle."

Annie's smile faltered, and she looked back down at the fruit she had been cutting up.

Had that been a pass?

"Yeah. Eloise said the HVAC company was waiting on some parts or something before they could hook up the unit." Annie picked the seed out of an orange slice with the tip of the knife. "Was there a space heater in your room? Kiki was supposed to bring one up."

And just like that they were talking about heating and air conditioning. It was worse than talking about the weather.

"I'll go look." Maybe he would find his brain too.

Jordy hadn't noticed the box in the corner of his bedroom both times he'd been in there. He picked it up and took it back out into the kitchen.

"Found it. We'll have you roasty-toasty in no time." He really needed to shut up.

Annie giggled.

At least her bar for humor was low.

The song changed, and a very familiar guitar intro filled his ear.

"A Sam song? Really?"

"This is the world's most perfect breakup album, and I will fight anyone who says otherwise." Annie twisted off the top of a bottle of red wine and emptied it into a pitcher. *"Washed your sins off my body, watched them circle the drain with my dreams. Come on."*

Jordy shook his head. "Yeah, but it's fucking sad."

"Are you telling me you don't intentionally hurt your own feelings?"

"Not by listening to Sam's music. It's...weird, I guess."

Annie scraped the fruit off the cutting board into the pitcher. "Yeah, I can see that. I can't watch Peter do sex scenes anymore."

"I haven't been able to do that for years. I cover my eyes."

"Logically I understand that it's fake, but watching your friend make those faces—"

"Oh, I get it." Jordy searched for a good place to put the space heater. "What's really disturbing is being at a wedding and having the couple's first dance song be 'Barcelona' and knowing what that song is about."

"What is that song about?"

"How Sam had a one-night stand in Barcelona that was so wild he won't tell me everything they did because he says I'd never look at him the same way again."

"That's pretty impressive considering…" Annie trailed off, blushing profusely.

It wasn't hard for Jordy to fill in the blank. He'd come by his reputation with women honestly with a lot of hard work on his back, his knees, and occasionally his feet—though his back didn't appreciate that move anymore. With any other woman, Jordy would have used that as a segue to get into her pants. There were a million avenues to take from that dangling thought. But this was Annie, and he wasn't supposed to go there. No matter how much he wanted to.

Fuck, he wanted to.

There was an outlet near the couch. A perfect spot for the space heater. Jordy plugged it in, hit the power button, and it whirred to life.

Then the power went out.

"What just happened?" Annie asked, a disembodied voice in the dark.

"The power went out."

"But why?"

"I don't know. Maybe we blew a fuse." Jordy pushed himself to his feet, digging in his pocket for his phone so he could use it like a flashlight.

"I'll go find the breaker box," Annie announced, and Jordy heard her collide with an end table a moment later.

"You know, if this was a horror movie, you'd already be dead," he told her, unlocking his phone. No service, which wasn't a surprise since most of Crane Cove and the surrounding area was a black hole. "Are you okay?"

"Yeah. I am starting to doubt my survival instincts, though."

Jordy found the flashlight function and turned the light in the direction of her voice. Annie looked sheepish. He made his way over to her, and together they began to hunt for the breaker box.

"Why did you come in earlier?" Jordy asked, putting his hand on the small of her back to guide her through the door to his room. These things were usually hidden in places like closets. "Did you know I was going to be here, and that was your really weird way of saying hi?"

She shook her head. "No. I thought you were Kiki dropping off supplies."

"So you decided to surprise her in the shower with a knife?" Jordy paused. "Actually, I could see her being into that kind of horror movie roleplay."

Annie laughed. "No, not that either. I didn't really think. I grabbed the knife because I thought you were an intruder and it seemed like my best chance to take you down."

"You definitely took me down."

"And when I tell this story at parties, I'm going to gloss over the fact that I did very little work and you took yourself down, and really emphasize that you're a massive professional football player."

"Sacrificing my reputation for your own street cred. I'm disappointed in you." Jordy tsked in mock disapproval and pulled open the closet door. "What are you doing here anyway?"

"Eloise invited me. What about you?"

"Graham offered to let me stay at the lighthouse."

"I would bet good money they both told Kiki and didn't tell each other." Annie pressed back against his hand. Or maybe he was imagining it. "At least I don't have to find the breaker box by myself."

Right. The box. They were looking for electrical stuff. He moved the light around the closet. "Do you see it? Sometimes they paint over them."

Annie leaned forward to look closer, and Jordy hated that it was dark because he bet her ass looked incredible in this position. But given how his dick jumped to attention at that mental image, it was probably for the best.

"No, I don't think it's in here. My room?" Annie suggested.

"Lead the way." He pointed the light at the door.

"Why do I get the feeling you're using me as a human shield?"

"Because if we're living in a horror movie, I want the killer to get to you first."

"Odds are I'm the final girl. Which means the killer is probably standing behind you," Annie pointed out, and Jordy fought the intense urge to look over his shoulder.

"Why would you say that? It's dark."

"If you get scared, you can always come sleep in my bed."

That was incredibly tempting. "Isn't it Horror Movie 101 that the couple having sex always dies?"

"Who said we're having sex? I said sleep."

Open mouth, insert foot. "Fuck. Annie, I'm sorry—"

She looked over her shoulder at him and he could faintly make out a mischievous grin in the low light cast from the edges of the beam. "Jordy. Calm down. I'm teasing."

Annie's room was smaller than his, and so was the closet. It didn't take more than a moment to locate the electrical box, which had been painted over.

"Hold this," he said, handing Annie his phone. It took some wiggling, but he got the door to open.

"Awww. This picture is cute."

His heart stopped. "Do. Not. Scroll. Through. Those."

"Your phone is locked, Jordy. I meant your lock screen."

Jordy took in a deep breath, trying to get some oxygen back to his brain. There were a lot of photos in his library he kept meaning to delete. His lock screen was innocent, though. It was the most recent photo he had of his best friends, when the four of them had been reunited in New York for a musical Peter had starred in. That had been almost a year ago.

"Right. Can you give me my phone back?"

"Scared I'll figure out your password is 0-0-0-0?"

He was now. "I need to see what I'm doing."

Annie passed him his phone. "Do you know what you're looking for?"

"My father was an electrician. If we did trip one of these by plugging in a single space heater, I'm going to be having strong words with Graham about who he hired to update the wiring." Jordy inspected the wiring. "So, do you want the good news or the bad news?"

"Good news. Always."

"The good news is Graham can keep his electrician. The bad news is that I think we lost power because of the storm."

"Or the murderer cut it from outside the house," Annie suggested.

"If you keep saying shit like that, I'm going to end up sleeping in your bed."

"That could work in my favor. You're a much bigger target."

Jordy scrambled for a comeback and came up blank. He could blame it on the fact that it was getting late, he'd had a long day, and frankly he didn't bounce back the way he used to, but really it was that Annie was smiling at him again and he wanted that to keep happening and he wasn't sure how he was doing it. Or if he even was. Maybe Annie just liked smiling.

The closet plunged into darkness as his phone died.

"Well, shit." Jordy pressed the power button again to be sure that it was really dead and not just faking it. "Now what?"

"My phone is back in the kitchen," Annie reminded him. "With the sangria. We could drink some wine, eat some cookie dough, and talk while we wait for the power to come back on."

"But that could be hours." What the hell was he supposed to say if they talked for longer than fifteen minutes?

"I promise not to talk about birds." Annie's hand landed on his tricep and slid down his arm to find his hand. The touch was innocent—so innocent that she didn't even take his hand, just hooked their index fingers together to lead him out of the room —but he felt it everywhere. Especially in his dick, which was getting whiplash from all the times it had risen to attention only to be smacked back down.

"You can talk about birds if you want to." He'd liked when she'd talked about birds before.

"If we run out of things to talk about, I will go full Professor Price," she said, navigating the room by the scant light from the windows. "So, Jordy, what brings you to Oregon?"

"Running away from my problems. You?"

"Same, actually."

"What problems do you have?" Jordy asked as Annie bumped them into the kitchen counter.

"I need a drink before we get into all of that."

So, Annie poured the drinks while Jordy made his way back to his room to strip the quilt off his bed, and then they met at the couch. Annie settled in on one end, Jordy on the other, and they arranged the quilt between them for warmth. Once he was settled, Jordy found his wine glass, curious about Annie's sangria recipe. He took a sip.

"Hey, Annie?"

"Yeah?"

"Is this just red wine and fruit?"

"Well, yeah. It's sangria."

He pressed his lips together to keep from laughing. "That's not how you make sangria."

There was a long pause on the other end of the couch. "It's not?"

"No. Sangria has brandy in it. This is wine with snacks."

"Does this mean I don't have to share my cookie dough?"

"That depends on the problems you're hiding from." Jordy took another sip of wine, relaxing back against the arm of the couch. "Spill."

Annie sighed. "My boyfriend of nine years and I broke up, I'm sort of unemployed, and I haven't had sex in almost a year."

The last thing made Jordy choke on his wine. "What?"

"I'm single, unemployed, and can't get fucked to save my life."

Jordy was baffled. "But how?"

"Well, after a while all the little things that were wrong in the relationship became a big thing, and I didn't want to fix that big thing." Her foot brushed his thigh as she shifted her position. "And the project I was working on ended, so I've been coasting for a few weeks doing side-hustle stuff. And, last but not least, I cannot seem to close the deal. Lots of mediocre dates, no sex." Her toes tickled his ribs. "So, what's your deal?"

Jordy squirmed away, unsuccessfully stifling a high-pitched giggle. "Don't do that. You don't want to talk about...all of that?"

"Not really, no."

"Fair enough." He took a deep drink of his wine, steeling himself. "I'm old."

"You're not that old. You're what...forty?"

"Thirty-seven, thank you." Jordy caught her foot as she tried to tickle him with her toes again. "By football standards, I'm basically a walking corpse."

"A zombie," Annie offered, and Jordy rolled his eyes, even though she probably couldn't see it.

"I should be past my prime, but I think I've got a few miles left on me. My team, however, is dragging their feet with my contract, and the draft is coming up..."

"You're worried you're going to be replaced."

"Worried is putting it mildly."

"So why are you here and not in Los Angeles?"

"It was suggested by several people close to me that I should maybe take a vacation until the dust settles. Probably so when I get the bad news the paparazzi don't get a photo of me exiting the grocery store with a cart filled with ice cream and alcohol."

Annie hummed her understanding. "That would definitely contradict the photo of you running."

"The what?"

"Nothing."

Was Annie looking at the photos of him that popped up online or in the tabloids? A thrill ran through him, hot and heady. Their kiss in December had been intense, but she had avoided him the next morning, so he had written it off as a drunken mistake on her part. Unless...

"Question," he began, searching for a delicate way to phrase his question. "When we kissed at the engagement party, were you, by any chance, still dating your boyfriend?"

"No, Jordy, you were not a homewrecker." Annie shifted again, pulling her feet back from where they'd been casually resting on his leg. "We'd been broken up for a few weeks. You were my first very clumsy attempt at getting over Jake by getting under someone else. Sadly, you were also my most successful attempt."

That baffled him. Annie was smart and funny and somehow easy to talk to even though she made him so nervous that his palms would sweat whenever he thought about her. Well, maybe not easy to talk to because he was doing a terrible job, but someone he *wanted* to talk to. Plus, she was beautiful. Tall, with an ass he wanted to sink his teeth into, and thick brown hair he wanted to run his fingers through. And those eyes...

"Was it a bad kiss? Am I really bad at reading signals?" Annie's question cut through Jordy's lust-filled fog he'd entered.

"What?"

"You and me. Was it a bad kiss? Were you humoring me? I'm a scientist, so I'm trying to figure out what I keep doing wrong, because the common denominator seems to be me. I know there could be countless factors, causation and correlation, blah, blah, blah, but... Is it me? Am I the problem?"

Jordy struggled for words like a fish tossed onto the shore struggled for air. His mouth opened and closed several times. What world was Annie living in where she thought the way he'd desperately pawed at her meant she was bad at kissing?

Annie plowed on. "I've been wondering about it for months, and it's easier to ask when it's dark and I don't have to see your face."

"You were drunk." Jordy was afraid if he didn't speak quickly, Annie would twist herself into a pretzel. "That's why I didn't go up to your room. That's why we didn't have sex that night. Or whatever."

"Oh." She sounded surprised or confused. Maybe both. "That's it?"

Jordy nodded, even though she couldn't see him. "That's it."

The sound of the wind and the rain pelting the small house ate up the silence that settled between them. Jordy finished his sangria and fished around the glass for the pieces of wine-soaked fruit at the bottom. What was he supposed to talk about now? What did they have in common? Annie seemed to have good taste in music. As long as she didn't bring up classical, he could keep up. Sam knew about classical. Tomorrow he should call Sam to get the lowdown about classical music so he'd sound smarter than he was. He only needed a few phrases to fake it. Did they have the same taste in movies? Movies were a safe, benign category.

"So, what's your favorite movie?"

On the other end of the couch, Annie laughed. "Nice segue.

Hmmm...probably *While You Were Sleeping*. Have you seen it?"

"Of course I have. I have three older sisters, and my parents made us rotate who picked the movie we rented every week. Between them and Peter, I have an impressive knowledge of Sandra Bullock romances."

In fact, his willingness to watch movies marketed to women had probably done more for his sex life than any smooth pickup line.

"Favorite Sandy B. movie?" Annie asked.

"See, this is a hard question. Because the knee-jerk reaction is *Miss Congeniality*. It's iconic. But *Practical Magic did* things to me. Like 'needed to put a pillow on my lap' things." Annie giggled. "But I think I gotta go with *Hope Floats*. I don't think people talk about it enough."

Annie's feet nudged against his thigh again. "That was a surprisingly thoughtful and thorough answer. I thought you were going to say *Speed*."

"I have depth. About the same as a kiddie pool, but it's there."

Annie laughed again, and Jordy would have made fun of himself forever to keep hearing that sound.

"So, what is your all-time *favorite* movie?" she asked.

"Easy. *Jurassic Park*. It was the first movie I ever saw in a theater. We went for my..." Jordy thought for a moment. "Eighth or ninth birthday. Blew my mind. Made me want to be a dinosaur scientist for a few years."

"A paleontologist?" Annie suggested. Jordy was grateful for the dark because he could feel his entire body blush. Of course he would forget that word around someone who actually knew it. Movies were supposed to be a safe topic where he could seem a little informed. Somehow he'd still managed to come off sounding like a dipshit.

"Yeah. That." He rearranged himself on the couch so he could lean back against the arm, their legs tangling and jostling for space under the blanket. "Never would've worked anyway. Too many fucking letters in those names. Why the fuck does pterodactyl start with a P?"

"Because ptero is Greek for wing, and the Greeks use P differently than we do in English."

He needed to stop talking. There was zero chance he was ever going to sound smart in front of Annie, and every chance he was going to make her think he was an idiot. Which might be true, but she didn't need to know that.

"I think *Jurassic Park* came out the year I was born," Annie added as the final nail in his coffin. He groaned.

FOUR

THE WIND HAD DIED DOWN and the rain was only a gentle pitter-patter against the windows as Annie tiptoed across the expanse of the tiny house toward Jordy's room. The moon was out, providing the smallest amount of silver illumination so she didn't destroy her toes on the furniture again.

She and Jordy had talked about movies, music, and TV shows for a long time in the dark, their legs intertwined under the blanket, until the power came back on a little after midnight. If they'd been on a date, she would have called Eloise after to gush. But instead of making a move, Jordy yawned, stretched, and mumbled something about having a long day.

"You know where to find me if you need me," he told her before he went to bed.

Annie rolled it over in her mind for hours as she laid in her bed, trying to decide if it was an innuendo. Because she did need him. She needed him to relieve the aching between her legs, to feel his weight over her, pressing her into the mattress. Or maybe she needed him under her, or behind her. The position didn't matter as long as he was *in* her. Which was illogical because her vibrator had better odds of giving her an orgasm.

Historically, partnered orgasms were disappointing compared to the ones she gave herself. Disappointing and rare. But given his extensive experience—chronicled to her as a warning, but she had taken it as a promise—Jordy was an ideal candidate to turn her sex life around.

Annie took a deep breath as she wrapped her hand around the cold metal doorknob to Jordy's room. The house was freezing. Going to his room in the middle of the night was all very innocent and practical if he wasn't ready to come out of his skin in the same way she was.

The door creaked as it swung open. Normally, this wouldn't have bothered Annie in the slightest. Doors creaked. But having them torn out from under her hand, causing her to stumble forward, was troubling. In the millisecond of motion, her brain fired through a handful of scenarios: the lighthouse was haunted and the ghost was strong; there had been an earthquake; a murderer really had been waiting for them and had already killed Jordy. She wasn't expecting to fall face first into a warm, solid chest with the faintest scratch of chest hair against her cheek.

They screamed in unison.

Jordy's scream tapered off into a low, rumbling laugh that felt good against her face and was heaven in her ears. Annie laughed too.

"We have to stop meeting this way," he chuckled, his hands resting on her hips. The heat from his palms soaked through the worn flannel of her sleep shorts. "You're going to give me a heart attack."

"I wasn't expecting you to be out of bed," Annie answered, smiling up at him even though he couldn't see her.

"You told me if I got scared I could come to your bed." Jordy didn't sound scared, and the way his thumbs were playing with the waistband of her shorts didn't feel scared.

She leaned into him, her hands sliding from his chest up to his shoulders. "You're scared?"

"Absolutely terrified. The power went out again. Didn't you notice?"

"Oh, I noticed." Annie noticed something at her hip level too, hard and insistent. "But that's not why I came over."

"It's not?"

"I'm cold."

Jordy was quiet for a moment.

"I think the problem might be these shorts," he finally said. Those wonderfully big hands moved over her ass, squeezing it gently. There wasn't enough oxygen in the world as he leaned into her, his fingertips hot against the skin just below the hem of her shorts. "They're not keeping you warm enough. I could warm you up. If you want."

"I want."

Annie had the length of time it took her to blink to regret that very eloquent statement—why couldn't she have said something sexy?—before Jordy's mouth crashed into hers with the kind of hungry desperation that set her body on fire. His hands moved lower to grip the backs of her thighs, and with a little hop, Jordy lifted her off the ground and her legs wrapped tightly around his waist. He grunted into her mouth, but never stopped kissing her. Any lingering doubts she had that he wanted her as badly as she wanted him evaporated like water in a hot skillet as the head of his cock tried to bury itself in her through several layers of fabric.

"Oh, yes, please," she moaned against his lips, "Please please please."

They crashed onto the mattress a few stumbling steps later. Jordy's body provided the exact weight she'd been craving, and when he rolled his hips against hers, she saw stars. Her back arched off the bed like an overdrawn bow as she chanted nonsense words that all added up to wanting and needing him as quickly as possible.

Jordy kissed and nibbled his way down the line of her pounding pulse, and it faintly occurred to Annie that she might have an orgasm like this, making out like frantic teenagers listening for the sound of the garage door. She dug her heels into the hard muscles of his ass—someone didn't skip leg day—and lifted her hips, trying to catch the blunt head of his cock again. The way he was shuttling his hard length over her clit was divine, but she needed him to fill her up so she could stop feeling hollow.

"Jordy..." she whined, threading her fingers through his thick blond hair and gripping it tightly, forcing him to look up at her. "Fuck. Me."

In the faint silvery light filtering in from the window, Jordy grinned at her. "Yes, ma'am."

Annie released his hair, and he sat back on his heels, feeling around in the pockets of his grey sweatpants for something. Quickly, she sat up and shucked off her sweatshirt, tossing it across the room. Cold air bit at her overly warm skin, and Jordy's hands stilled as he openly stared at her.

"Were you not wearing a bra this whole time?"

"I can't believe it took you this long to notice," she said, lying back to push her shorts off.

"I was distracted." He pulled a condom out of his pocket, and smug pride found some space inside of Annie beside all the lust. He'd had the exact same plan she'd had, though a bit more prepared.

"Distracted by what?" Her shorts and underwear landed on the floor with a soft thump.

"Your shorts. And these socks." Jordy ran a hand up the back of her calf. "The socks stay on, by the way."

"My socks?" Annie laughed, knees falling open to encourage him to hurry up.

"The duckies are too cute."

"They're mallards," she corrected. "Take your pants off."

"Yes, ma'am." Amusement laced his words, but Jordy hopped off the bed and hooked his thumbs into the waistband of his sweatpants. "If this is a striptease, I'm going to need a beat of some sort."

"If you tease me anymore, I'm going back to my vibrator."

His eyebrows raised, clearly interested. "Okay, we're going to explore that addition another time."

"There isn't going to be another time if you don't get naked right now."

"So bossy."

With a decisive push, Jordy's sweatpants fell to the floor, and half of Annie's IQ points went with them.

Big. Beautiful. Perfect.

Those were the only three words that her brain made. All her years of scientific study, and that was the best she could do. Because it was big, but not intimidating, mostly straight with a tiny upward curve. If she had gone into a store and seen his dick on a shelf, she would have bought it.

"You could make a fortune if you made a mold of that thing."

"There's a retirement plan I hadn't considered."

"You should definitely consider it. I'd buy one in every color."

"What would the slogan be?" he asked as he rolled the condom down his length. Annie was mesmerized by the motion. It wasn't until he prompted her with a "Well?" that she remembered there was a question.

"Fuck like a champion. Obviously."

"Obviously?" The mattress shifted under his weight as he climbed back onto the bed, positioning himself between her knees before grasping her hips and pulling her to him. "You think that's what I'm going to do right now? Fuck you like a champion?"

Annie's pulse was officially beating between her damp thighs. "God, I hope so."

Jordy nodded, but then something in his expression shifted that made Annie nervous. He was thinking. Her pool of experience was roughly as deep as a teaspoon, but a man thinking when he was supposed to be fucking couldn't be a good thing.

"I do get checked. Regularly. Nothing to report."

It took Annie a moment to realize that he was referring to STI checks. Her brain had gone warp speed down a very nasty road where he was having second thoughts about having sex with her, and she had been preparing her self-esteem for a fatal blow. This had been nowhere on her radar. The amount of people she'd been intimate with didn't use up all the fingers on one hand, and the majority of the last decade had been with the same person. Somehow she'd jumped from flag football to... well...what Jordy played. Apparently the rules were different here.

"Oh. That's good to know." How the hell was she supposed to say this without it being awkward? "I had my cervix swabbed three months ago at my annual, and everything came back normal."

Smooth.

"I pee in a cup and get my blood drawn. The nurses always tell me I've got great veins."

Grateful relief washed over Annie. Jordy hadn't laughed or made fun of her fumble. He simply joined her in the awkward moment.

"The phlebotomists are definitely hitting on you," she told

him, hooking her legs around his hips, futilely trying to pull him into her. "I don't blame them. You're hot. Now please fuck me."

"Why are you in such a rush?" he teased, effortlessly sliding a finger inside of her instead of his cock. It would have been frustrating if he hadn't immediately found a spot that made her buck up against his hand.

"Fuck," she moaned as a second finger joined the first. "Um...what was the question again?"

"Why are you in such a rush for me to get it over with and fuck you?"

"You know it's really hard to think when you—oh, *god*." Either she had a hair trigger tonight or Jordy actually knew what he was doing. Maybe a combination of both. Because the moment his thumb found her clit, a tiny shiver of an orgasm pulsed through Annie. Nothing earth-shattering, but enough to make her want more.

"There you go," he purred, self-satisfaction dripping off every syllable. His fingers kept their rhythm, building the pressure that would blossom into another orgasm if he didn't stop. "Still want me to hurry?"

"A—*ohmygod*—a little."

"Why?"

Annie arched, so close she could taste it. "B-because I don't want you to change your mind again."

His fingers slowed, and she whined as the sensation that had been making her blood crackle instantly faded. "I didn't change my mind, Annie. I wanted to fuck you. Are you drunk right now?"

She shook her head rapidly. One and a half glasses of "snack wine" as he'd called it. Not drunk. Not even buzzed anymore. She'd crossed the tiny house to get to his room sober enough to go to church with her grandma.

"Then you've got nothing to worry about." Jordy continued to lazily stroke her. "Still want me to hurry up and fuck you?"

"Please."

"Any hard nos or requests?"

Annie's mind blanked. And not just because his thumb was rubbing her clit in a way that made her squirm. She had been with Jake for nearly a decade, and he had never asked her what she wanted in bed. The few times she had asked to try something, he'd been sulky and offended. Annie had stopped asking and accepted that her sex life was going to be two minutes of foreplay and the same three positions for the rest of her life. Sex wasn't the most important thing in a relationship. It was a bonus. Sometimes that bonus happened to be the Jelly of the Month Club.

"I have no idea."

"What usually works?"

"My vibrator."

Jordy looked at the door, and Annie tightened her legs around his hips.

"Don't you dare leave."

"I can go get it," he offered as she had another shivering orgasm that made her nerves tingle.

"You're doing great. I can get it after we're done."

"If you think you're going to need to sprint out of my bed through a freezing house to finish yourself off, I'm not doing great," Jordy argued. "Tell me what you want, Annie."

Annie groaned, half out of frustration and half from pleasure. "I don't know. If I'd known there was going to be a quiz, I would have studied."

Jordy chuckled, bending down to kiss her throat. "I bet you would have aced it, smart girl." His lips ghosted over a spot beneath her earlobe that gave her goosebumps. "How do you want me to fuck you? Hard? Fast? Do you want to role play? I'm the bad student, and you're going to help me study for the big test?"

"I never fucked anyone I was tutoring."

"Really? Hands-on studying was how I passed Anatomy."

Another small, shuddering orgasm rolled through her. With every stroke, Annie became more sensitive and desperate. She lost the trail of their conversation, need overriding any follow-up questions about his collegiate study habits.

"Jordy," she whined.

"Come on. I'm giving you permission to boss me around. Tell me what you want. Beg me to fuck you until you're a stupid mess who can't walk right because I pounded you into the mattress."

She clenched around his fingers. "That. I want that."

"Use your words."

"Fuck. Me."

"Bossy."

Jordy caught her mouth before she could give him a piece of her mind, kissing her in the kind of hungry, demanding way that made her lose her faculties. It was hard to be frustrated with a man who kissed like that.

There was a split second, suspended in the time it took him to withdraw his fingers and replace them with the tip of his cock, where it occurred to Annie that she could be very bad at this and Jordy might have a terrible time. Yes, he had been very sweet so far, but all that experience that had made him seem like the ideal candidate for sex came with a mountain of expectations. The Everest of expectations. Who the hell did she think she was trying to climb Everest when she only had experience hiking beginner trails?

Then he filled her with a commanding snap of his hips, and Annie forgot about mountains and expectations. She moaned into his mouth and dug her heels into his ass—such a great ass—

trying to take him deeper faster. Mercifully, he took the hint and the bed began to squeak beneath them, the metal headboard clanging against the wall. Getting pounded into the mattress had not been an empty promise.

Annie held on for dear life, trying to ride the waves of pleasure as they crested over her body, but she was constantly yanked into the undertow where she couldn't think, only feel. Her entire existence was distilled down to the sharp, twisting pleasure building in her body until she couldn't take it anymore and she snapped. Annie screamed into Jordy's kiss as she came, one hand fisting his hair tightly, the other hand clutching the back of his neck in a vice grip.

His pace didn't slow. It barely faltered. If anything, her orgasm made him go harder and faster, and Annie wasn't sure if her next orgasm was fresh or a riotous continuation of the first. She broke their kiss, adding gibberish praise and encouragement to the cacophony of noise the bed was making.

Yes, yes, yes. More, more, more.

Jordy buried his nose in the crook of her neck, and the swipe of his tongue there made her shiver. A sharp pull at the skin there, counterbalanced by him rolling her nipple between his thumb and forefinger, and Annie clenched around his cock again. He stiffened against her, shudders shaking his body.

Silence settled over them like a warm blanket. Annie ran a soothing hand up and down Jordy's back. Aftershocks made him tremble, and those little tremors set off shivers in her, too. She felt like a glow stick: broken, shook up, and radiant.

And light. So very, very light.

She looked down at her body to make sure she wasn't glowing or floating.

Soft lips pressed against the warm spot on her neck.

"We need to get some ice on this," Jordy murmured, his voice slow and thick. Another kiss to the same spot.

"Ice on what?" Annie asked, stretching her arms above her head to make sure her limbs still worked. She felt more like unset Jell-O than a person.

"I got a little carried away, but it's nothing some ice now, maybe a warm compress later, and some makeup won't fix."

It was embarrassing how long it took her brain to catch up.

"Jordy...did you give me a hickey?"

"I don't think it's that bad. It's kind of hard to tell in the dark, but I'm going to assume that's a good sign." He kissed it again. "Sorry." He didn't sound very sorry.

"If you hadn't been handing out orgasms like Halloween candy, I'd be very mad at you right now."

"But since you got to go trick-or-treating, we're cool?"

"Eloise might have a scarf I can borrow. I can tell her I'm thinking about becoming a flight attendant."

Jordy snorted and rolled off of her, reaching over the edge of the bed for his sweats.

"Where are you going?" Annie asked, pulling the covers up to her chin. Was she supposed to be getting dressed too? She probably was. Too bad she'd flung her clothes god knows where.

"Errands," he said. "Dispose of condom. Get you some ice. Get us some water. Maybe fish some of the fruit out of the wine for a snack so I can do this again in twenty minutes."

Twenty minutes later, Jordy was breathing heavily next to her, dead to the world. He'd said he was going to shut his eyes for a moment, and less than two minutes later, he was out cold.

She wasn't sure what to do. Did she stay? Did she go back to her room? When he woke up in the morning, was he going to be weirded out that she stayed, or disappointed that she left? He was big, and warm, and solid, and every long-term-relationship-honed instinct she had told her to cuddle up and make herself at home.

That solidified her decision.

Annie found her clothes, made sure Jordy was covered by the blankets, kissed his forehead—he didn't even flinch—and then tiptoed across the house back to her room. Using the flashlight on her phone, she opened the electrical box and flipped the main breaker. The space heater Jordy had insisted be set up in her room hummed back to life.

FIVE

WAKING up cold and alone wasn't a new thing for Jordy. He was used to it. In fact, he usually preferred it. Back home, he had what he and Sam called "The Cinderella Rule"—gone before midnight. Either they or the person they were having sex with needed to be out the door by midnight. It was exponentially harder to get rid of someone after that. Still there in the morning? Good luck getting them to leave before noon.

So it came as a shock that he was disappointed Annie wasn't still in bed next to him.

The last thing he remembered was telling her he was going to close his eyes for a moment. Her head had been on his chest, her fingertips tracing invisible patterns on his skin, and the whole thing had been so damn comfortable that it had lulled him straight to sleep. The human version of a sleeping pill, without any of the side effects.

Maybe some side effects. His left quad was achy.

Jordy stretched his arms above his head, twisting his hips to crack his back. Tension eased out of his body as he held the pose on one side, and then the other. Had he reached the age where he needed to warm up before sex?

No. He could blame this on spending most of the day before sitting on his ass traveling.

It was a good thing Annie wasn't in bed with him. She would have said something awkward and adorable, and it would have been so fucking cute that he would have rolled her over, grabbed her by her hips, and fucked her until she was screaming his name like it was the only word she knew or he pulled something, whichever came first.

Jordy needed a cold shower.

The sound of soft singing lured him out of his room like a sailor following a siren. In the kitchen, Annie was filling a tea kettle with water, dancing in place to whatever song was playing in her headphones. He watched her for a minute, hands in his pockets, a strange floating feeling in his stomach, similar to standing in the tunnel before big games.

Nervous. He was nervous.

How was he supposed to approach this? He'd given her a damn hickey the night before, swept up in an overwhelming need to mark her, to leave evidence that he had been there. Did he tap her on the shoulder? Smile politely and maintain a respectful distance? Pretend it had never happened because he had woken up alone and maybe it was a one-time thing?

Annie looked over her shoulder, blushed, and smiled shyly.

Jordy wasn't in control of his feet again, and like the night before, they carried him across the room of their own volition. Annie put the kettle on the stove as he leaned against the counter, watching her. Same shorts, same socks, same purple University of Washington sweatshirt as the night before. Her brown hair was gathered into a messy bun on top of her head, so he was able to see the bite mark peeking out. He hooked his finger into the collar of her sweatshirt, pulling it down to get a better look. His thumb brushed the fading bruise.

"It doesn't look fresh," Annie commented, her cheeks rosy.

Why did that make him want to make it look fresh? More obvious.

"I can say it happened before I got here, if anyone asks," she added.

And that was why he couldn't make it bigger and darker. People would ask questions. Specifically Graham and Sybil. He could lie to Graham easily, but he had a sneaking suspicion that Sybil wouldn't buy whatever flimsy excuse he could come up with. She would stare at him until he caved, and then she would make good on her promise to use those rusty gardening shears.

"You'll need a good story," he warned her. "They'll want the juicy details."

"His name was Mark. Great kisser. Mediocre sex."

Jordy bristled. "Mediocre?"

Annie tapped the tip of his nose. "Not. You."

He relaxed. "Been thinking about your story?"

"I did go on a date recently with a guy named Mark."

"Great kisser and mediocre sex?"

"Aggressively mediocre kisser and no sex." Annie reached behind him for a small wooden box. "You're the first person I've had sex with in a really long time."

That should not have made him want to puff out his chest and strut around the room, but it did.

"Glad I could help you end the drought."

Annie's cheeks flooded with color again as she leafed through the tea bags in the box.

"About that drought..."

There was that feeling again. Dry mouth, fluttery heart, rolling stomach. She was going to tell him that the sex had been great, but ultimately a mistake. She was a long-term kind of girl, and he was a short-time kind of guy. Fun but impractical, like high heels that were a little too tight. He had heard it all before, so often that he could have provided a fill-in-the-blank form.

"Last night was..."

"Good?" he suggested, folding his arms under his chest, wishing he had bothered to put on a shirt before coming out. Getting let down easy was less embarrassing when he was fully clothed.

Annie shook her head. "No." She frowned, and his stomach changed its address to the space between his feet.

"I'm sorry," she groaned, covering her face with her hands. "I'm trying to find a cool, casual way to say this, and I can't. It was amazing. Five stars. Ten out of ten. Would write a letter of recommendation."

"A letter of recommendation?"

"References are the way of the future. No one should take their pants off without them. 'Rocky start, but takes direction well. Lots of growth potential.' I'd give that a shot."

Jordy laughed. The sound burst out of him in a bark and echoed around the room.

"Was it a rocky start?" he teased, most of the tension drained from his body.

"Oh, no. You are a seasoned professional, sir. Very skilled." Annie shut the tea box without selecting a bag. She must have noticed at the same time he did, because she quickly reopened the box and grabbed a bag at random. Sleepy Time Tea, complete with a drowsy bear in a nightgown stared up at them from the counter. "I think we should keep fucking."

She lobbed it out like a grenade. Jordy wasn't sure if he was supposed to fall on it or run and duck for cover. Or kick it to see if it was actually live.

"You think we should keep fucking?" he repeated, convinced he'd heard her wrong.

Annie flushed from the top of her forehead down to her neck. "It's okay if you say no. I'll understand. It's just...I had a really good time last night and I hope you did too and since we're both here for the next few weeks, it's convenient. We don't even have to leave the lighthouse. And after the wedding, we go our separate ways. Easy as that. No strings attached."

Jordy's brain was still trying to catch up. When she was nervous, Annie was a verbal traffic accident waiting to happen; she blew through intersections and stoplights, careening towards her point at one hundred miles per hour. And the fact that she was talking about having sex with him for a few weeks? It was a miracle there was enough blood left in the upper half of his body to power his vital organs.

She crashed on. "Do they call you the King of the One-Night Stand because you want to keep things casual or because they don't come back for a second night? Have I been getting such subpar sex that what I think is amazing sex is actually *meh*? Or am I breaking a rule by asking for more? Because we can pretend I never ask—"

He kissed her. It was the only way he could think to stop her runaway mouth and assure her he was interested without fucking it all up by speaking. Her teeth scraped his bottom lip as her last syllable got muffled against his mouth. Sparks skittered down his spine to the tip of his rapidly hardening cock.

One way or another, this woman was going to be the death of him.

There was the briefest flash of surprised hesitation from Annie before she melted against him like they could become one person, her fingers tangling in his hair to bring him closer. As soon as her mouth opened, he slipped his tongue inside and they moaned in unison. This felt good—*she* felt good.

Annie was an easy person to be around; easy to talk to, easy to look at, easy to kiss, easy to fuck. A few weeks of easy was what he needed. No strings, no distractions. Outside of this— the groping hands and heated moans—they didn't make any sense. She was a scientist with a doctorate, and he played foot-ball. Different worlds was an understatement.

He pressed her back against the counter, grinding himself against her. Annie broke their kiss with a moan.

"Oh my god," she panted, and wiggled her hand between them to grasp his rock-hard length through his pants. "Is this all for me? Was it something I said?"

His tombstone flashed before his eyes. *Here Lies Jordy Taylor, Killed In His Prime By A Sexy Scientist.*

"You are so bad," he mumbled against her mouth, and boosted her up onto the countertop.

Annie giggled, and the sound did something weird to his heart. It had been pounding, working overtime redirecting blood flow, and then it fluttered, like it was laughing in response.

Was he having a heart attack?

Her hands slipped from his hair and trailed down his shoulders, her fingertips tracing muscles as she found them. Annie sighed contentedly.

"If this is a dream, don't wake me up."

She kissed him once, pulling back before he could deepen it, then kissed his cheek, his jaw, and then began working her way down his neck. Jordy tilted his head to the side to give her more room. He loved having his neck kissed, and for some reason, it almost never happened. Excited goosebumps broke out over his skin as Annie licked his pulse. He gripped her hips and pulled her closer. She responded by wrapping her legs tightly around his waist.

This was going to be an excellent few weeks.

Sharp pain that dissolved into liquid pleasure radiated out from the juncture of his neck and shoulder, suspiciously under Annie's lips.

She'd bitten him back.

The sharp scream of the tea kettle made them both jump.

A nervous laugh filled the new space between them.

"That was a yes. In case that wasn't clear," Jordy said, turning off the burner and moving the kettle.

Annie pressed her thumb into the blossoming bruise she'd created, not trying to wipe it away, but like she was trying to make sure it would stick.

"Now we match."

Curious, Jordy left the safe harbor between her legs and went to the bathroom to see her handiwork for himself. She'd gotten him good. The hickey was darkening to a deep purple, and it soothed something right beneath his sternum.

Now we match.

SIX

ANNIE COULDN'T TAKE her eyes off Jordy's ass as he walked to the bathroom.

How the hell had she convinced someone with an ass like that to fuck her? It defied all logic. Up was down, and down was sideways. Because someone with an ass like that should not be lowering themselves from their spot on Mount Olympus to even speak to her.

She was out of her depth and wildly out of her league. A nice accountant was more her speed. Safe, predictable, and a little boring. He would wait a respectful amount of time before awkwardly feeling her up and never give her a hickey.

Annie's hand passed over the bite mark on her neck. It was a good thing Jordy was a short time thing, because just kissing him got her so wound up she could feel her heartbeat in her toes. More than a few weeks of this and she was at risk for serious cardiac complications.

They needed rules. Quickly. Because as Jordy exited the bathroom and started back towards her, every rational, self-preserving instinct evaporated from her body and biology took over. The base parts of her brain that normally remained dormant—those instincts that had kept the human race going for millennia—screamed that she needed his genes swimming in her pool. That his babies were worth risking her life to carry and care for.

Her legs fell open as he stepped back into his natural place between them.

Rules. Boundaries.

The animal part of her brain didn't want those. It was both mollified and jubilant at the bite mark she'd left on his neck. It was a purple billboard that shouted, "I licked it, so it's mine." A neon sign warning other potential partners away.

Rules. Boundaries.

Jordy's massive hands gripped her hips and pulled her flush against him.

Rules and boundaries could wait.

Her stomach, however, could not. Jordy was midway to kissing her when her stomach rumbled like distant thunder, and he froze. He looked down at her stomach.

"Was that you?"

Annie's cheeks burned. "Maybe?"

"That's actually kind of impressive." Jordy chuckled and put his hand on her belly. "I should feed you so I can fuck you."

Annie wanted to say that she was fine with the order being reversed, but her stomach wouldn't tolerate only being filled with butterflies.

"I guess I have a few weeks to have kitchen counter sex."

Jordy grinned at her, his eyes flitting to her mouth quick as a hummingbird's wings. Down, up, down, up. He seemed unsure, so she curled her hand around the back of his neck and brought him in for a deep, toe-curling kiss. There was a heady thrill in having an attractive man melt against her.

Her stomach growled again before she could convince herself that food was unimportant.

. . .

THEY SETTLED on a restaurant called Queens.

Jordy and Annie were shown to a teal-and-bubblegum-pink booth and handed menus that sported a giant pink neon flamingo. There was a jukebox near the bathrooms and a kitchen-facing counter with alternating pink and teal stools. The whole place felt like a technicolor trailer park fairy tale directed by Wes Anderson.

"Have you ever been here before?" Annie asked, opening her menu. She'd had time to cool down since she'd tried to convince him to fuck her on the kitchen counter. Her brain was semi-functional again, which wasn't necessarily a good thing. She was spiraling now that her reproductive organs were no longer in charge of the show. Once the biological imperative was removed from the equation, so was her courage.

Who the fuck did she think she was?

"No, but I heard good things."

While Jordy studied the menu like she was going to ask him to present on it later, Annie studied Jordy. He was handsome, with lovely smile lines that crinkled the corners of his eyes every time he chuckled at one of the puns on the menu, and a few strands of silver hair threaded through his thick blond mop that shimmered in the sun if he moved his head just right.

Why had he agreed to her harebrained scheme? Sure, it was sex he didn't have to work for, but Annie very much doubted Jordy Taylor had ever worked hard to get sex. Women threw themselves at him. *She* had thrown herself at him. Twice, if she was going to keep score.

"Did you see the salad?" he asked, pointing three-quarters of the way down the right-hand page of the menu. "Don't Stop Be-leaf-in'. I love this place."

A wide, amused smile crinkled the corners of his blue eyes,

and Annie wanted to crawl across the table, plant herself in his lap, and kiss those wonderful wrinkles.

This was why she needed rules and boundaries. Without them, her brain and her womb were going to team up against her and try to break her heart by convincing her that Jordy was The One. It wouldn't be hard to fall in love with a kind, respectful, funny man who could at least pretend to listen when she talked and gave Grade A orgasms.

"I think we should revisit our deal," Annie said, folding her menu shut.

Jordy's cheerful smile faltered and then faded away entirely. He folded his hands on top of his open menu.

"Which part?"

"All of it."

Talking to him had been easier in the dark when she couldn't scrutinize every facial muscle twitch. The urge to say every thought careening around her brain, to let him pick through the wreckage of words to find her meaning, to confuse him with her stream of consciousness so they were on a level playing field, was overwhelming.

"This is only until after the wedding," she said, her thumbnail picking at the part of the lamination that was coming apart.

"You mentioned that earlier." Jordy slouched on his side of the booth.

Annie clenched her molars to stop herself from sprinting to the finish line of this conversation.

"It's not like we work outside of this"—she snapped her fingers a few times to conjure the word she wanted—"*situation*, anyway. In three weeks, you'll go your way, and I'll go my way, and we never have to see each other again."

"One of my best friends is marrying your cousin. There's a chance we'll see each other again."

"But there won't be anything between us."

Jordy shifted, looking around the room. Maybe she could speed up a little bit. This was probably all very obvious to him.

"I don't want anyone to get confused. Three weeks. Just sex. No sleepovers, no more than ten minutes of post-coital cuddling, no kissing except to express sexual interest, and no obligation to continue if the other person changes their mind or loses interest."

There. She'd even left him an out.

"We call that last item consent." Jordy sighed, raking a hand through his hair, and then sitting back with his arms crossed across his chest. "Is that it?"

Annie ran the list over again, then nodded. "I think so."

"Am I allowed to add some things?"

"Of course," she said brightly, though her stomach pitched violently.

"We keep this between us. No one else needs to know. That way it's not awkward in the group later."

She nodded. "That's probably for the best. Peter would have a field day."

"Exactly. And as long as we're"—Jordy waved his hand between the two of them—"it's just us."

Annie frowned. "You want to be monogamous?"

"It's for safety," Jordy insisted.

That made sense. Safety, not because he had developed any kind of fledgling feelings for her in the last twelve hours. This was exactly why they were having this conversation. Because without the rules and boundaries laid out between them, she might have spun his request for exclusivity into a confession of interest. Jordy could have anyone he wanted; she happened to be exceptionally convenient and extremely willing.

"Monogamy it is." She opened up her menu again, feeling marginally more settled about their situation now that they'd had a real conversation about it, instead of one where she gave him a hickey.

"Like the birds."

Annie's pulse fluttered. She looked up at Jordy, the shadow of a smirk hiding in the corners of his mouth. "You remembered?"

"Birds mate for life, right?"

"Not all birds. Actually, not even most birds. They're only monogamous for a period of time—like us."

Jordy's cheeks turned rosy. "Right. That makes sense."

The urge to keep talking bubbled up again, but Annie was saved by the presence of a man who looked like Santa if Santa did home gym commercials. Buff Santa wore a teal T-shirt with the pink Queens logo on it, and his pink oval name tag proclaimed his name was Leo.

"Good morning, lovebirds," he said. "What can I get started for you?"

"The biggest mimosa you can legally serve me," Jordy answered.

THE BIGGEST MIMOSA LEO could legally serve Jordy came in a goblet with a pink flamingo stem and arrived one more self-esteem-bruising bird lecture too late. Because, as Annie had happily pointed out, they weren't lovebirds—because they mated for life—but more like flamingos, who only mated for a year and then broke things off. Jordy normally loved her bird lectures—she had given him one on the drive down from the lighthouse about pelagic cormorants and how they were misnamed because they didn't go far from shore—but when they were used to illustrate how utterly incompatible she thought they were, he wished she would just stop talking.

This should have been his dream scenario: a gorgeous woman wanted to have as much sex with him as she could, and sex was all she wanted from him. In three weeks, Dr. Annie Price was going to go do whatever smart people with bird PhDs did, and he would go back to Los Angeles to hopefully play another season with the Phantoms. So why did he feel so fucking awful?

Jordy took a hefty swallow of his mimosa.

Annie picked up her flamingo-shaped mason jar, examining it closely. She'd ordered a carrot, orange, ginger, and turmeric juice dubbed the Bugs Bunny. At least he'd gotten a giggle out of his "What's up, Doc?" joke.

"Do you think I could smuggle this out in my purse?" she asked, placing the straw between her lips, her hazel eyes glittering with mischief as they met his.

Jordy tried not to imagine her sucking on his cock instead and failed.

"Liberating the local wildlife?"

Annie nodded, a devilish grin blooming. "This is a public service. Completely altruistic."

Jordy made a mental note to look up "altruistic" later. He'd heard it used before, but he'd never cared what it meant until Annie said it.

"So, what are we doing today?" Annie asked. "Or, um, what are you doing today? It doesn't have to be us. We don't have to hang out. Should we be hanging out?"

"We can hang out," Jordy reassured her. He wanted to hang out with her. How else was he ever supposed to learn words he could use to beat Peter at Scrabble?

"But *should* we be hanging out?"

Jordy raked a hand through his hair and took another hefty swallow of mimosa. "Why not?"

"Because we could end up developing feelings."

"Are you worried about developing feelings, Dr. Price?"

Annie's cheeks flushed the same shade of pink as her novelty glassware and she became very interested in her straw. "No, I guess not."

"Then that settles it. We can hang out and be friends." *Friends* felt awful in his mouth, like chewing someone else's old bubblegum. "What are we doing today?"

Annie shrugged. "We should probably get groceries, unless you like subsisting on cookie dough."

"Tempting, but not enough protein."

She grinned at him. "So groceries, then I need to check on Eloise at some point to make sure she hasn't decided to throw herself into the ocean because her mom has gently *suggested*"— she paused to emphasize that these were not suggestions— "another potential change to make the wedding better."

"Sandra strikes again." Jordy shook his head.

"You know Eloise's mom's name?"

"It's become a bit of a catchphrase in the group chat," he admitted.

Annie snorted. "Do you have anything you need to get done?"

"Work out. Bug my agent. Make good on my promise to fuck you on the kitchen counter." Jordy shrugged, pretending like Annie's deep pink flush didn't thrill him. "Maybe take a nap."

"So I rank below physical fitness and work, but above sleep. I think I can live with that."

"I'd say you're equal with physical fitness. Fucking you doubles as cardio."

ANNIE'S CAR was so old it didn't have Bluetooth. Jordy's first car had had an 8-track, but somehow her still using an aux cord to play music off her phone blew his mind. He changed the playlist at her request, and it took every bit of willpower he had to not go through her phone while it was unlocked. Did she have nudes? Annie didn't seem like the kind of person to take nudes, much less keep them stored on her phone for easy use, but then again he hadn't expected her to show up at his door the night before either. She was full of surprises. And why was her ex texting her? The name *Jake* had popped up several times when they had passed through a patch of cell service, and it was killing Jordy in slow increments not to know what they were talking about. Just friends? Hoping for reconciliation? Still finding items that needed returning?

"Do you mind if we stop and get coffee?" Annie asked.

Jordy put her phone in her cup holder. "Why didn't you get coffee with breakfast?"

"Because it's not Stardust," Annie said, following the signs for Historic Downtown Crane Cove. "It will only take a minute."

"It's fine. I wanted to see the twins about a tractor tire."

"Why do you need a tractor tire?"

"To work out," Jordy explained. "Crane Cove doesn't have a gym."

Chase and Cole McMahon, who owned Cranberry Brothers Brewing, had mentioned once that they lived on a farm, so it stood to reason that they might have a tractor tire laying around. He was not running a silly errand to avoid seeing Sybil.

It was a little bit because he was avoiding seeing Sybil.

Jordy had no doubt that Sybil would take one look at him with Annie and *know* the things they'd done. It didn't matter that they'd covered their matching hickeys. Sybil would know, and then his nuts would be toast.

"There's a Sit and Be Fit class at the community center,"

Annie told him as she parked her car at the end of the closed-off street. "So you don't hurt your geriatric knees."

"There's nothing geriatric about my—" Jordy's indignation fizzled when he saw the grin Annie was fighting. She was teasing him.

He unbuckled his seatbelt, leaned across the center console, caught the back of her neck in his hand, and kissed her.

No kissing except to express sexual interest? Biggest fucking loophole he'd ever seen.

It wasn't a long kiss—people might see—but Annie's lips were soft and inviting, and Jordy lingered longer than he should have. Her hand came to rest right over his heart, and he started to pull back, only to have Annie's light touch turn into a death grip on the worn material of his sweatshirt. She recaptured his mouth, kissing him with the kind of earnestness that lit up his senses in a way he'd never known.

Annie relinquished his lips, but not his sweatshirt, resting her forehead against his. "You broke the rules," she told him, her voice whisper soft.

"Nah," he said, stroking her cheek with his thumb. "I stayed inbounds."

"You're only supposed to kiss me—"

"To express sexual interest," Jordy interrupted. "I know. I was listening."

Color spread across Annie's pale cheeks. "Oh."

She released his sweatshirt, then checked her appearance in the visor mirror, adjusted the high neck of her quarter-zip sweater and arranged her hair to ensure her hickey was covered.

Fuck, she was pretty.

He needed to get out of the damn car.

"Did you want a coffee?" Annie asked as they stepped onto the preserved brick street that ran through historic downtown Crane Cove.

It was on the tip of his tongue to say "Yes, but please don't tell Sybil it's for me so I can keep my nuts attached to my body" when Graham pushed open the door to Stardust Coffee, a full cardboard drink tray in his free hand.

It was amazing what a year of being happy could do to a person. Jordy had never really noticed how tightly wound and miserable his friend was until Graham had sold his booming tech company a year and a half ago to relocate for love. In eighteen months, Graham seemed to have gotten younger.

"Annie!" Graham beamed at her. "When did you get to town?"

"Last night," she answered, and pointed to the coffees he was carrying. "Have you developed a serious caffeine dependency?"

"Staff meeting. We bribe them with treats. You'd think the paychecks would be enough."

"Money can't buy everything," Jordy said, and Graham did a double take.

"When did you get here?" he asked, his face a mixture of shock and confusion.

"Last night."

"No, to here. Right here. This sidewalk," Graham clarified.

"Same time as I did," Annie answered. "I wanted coffee, and he needed to see the twins about a tractor tire."

Graham looked from Jordy to Annie, then back again. "So you didn't show up together?"

"No, we did." Annie looked up at Jordy. "What kind of coffee did you want?"

"Iced white chocolate mocha with two pumps of caramel," he told her. Then he dug into his pocket for his wallet, giving Annie the same firm glare he had given her at breakfast when the check came, and handed her his credit card. They were in wildly different tax brackets; he wasn't going to let her pay for anything.

"Be careful in there," Graham warned her. "The bird watchers are having their post-walk coffee."

Graham waited until Annie went inside to turn on Jordy.

"You have thirty seconds to explain what parts of 'off' and 'limits' were unclear. What's going on? Why are you together?"

Jordy shoved his hands into his pockets, looking at the wooden sign that hung above the door. "What's going on is you're really shitty at scheduling, and we went out for breakfast because there isn't any food in the lighthouse," he explained, picking his words carefully so he wasn't lying to Graham. "Both 'off' and 'limits' were very clear."

"You're both at the lighthouse?" Graham paled.

"We talked about it, and we're both fine with it. She's got her bed, I've got mine. No sleepovers."

Not that he didn't want to revisit that clause of the verbal situationship contract, if for no other reason than having wakeup sex.

Graham raised his eyebrows in disbelief. "No sleepovers?"

"No sleepovers." For good measure, he even crossed his heart.

Graham checked his watch. "I am officially late for staff, but I just wanted to say…" he sighed. "Annie is a sweet girl with a big heart. If you fuck around with her, she's going to get attached, and I don't want to have to let Sybil hurt you. So keep it friendly, okay?"

"I can keep it friendly. I'm an extremely friendly guy."

"That's what I'm worried about. I've seen how friendly you can be."

"You said it yourself. Annie is a sweet girl. Sweet girls aren't interested in me," Jordy reminded him. "All we've got in common are Sandra Bullock movies, so stop worrying about us."

Over Graham's shoulder, Jordy could see Annie at the end of the bar waiting for their coffees, talking to two very eager and enthusiastic-looking senior citizens wearing hiking gear. She caught sight of him looking at her, smiled, and gave a small wave. Jordy's heart skipped. If all they had in common was Sandra Bullock movies, he was ordering her entire career on DVD.

SEVEN

THE BEST VIEW in Crane Cove was through the lighthouse kitchen window: Jordy Taylor, shirtless, doing a bodyweight workout as the sun went down. Annie was so busy watching him that she narrowly missed cutting her finger instead of the onion. The man was *distracting*. One hundred push-ups, and she wanted to crawl into the freezer to cool off after watching the muscles in his arms flex.

Rain drummed on the roof, and Jordy grabbed his shirt and headed for the house.

So much for having dinner done when he was done with his workout. She'd barely made any progress on the onion.

Annie tried to look like she had been chopping and not lusting after him when Jordy came inside. She tossed the root end of the onion into the trash and used the motion as an excuse to look at him. He used his T-shirt like a towel to wipe his face, and Annie's eyes followed a drop of water or sweat as it traveled down his torso and settled in his belly button.

Was it hot in here, or was it just her?

"I thought you'd be done," Jordy teased as he toweled off his arms, chest, then stomach.

"I had to wash all the produce we bought," she explained. Not a lie, but she had washed an apple for so long while watching him that the sticker disintegrated.

"Mm-hmm." His smug grin was proof she wasn't half as sneaky as she thought she was.

He went to the closet that hid the washer and dryer and dropped his shirt into the washer, then came back to the kitchen and settled his hands on her hips. The chill from his skin seeped through her leggings, and then he tucked his fingers into the waistband and she jumped.

"You're freezing!"

"Want to warm me up?" His teeth scraped her pulse and shivers ricocheted down her body.

Annie tilted her head to give him more access to her neck while she fumbled for the red bell pepper. "I thought you were hungry."

"I am," he murmured, nibbling her neck, "but I want you for an appetizer."

She pushed her ass back and had no trouble locating his hard cock. It baffled her that he wanted her when she was wearing her alumni sweatshirt, leggings, and cozy duck socks, but she couldn't argue with the empirical evidence grinding against her.

Chicken gnocchi could wait.

Annie turned her face toward his and caught his mouth. They moaned in tandem when his tongue touched hers. Jordy smelled like sweat, rain, and cold air, not a combination she normally liked but on him it smelled like the promise of adventure. One chilly hand creeping into her underwear while the other one stole up her sweatshirt was more like a guarantee.

"Tell me what you want," he coaxed, his nose brushing against hers. Those big hands were just shy of where she wanted them, and when Annie tried to tilt her hips, he moved that hand away. "Use your words."

She gave a small, pathetic whine. "Touch. Me."

The cold of his fingers was a sharp contrast to the heat of her pussy and Annie gasped when he touched her. He toyed with her, sliding two fingers in and out easily, and then using that wetness to circle her clit. She arched, stretching onto her tiptoes, anything to get more.

"Jordy..."

He palmed her breast through her sports bra. "My room or your room?"

"Fuck, I don't know. You're playing with the off switch to my brain and asking me to make decisions."

Jordy pressed his nose against her neck and chuckled. "Do you want to try your bed tonight?"

"Yes."

"I'll give you a fifteen-second head start," he said, withdrawing his hands from her clothing. Annie wanted them back. But she wanted his cock inside of her more, so she hustled to her room, wiggled out of her sweatshirt, and tossed it in the general vicinity of her suitcase.

"Getting started without me?" Jordy teased. Annie turned, thumbs hooked into the waistband of her leggings, ready to push them down, and saw him standing in the doorway, grinning, a condom in his right hand. At least he was always prepared.

"You already had your shirt off," Annie pointed out. "I was catching up."

Jordy moved through her room like he belonged there. He plopped down on her bed, laid back against her headboard, and crossed his ankles like he was settling in for a show. What was it like to have that much confidence? The lights were on, and her courage was fading.

"Take your shorts off," she told him, and he complied

without hesitation. Underwear, too. He returned to his reclined position, this time with his cock in his hand. Slow, hypnotizing strokes worked his shaft, and she tried to memorize how he touched himself so she could make him moan and writhe.

"I was thinking about you today."

That caught Annie off guard. "Why?"

"Actually"—Jordy's breath caught as she pushed down her leggings—"I was thinking about your socks. Got any other birdies I could see?"

"Nah, just the mallards," she answered, hopping awkwardly out of her pants. Next came the sports bra, the least sexy bra on the planet. It joined her sweatshirt in the corner. "But if you want to see some birds, I'm going birding in the morning."

"Sounds cool."

"It's early," she warned, joining him on the bed. The speed at which he abandoned his dick in favor of touching her made her giddy. His face was between her boobs faster than she could say "tit."

"That's fine." Jordy kissed the inner curve of her left breast. "How do you want me to fuck you?"

If Annie thought the only off switch for her brain was her clit, she was wrong. Because while she tried to decide what she wanted, Jordy flicked his tongue across one nipple while teasing the other one between his thumb and his forefinger. All higher brain function ceased, and the fog of lust settled over her again.

"Good" was her extremely intelligent answer.

He sucked her nipple into his mouth and hummed his amusement. "Mmm...want to ride my cock?"

"Are you going to keep playing with my boobs?"

"Uh-huh."

Fuck the unflattering angle. "I'm in."

Jordy grabbed the condom, and as soon as he had it on, Annie straddled him. She reached between them, grabbed his cock by the root, and then lowered herself down on his length. It happened in fractions. She wasn't as ready as she'd been the night before, but she was impatient. And the stretch as her body worked to accommodate him was divine.

"You feel so good," she sighed as she reached the base. Three weeks of fucking Jordy was going to be almost as good as winning the lottery.

The first roll of her hips made them moan.

Annie found a steady rhythm while Jordy played with her nipples. It felt great, but not good enough. She was standing on the precipice but couldn't figure out how to get over the edge. And it wasn't that Jordy wasn't trying his best below her, but even his thumb on her clit wasn't doing the trick. Top had been a bad idea. She didn't have Jordy's stamina and her brain wouldn't quite turn off, concerned that he was not having a good time because she wasn't orgasming.

"I don't know if this is working," she said, stopping in exhausted frustration. "I'm sorry."

"Don't be sorry," he soothed, stroking her thighs. "Do you want to try your vibrator? That might help. Or do you want to be done?"

Annie didn't want to be done. She wanted to come on his cock. "You won't be offended if I grab it?"

Jordy scoffed. "Fuck no, I won't be offended."

Her vibrator was in a cute little pink case in the bottom of her bag. It wasn't big, just a clit stimulator, but it packed a punch. Annie took it out and turned it on to make sure she'd remembered to charge it. The buzz startled Jordy.

"How strong is that thing?"

"It does the trick." She straddled his hips again. "If this doesn't work, it's not you, it's me."

"If this doesn't work, we've got three weeks to find something that does work." Jordy notched the head of his cock inside of her.

She sank down his cock easily this time. "Mmm...it really does feel good."

The first touch of her vibrator was like touching an electric current, and she clenched hard around him. Annie tried to find her rhythm from before, but it was hard to keep her vibrator in a spot that felt good and move at the same time.

"Don't worry about me," Jordy said, squeezing and kneading her ass. "I'm having a great time. Use me."

So she did. Annie barely moved and let her vibrator do 98% of the work. The tense, clenched pleasure from before returned, and as the anxiety that she wouldn't be able to finish began to settle in, Jordy pinched her nipples and that was it. A breathless cry choked her throat as her body shuddered relentlessly. When it became too much, she dropped her vibrator on the bed and collapsed onto Jordy.

"Hold on," he grunted, and grabbed her hips. He pounded up into her for maybe fifteen seconds before she vaguely felt his cock pulse inside of her.

The only sound for a minute was their breathing, then Jordy asked, "So how many colors does that thing come in?"

EIGHT

JORDY KNEW he had made a crucial mistake when Annie woke him up at five twenty-five in the morning. The sun wasn't even up. If he had doubted for even one second that she was smarter than he was, this was proof, because he hadn't been listening to the activity he had agreed to the night before. Annie had been in the middle of taking off her bra when she asked, and the only thing his brain understood at the point was tits. That was how he'd ended up trudging up a gentle incline through some woods a bit north of town in the early hours of the morning with a pack of wily senior citizens armed with binoculars.

She'd tricked him.

And he'd let her trick him again if she'd take her top off and let him look some more.

"Are you having fun?" Annie asked for the seventh time since they'd started up the trail.

"Yes," Jordy answered. It wasn't a lie. Annie was wearing leggings and walking in front of him. He was having a great time.

"You don't look like you're having fun." Annie played with

the excess strap on her backpack, sliding the black nylon through her fingers. "You seem...tense?"

Jordy was tense. But it had nothing to do with hiking—if stopping every thirty feet to look up in the trees could be called hiking. His problem was twofold.

First was that when Annie had woken him up that morning, bounding all her wonderful softness into his bed with the grace of an adolescent puppy, he had thought she was waking him up for a very different reason. After he had gotten her to clench around his fingers, her wetness coating his palm, she'd informed him they were most definitely going to be late. There had been no satisfaction for the aching, throbbing state of his cock because there had been no time.

Secondly, his call with his agent the day before had been less than encouraging.

"Jordy, I told you I'd call when I had news."

"Well," he'd said, *pacing the packed gravel parking area in front of the light house, "I don't believe no news is necessarily good news. What are the updates?"*

Priya had been quiet long enough for his heart to migrate up to his throat. "They want to table discussions until after the draft. Jordy, I think we need to revisit seeing if other teams are interested. I know other teams are interested. Detroit—"

"I'm not going to Detroit."

"Fine," Priya growled, annoyed. *"Your joints would never survive the winter anyway. What about Miami? Lots of old folks go there to retire."*

"What's wrong with my joints?"

"Nothing, I hope. But I need you to start becoming comfortable with the idea of moving boxes, okay? I'm going to keep working on the office to give us what we want, but I think it's time we get realistic."

Realistic.

That word tumbled around his brain like a pair of dirty sneakers in the dryer. What was he supposed to do without football? Who was he if he wasn't the Los Angeles Phantoms quarterback?

God bless Annie for distracting him.

"I'm fine," he told her, pressing his thumb into the crease between her eyebrows. "Don't worry about it."

"Anything I can do to help?" she asked, still playing with her straps. And her playing with her strap was a third problem because his brain could make anything obscene.

Was there a good way to ask her to repay the favor from that morning?

"Because, you know, I don't think they would notice if we snuck off for a few minutes," Annie said, looking down the trail where the bird watchers had clustered around someone's long lens camera to admire a picture.

His cock jumped to attention. Any curiosity about the camera withered and died.

"I don't have a condom," Jordy mouthed, on the off chance someone had their hearing aids on high.

"Where's your imagination?" She winked, and pointed up the trail.

Jordy would have followed her into hell.

"So, how much of the rumors are true?" Annie asked when they were a safe distance away from the group. She stepped off the trail into the woods.

"You're going to have to be more specific," Jordy answered, picking his steps carefully so he didn't roll an ankle. No one would be able to carry him back to the parking lot, and he didn't want to wait for either the McMahon twins or the Forest Service to come save him.

"The ones about how you're a..." She looked over her shoulder and wiggled her eyebrows at him.

Jordy tried to keep a straight face. "Are you slut-shaming me?"

"Slut-acknowledging. I don't think you're ashamed."

"Why do you want to know?"

"Because"—Annie paused to navigate a large tree root that Jordy chose to walk around—"this is all new and exciting to me, and if the rumors aren't true and you've showed me your best moves..."

"Are you bored of me already? It's been two days. We've had sex twice, and then there was this morning."

"I really liked this morning, even if it did make us late." Annie grinned at him. "Just saying yes where you're concerned has really worked out in my favor." She stopped, assessing a tree, and then looked back towards the trail. "I think this is the spot."

"You didn't answer my question." Jordy took off his backpack and set it on the ground. Annie was watching him, so he took his next twenty steps slowly so he wouldn't embarrass himself by sprinting toward her. When they were toe to toe, he cupped her jaw, running the pad of his thumb across her lower lip. "Are you bored of me already?"

"No. It's just that I spent the last decade thinking sex was a boring thing meant to be endured and you're..." She lost her train of thought, her eyes following his forearm as he rested it against the tree trunk above her head. The way they slid down the rest of his arm, visibly tracking the bump of his bicep through the gray cotton of his long-sleeved shirt, made him dizzy. When she caught his eyes again, her pupils had dilated noticeably. "You're exciting."

Then Annie took his thumb into her mouth and sucked.

A shudder started in his shoulders and rolled through his body, pooling in his groin.

And just when he thought he couldn't get any harder, she turned the tables on him, taking advantage of his dazed state and spinning them so he was the one pinned against the tree. Then she sank into a crouch and curled her fingers into the elastic waistband of his shorts, looking up at him for permission.

"What are you doing?" he asked, even as his hand wrapped around the base of her ponytail. Why had he said that? It was obvious what she was going to do. But they hadn't done oral yet. It had never come up. What the hell had he done to deserve this?

"Tell me what you want," she said, echoing the phrase he had used with her.

What were words? How the fuck was he supposed to string a coherent sentence together when her fingers were touching his skin mere inches from his dick?

"Please."

"Please what?" A coy grin that made him lightheaded flashed across her lips.

"Please suck my dick."

"Good boy."

And then she pulled down his shorts.

STILL PERFECT.

Annie sighed as she wrapped a hand around the shaft, giving it an exploratory pump. There had been a brief moment where she thought she had fucked everything up by trying to take charge. That despite all the times Jordy told her to tell him what she wanted he wouldn't like it if she actually tried to do it.

She looked up to see him watching her with a potent mixture of lust, anticipation, and awe. Like he couldn't believe this was happening to him. Which was hilarious, because this couldn't be his first public blowjob. Annie doubted it was even his first woodland blowjob. How many birds and squirrels had watched him blow a load?

Probably a lot.

Annie felt bad. So far all of their sexual encounters had been Jordy heaping loads of pleasure onto her, and her not doing a lot more than spreading her legs and begging him to fuck her. It was lopsided and unfair. Not that she thought he was having a bad time, but he deserved more than what she had given him so far.

Plus, his penis really was perfect.

A bead of precum formed on the tip, and she licked it off, letting the salt bloom on her tongue. Jordy groaned, and his head fell back against the tree trunk.

"Fuck," he groaned, goosebumps appearing on his thighs.

Annie took the head in her mouth and swirled her tongue around the crown. A desperate whimper was her reward.

There was something incredibly intoxicating about having *this* man come undone while she slid her mouth up and down his shaft. It was a fun experiment to see what made him moan—any tongue action—and what made him shiver—humming as best she could when he was far back in her mouth. One of his hands was tightly wrapped around the base of her ponytail, but he wasn't guiding her. It was just there because he needed something to hold onto. He bit the back of his other hand to keep himself quiet. Or at least quieter.

"A-annie," he gasped, his voice catching on the first vowel sound. "I...I'm...oh Jesus..."

Was it a little evil to make him lose his train of thought by sucking hard enough to hollow her cheeks? Yes. But it was fun.

"If you keep doing that I'm going to—"

It was her fault for tempting fate. Another swirl of her tongue, and his cock began to pulse in her mouth. And while the look of ecstasy on his face was great, Annie remembered something very important: while precum was fine, she never let anyone finish in her mouth because she hated how it tasted.

And now her mouth was full.

"Oh fuck," she said, but it came out all rounded vowels. Was she supposed to swallow? Would he be offended if she spit? Did all the other girls swallow and that's what he was expecting and if she didn't swallow all the fantastic partnered orgasms would end because he was going to find a girl that *would* swallow?

"Holy fuck, that was—Annie, are you okay?"

"I don't know what to do with it." All rounded vowels again.

"You either spit or swallow." Jordy pulled up his shorts, carefully tucking his softening cock back inside. "Or hold it in your mouth forever, I guess?"

Annie groaned, her distress multiplying rapidly with every passing second. She looked around, like the answer was hidden behind a bush or the next tree trunk over.

"Spit."

It was a command, and Annie gratefully spit it all out on the forest floor. The taste remained, not lingering but overwhelming. Jordy crouched next to her, rooting around in his backpack for his water bottle and handing it to her. She took a big mouthful, swished it around, and spit again.

"Sorry. It's not you, it's—"

"Hate the taste?" A lazy, satisfied grin played at the corner of Jordy's mouth. "You didn't have to take it in the mouth."

"I know. It surprised me."

"I tried to warn you."

"Call me Icarus." When he frowned, Annie clarified. "I got cocky."

"Ah." Jordy took back his water bottle and took a deep drink. "So I'm exciting, huh?"

"Tip-top of the rollercoaster." She held her hand out for his water bottle. "And very sweet. Who knew watching you listen to lectures about the local fauna from a retired science teacher would make me horny?"

"That's what does it for you? All my moves, and I only needed to let Bernie tell me about hairy woodpeckers?"

Warmth spread through her body, radiating from her chest and diffusing into sparkling happiness. "You remembered the name of the bird?"

"Well, yeah. It kind of sounds like something you'd call your—"

Annie laughed so loudly a few birds left the branches they had been sitting on and flew away. Of course Jordy remembered hairy woodpeckers because it sounded like a euphemism for a penis.

"Wait until I tell you about the tits and boobies."

"Annie!"

"Annie!"

"Annie, where'd you go?"

Shouts filtered through the trees from the trail. With a grunt, Jordy stood, and held out his hand to help her up. "Should I be offended that they're only looking for you and not me?"

"Who else would settle their birding arguments?"

"I could do that." Jordy shouldered his backpack.

Annie pulled out her hair tie to fix her ponytail. "So you can tell the difference between an iron-billed wooflespoof and a least vermilion flycatcher?"

"No, but I could learn."

"Really? Because the least vermilion flycatcher is extinct, and the iron-billed wooflespoof doesn't exist."

Jordy rolled his eyes, then caught the back of her neck, drawing her in for a kiss. She tried to remind him that her mouth still tasted like his cum, but his lips were on hers too fast, and his tongue swiped over hers without a care. Annie moaned.

The problem with Jordy was that she went from reasonable woman to wanton in 0.6 seconds. His hand cupped her breast, and he dragged his thumb across her nipple. The sensation was muffled by her sweatshirt and sports bra, but it lit her up and she pressed against him. Her self-control never stood a chance.

"*Annie!*"

Birds threw themselves out of the trees to escape the sound.

"They're going to be calling the Forest Service if we don't head back," Jordy mumbled against her lips, sneaking in a few more kisses.

"You're a terrible, awful, no-good tease, Jordy Taylor," Annie panted.

"Payback for walking in front of me in these pants," he told her, running two appreciative hands over her ass.

"We're coming back!" Annie yelled toward the trail, shaking her head at Jordy, unable to keep a smile off her face.

"What were you doing off the trail, Dr. Price?" Bernie asked when they rejoined the group on the trail.

"I thought I saw something."

"Oh?" The entire group craned their necks in unison, like a group of elderly flamingos. "What was it?"

And before she could answer, Jordy did.

"An iron-billed wooflespoof."

NINE

MONDAYS WERE for Wine and Whining.

It was Annie's favorite Crane Cove tradition. Every Monday night, Eloise got together with Sybil and Connor to drink wine and whine about the start of the week. And there were snacks.

Annie had tucked herself into a corner of Sybil's big, blue velvet couch, a glass of red in one hand, and a plate of strawberry rhubarb pie on her lap. Connor was sitting on the floor in front of the coffee table, a stack of papers to be graded in front of him, scrutinizing the crust on the pie.

"I wasn't sure about the hydration after I rolled it out," he said, poking at the bottom layer with his fork. "It's kind of tough."

"Shut up. It tastes great." Sybil poked him in the side with her foot, then drew her leg back up under her. She was sitting cross-legged in her wingback armchair, the sleeves of her large red cardigan pushed up to her elbows, her red hair thrown haphazardly into a toppling bun, and Annie thought she looked tired. But that could be because Sybil got to work at six a.m.

every day and they were treading dangerously close to her bedtime.

"You're the only one that notices," Eloise reassured him, drinking her red wine through a straw on the other end of the couch. The infamous wedding binder occupied the space between Annie and Eloise, brought on the off chance there was a wedding planning emergency.

"Why are you doing that?" Sybil asked, pointedly looking at Eloise's glass.

"My mom called today and reminded me that red wine stains teeth. She's worried about my photos."

"Sandra strikes again," Annie said under her breath.

"I think you should get those fake teeth where most of them have fallen out and take a special set of photos with those in," Sybil suggested, "then get them printed on mugs and give them to her for Christmas."

"The worst possible use of resources." Connor shook his head at her. "Who raised you?"

A tense, pointed look passed between them before Sybil answered, "Wolves. And then your mother came in and batted clean-up."

"And what a horrible job she did."

The look that passed between them this time was warm, almost familial affection. The first time Annie had met Sybil and Connor at a Wine and Whining, she had thought there was something going on there because of the ease of their relationship. Eloise had assured her that they were just friends. Annie had watched them closely for signs of a blossoming romance, but there was never anything there. There were no surreptitious looks or lingering touches. They laughed a normal amount at each other's jokes. And they never looked around a room to check on where the other person was.

"How's job hunting going?" Eloise asked Annie.

"The last time you looked for a job, did you want to take a long walk off a short cliff?"

"The last time I looked for a job, I was drunk." Eloise toasted Annie with her wine glass. The last job Eloise had applied for was to be the manager at the Crane Hotel. It had worked out incredibly well for her since she had eventually gotten a business and a fiancé out of the deal.

Annie hated job hunting. Ornithology was incredibly competitive. What was impressive to her friends and family was not necessarily impressive to departments and hiring committees around the country. It had been months, but she was still kicking herself for giving up a research trip opportunity to Peru with a well-known ornithologist who was friends with her doctoral advisor. Jake had discouraged her from taking it because he didn't know where his residency would be, and did she really want to leave for an entire summer when they might be in the middle of moving? After they broke up, she called to see if she could still go, but the position had been filled.

"Maybe that's what I need to do. Get good and drunk and start sending my resume to random open positions. Pass the bottle, Sybil." Annie held out her hand.

Sybil picked up the bottle and brought it to her chest. "How are you getting home if I let you get drunk?"

"Jordy will come get me."

All the sound and a majority of the air left the room. The small hairs on the back of Annie's neck stood up. Sybil stared at her like she knew that Annie's version of a nightcap all weekend had been Jordy's dick.

Without a word of explanation, Sybil put the wine bottle back on the end table, then got up and left the room.

"I thought Jordy and Graham were hanging out at the brewery?" Eloise frowned. "How do you know he's not saying the same thing to the twins right now while he gets drunk?"

"Because," Annie said, becoming very interested in the contents of her wine glass, "he told me he would come get me if I needed him to. He even put his number in my phone."

Connor chuckled. "That smooth motherfucker."

"What's smooth about him giving me his number to be my taxicab?"

"This feels like revealing a magician's secret." Connor set down his red pen. "You have his number so it feels like you're in control, but he's positioned himself as a good guy no matter how you use it. If it's 'hey, thanks for giving me your number but I made it back safely,' he's a good guy. If he has to pick your drunk ass up off Sybil's couch, he's a good guy."

"Or he's just a good guy being nice to a friend?" Annie suggested. "Not everyone has an angle."

"He is a good guy and a good friend," Eloise agreed, then added, "and an unrepentant flirt."

"What's wrong with flirting?"

"I was trying to be nice about it." Eloise laughed. "Casanova would ask Jordy for pointers."

Annie's cheeks burned. What would Eloise think of her if she knew that Annie was the one that had made the first move? Or that all Annie could think about was how to get Jordy naked next? Hell, he didn't even have to be naked. Pants down. That was it. And the more she got to know him, the worse it got. Because Jordy Taylor *was* a nice guy. Full stop. No qualifiers.

Sybil came back into the room, a full bottle of wine in one hand and a pair of long, sharp garden shears in the other hand. She handed Annie the bottle of wine, and then sat down in her chair, setting the shears casually on the end table.

"So, Connor, how's being in charge of prom committee going?"

Connor groaned.

. . .

"THE RSVPS ARE GETTING out of control," Graham told Jordy. They had claimed two stools at the end of the bar and were nursing their beers. "Three weeks out, and I thought it was safe to bring up the security issue. Now all these people that said no are changing their minds and Eloise doesn't want to offend anyone and Sandra—"

"Strikes again," Jordy finished for him, reaching for the popcorn between them. "What security issue?"

"You idiots." Graham shook his head. "I want our guests to sign NDAs before they come so that way if someone leaks the bridal party to the press and a helicopter shows up, I can legally nail their ass to the wall."

"Call me stupid, but I don't understand what happened with the RSVPs."

Graham sighed and combed his fingers through his hair. "I had to explain to Sandra why I wanted NDAs and she must have bragged that there were going to be *celebrities*"—the word dripped with sarcasm—"at the wedding."

"How did you make it over a year without your mother-in-law finding out who your friends are?"

Graham shrugged. "I just called you Peter, Sam, and Jordy. I don't brag about you to strangers."

Jordy chuckled. "So what are you doing about it?"

"I don't know. If Eloise wants me to be the bad guy, I'll be the bad guy. But it's her mom, and it's a weird relationship." Graham picked up his beer. "We should've fucking eloped."

In his pocket Jordy's phone buzzed several times. Cell service in Crane Cove was notoriously crappy, so it wasn't unusual for text messages to be delivered in batches minutes or even hours after they had been sent. One message was from a woman in LA that he'd hooked up with before. She was single again and wanted to know if he wanted to hang out. The next one was from Sam.

SAM I AM:

Fuck this shit. I give up.

It was nice to know he was trying to write again.
And finally, a series from Annie.

HEAD BIRD NERD:

I had wine.

I had more wine.

I made a list in my notes app of sex thongs I
want to try.

Things. Not thongs.

Pop quiz: How fast can you take your clothes
off? I want to see that peacock.

That's not what I wanted to say. Duck
autocorrect.

"I think I have to go pick up Annie."

SYBIL'S HOUSE looked different from what Jordy had
pictured. For one thing, there was not a single clap of thunder
with an accompanying bolt of lightning to warn visitors that the
owner was terrifying. Instead of a Gothic castle with gargoyles
and an alligator-infested moat, it was a quaint bungalow with a
gigantic tree in the yard. Unsuspecting kids came trick-or-
treating here because it looked so normal.
  He knocked cautiously on the door.
  "It's open!" called a voice from inside.
  It felt like a trap, but Jordy opened the door anyway.
  "Jordy!" Annie cried, beaming at him with the kind of

wattage that could light up a city. "Connor made pie. You should have some."

"Any chance we could take it to-go? It's past this old man's bedtime."

Jordy didn't want to stay any longer than he had to. Sybil was casually sitting in a wing back armchair with a pair of very sharp-looking garden shears on the end table next to her. His balls reflexively tried to retreat into his body.

"You can take the dish as long as I get it back," Connor said, packing a thick stack of papers into a backpack.

"This feels like a sneaky way to get me to wash your dishes." Annie pushed herself up from the couch. The funny thing was, she *looked* sober. If he hadn't spent the entire weekend with her listening to her talk, Jordy might not have noticed the slight slur in her words.

"Guilty as charged." Connor smiled at her, and Annie giggled. Directed at another man, the sound felt like a flag on a scoring play that took the ball ten yards behind the line of scrimmage. Jordy clenched his jaw, shoving his fists into his jacket pockets.

Jealousy wasn't a cute look.

Annie picked the half-full pie plate off the coffee table and brought it over to him.

"Strawberry rhubarb," she told him, dipping her finger into the filling that had fallen out when they were cutting slices. And because he lost his fucking mind whenever Annie looked up at him with those sparkling blue-green hazel eyes, he sucked her finger clean when she pressed it to his lips. For the span of time it took him to swirl his tongue around the tip of her index finger, it was only the two of them in the room. No one else existed when her cheeks and chest flushed pink.

The spell was broken by Eloise loudly slurping the remaining drops of her wine through a straw.

"We should get going," Annie said, unable to blink away the slightly dazed look she'd acquired.

They were almost down the front porch steps when Sybil caught up with them.

"You forgot your coat," she said to Annie, holding out her green raincoat. In her other hand, Sybil held her garden shears.

"Isn't it a little late for gardening?" Annie asked, looking up at the moon.

"Never know when you're going to need to do a little pruning," Sybil answered, looking straight at Jordy. He took a half step behind Annie.

"I'm going to get you a hummingbird feeder," Annie declared, and then launched into a hummingbird lecture on their way to the car.

"And rufous hummingbirds migrate farther than any other North American species. They winter in Mexico and fly back to Alaska every spring. Can you imagine?"

Jordy opened the passenger door for her and held the pie plate while she sat down. "I hope they get frequent flier miles."

They had officially left Crane Cove by the time Annie stopped talking about hummingbirds. The car fell into its first silence in over five minutes. Jordy searched his brain for something interesting to tell Annie, but came up empty.

Then she giggled.

"What's up, Doc?"

"Nothing," she said, but she raised and lowered her hands, and laughed again.

"Something is funny."

"Schrodinger."

The name sounded familiar. "The piano kid from Charlie Brown?"

"No, the cat guy."

"...That sounds kind of kinky."

Annie snorted, then snorted again before dissolving into another fit of giggles.

"You're thinking of Schroeder. Schrodinger was a scientist who said if you put a cat in a box and sealed it, the cat is both alive and dead because you don't know."

"Whoa. That's kind of fucked up."

"He didn't actually put a cat into a box."

"Still." Jordy shook his head. "What made you think of the cat guy?"

"Gravity," she answered, dropping her hand onto his thigh. "I feel heavy and light at the same time. Like I could float away, but my head is anchoring me to the ground."

"I think you're just drunk, sweetheart," Jordy told her, putting his hand over hers.

"What makes you think I'm drunk?"

"I got a seven-minute lecture on hummingbirds, and you told me about Schroeder's cat."

"Schrodinger," Annie corrected, and squeezed his inner thigh. "And I would've said that all sober."

"So you agree that you're drunk?"

"No, I'm not sober. There's a difference. Like squares and rectangles."

"All drunk people are not sober, but not all not-sober people are drunk?" Jordy guessed. After three days, he was starting to speak Annie.

"Exactly." Her hand tried to creep higher on his thigh, but he laced their fingers together instead. She pouted. "I want to touch you."

"I want you to touch me too, but you can't right now because you're not sober."

"But it's nothing we haven't done before," she reasoned. "And you're getting hard."

It was true. The proximity of her hand to his dick triggered a directional change in blood flow. All roads now led south. His body didn't care about the things his brain cared about; Annie's hand was close and she wanted to touch him. Bringing up even the vaguest mention of the things they'd done before didn't help either. They hadn't even gotten creative yet, and he was excited.

"I get hard around you a lot, but that doesn't change that you're not sober and I'm very sober," he reminded her, using her own phrase against her. "No hands under clothes when you're under the influence."

"But if I take my clothes off, your hands aren't under my clothes."

Jordy snorted and turned down the lighthouse driveway. "I bet you were a really fun kid."

"I was obnoxious." She squeezed his thigh as he parked the car. "Can we at least make out? I missed you tonight."

How the fuck was he supposed to say no to that?

TEN

ANNIE WOKE up face down in a pillow, starfished in the middle of her bed wearing a T-shirt that did not belong to her. In the corner of her room the space heater whirred, keeping the small space comfortably toasty. She knew she hadn't been in the right headspace the night before to turn it on, which meant Jordy had after he had tucked her into bed and promised to fuck her silly in the morning if she was still horny.

She was definitely still horny.

Annie rolled onto her back, stretching her arms above head and arching her back. The scrape of cotton over her nipples made her shiver. Everything was sensitive. It was Jordy's fault. They'd made out on the couch, and true to his word, he had kept his hands over her clothes. Didn't mean he hadn't worked her into an unsatisfied mess. Riding his thigh hadn't helped, either.

She needed to change her underwear.

There was a growing pile of dirty clothes next to her suitcase. Claiming she was out of pajamas was how she had finagled the shirt from Jordy. It smelled like clean cotton instead of him, which was a disappointment. Drunk horny Annie had wanted to be wrapped up in his scent. Sober horny Annie wanted that too.

Sober Annie could also admit that Jordy had been right to hold a firm line with her the night before. She would have suggested and agreed to things that were a little embarrassing in the bright morning light. Annie froze with her clean underwear halfway up her legs. She *had* suggested things that were a little embarrassing. Anything to get him to fuck her. His commitment to her safety and comfort was both endearing and disappointing.

She dug through her pile of dirty clothes for her duck socks. Jordy loved her duck socks.

Outside of her room, the little house was cold. Goosebumps sprang up on her bare legs and her nipples had hardened into chilly points the moment she opened her bedroom door. Jordy was sitting at the small dining table, his back to her, watching a football game with no sound on his laptop while he ate breakfast from a bowl. The hood of his black sweatshirt was up, and she resolved to find a second space heater so he wouldn't be so cold at night.

Oatmeal, brown sugar, blueberries, and a drizzle of honey. That's what the great Jordy Taylor ate for breakfast. When they had gone to the grocery store, he had admitted that he didn't know how to make anything he couldn't toss in the microwave. In Los Angeles, he had a private chef that came to his house twice a week to meal-prep for him. Then he had juggled eggs in the dairy aisle to make her laugh.

Annie tugged off his hood, and he jumped. Of course he had his headphones on so he wouldn't wake her up. If Eloise, Sybil, and Connor knew this side of Jordy, the guy that tucked her into bed when she had too much wine and moved quietly in the mornings to not wake her up, they wouldn't think he had so many ulterior motives with her.

Well, maybe he did, but they were nothing compared to her ulterior motives with him.

"Good morning," she said, stepping over his legs and straddling him. Jordy pushed back marginally to give her more space, his eyes sliding down her body as he hung his headphones around his neck. Between them, Annie felt him pulsing to life through the thin cotton of her underwear and the thick cotton of his gray sweatpants.

"Morning," he answered, cupping and squeezing her ass. He had done the same thing when they made out, and it made her wet. "How are you feeling?"

"Horny." Annie rolled her hips to emphasize her point. Jordy's eyelids fluttered closed as he moaned.

"You're always horny." He caught her mouth in a deep, hungry kiss. He tasted sweet from his breakfast, and when he pulled away, the mix of blueberries and honey lingered on her tongue.

"Hop up on the table," he instructed, releasing her ass to push aside his bowl and laptop.

Annie did as she was told, shivering once she lost the warmth of his body. The table was cold under her ass, too. Jordy looked her over again, his eyes pausing on her breasts for a long time.

"I can't decide if I want you to keep the shirt on or not," he finally said, grasping her ankles and putting her feet on his strong thighs for support. "Because you've got great tits, but making you scream while you wear my clothes is hot as fuck."

Annie clenched around nothing. How did he do this to her? Because when he ran his hands up her legs and pushed her thighs apart, she felt powerful. This man who had no problem finding someone to fuck wanted to fuck *her*. The underwear that had been clean five minutes ago definitely needed to be laundered now.

Jordy pushed up the hem of his T-shirt, placing open-mouthed kisses and teasing scrapes of his teeth over her belly, working his way lower each time. His fingers hooked the elastic waistband of her underwear and started to ease them down her hips.

"What are you doing?" Annie asked breathlessly when he kissed the skin right above her pubic hair.

"Having a balanced breakfast. Lift your ass up for me."

There wasn't enough air in the room and her chest had somehow become too small for her heart to beat properly. She tried to close her legs, but his arms were in the way.

"You don't have to do that," she said quickly.

Jordy's forehead creased into a frown. "Do you not want me to?"

Annie hesitated. "I don't want you to do anything you don't want to do. I don't want you to feel...obligated."

He stared at her.

The words spilled out of her in a long stream, with hardly enough space between them to breathe. "Because I know guys don't really like to do that, that it's just a means to an end and you can have the end without the means. I'm more than ready to go. You can check."

His thumb slipped into the crotch of her underwear, gliding through her wetness easily before rubbing her clit in slow, torturous circles. She was already aching for him. She'd been aching for him all night.

"Jordy..."

"Do you not want me to go down on you because you don't want me to or because you think I don't want to?"

Her cheeks burned. "Jake didn't like it. He said guys only did it so women would do stuff to them."

Jordy took a deep, calming breath. "Annie—wait, what is that short for?"

"Roxanne."

His eyes widened, sending his eyebrows upward. "Holy shit."

Annie wanted to squirm. And not just because he had an incredible ability to hold a conversation and edge her at the same time. "What's that supposed to mean?"

"That Roxanne is a fucking sexy name and it's perfect for you."

Warmth spread through her body. "Why did you want to know?"

"Because this is serious, and serious means full names." Jordy kissed her knee. "Roxanne, your ex is a jackass. And an idiot—"

"He's a doctor."

"Fine. Dr. Jackass doesn't speak for all men. He sure as shit doesn't speak for me. I want to eat you out right here, right now. If you don't want me to, that's fine and I won't. But if you're saying no because you got it twisted that I don't want to and I'm somehow making a sacrifice, that's bullshit."

"You never have before," Annie said quietly.

"Because every time we get frisky, you go diving for my dick. You're a cock-seeking missile, Annie."

Her laughter melted into a moan as he pressed on her clit. "Jordy..."

"I want to go down on you. I want to taste you all day long. I want you to forget everything that asshole ever told you. Tell me what you want, Roxanne."

Annie sank her teeth into her bottom lip. This should be easy. All she had to do was ask, and Jordy would do the rest. She *wanted* him to do it. As wound up as she was, it would probably take mere minutes until she went off like a bottle rocket. But Jake's voice still whispered in the back of her mind that no guy actually liked doing this, that it was a boring chore.

"I want to make sure you have a good time too."

"I'm about to have the time of my life, sweetheart," Jordy said with an easy grin. "Tell me what you want me to do to you, and I'll do it."

Be bold. Be brave. Jordy liked it when she asserted herself.

"I want you to eat my pussy."

"That's my girl." Jordy tugged her underwear off, and they disappeared into his pocket. "Just relax. I've got it from here."

Annie let her legs fall open again and waited for Jordy to dive in. Instead, he kissed the bend of her knee, then the freckle on her inner thigh, acquainting himself with her body like it was the first time he had ever seen it. She was exposed, and he was taking his fucking time.

Why was she surprised?

"Jordy," she whined, threading her fingers through his hair. "I thought you were going to eat me."

"This is part of the experience. Don't you love the antic"— he looked up at her from under his lashes, holding the silence until she thought she would burst—"ipation?"

"Is Jordy short for something?"

"Jordan."

"Jordan, stop fucking around."

He chuckled, lowering his face to where she was open and soaked because of him. "Bossy," he said, blowing gently on her sensitive clit. Pleasure shot through her body, and she shivered. She couldn't see it, but Annie could feel the smug smirk of self-satisfaction on his face. Then he flicked his tongue over her clit, and she gasped.

"More." It was half plea, half demand, and one hundred percent effective. Jordy got to work in earnest, licking and sucking, his happy moans and sighs of blissful contentment doing more for her arousal than anything he was doing with his mouth.

"So fucking good," he murmured against her skin, then dipped his tongue inside of her again. "Fuck, I love that."

Her orgasm built slowly because she didn't know how to direct him. It had been almost ten years since anyone had been face-first between her thighs, and certain things that felt good with fingers didn't feel as good with a tongue. They still felt good, just not the same. But Jordy was persistent and patient and talented. Not that she had a lot to compare to, but it didn't take a PhD in art history to appreciate the paintings in the Met or the Louvre. When it finally came, it rolled through her body like a locomotive: big, powerful, and rattling her to her core. He kept going, even as her knees squeezed the sides of his head, until her vocal praise was unintelligible.

Annie shivered, her muscles twitching as Jordy gave a few gentle, parting licks. She could have floated away on a gentle breeze like a downy feather.

"I can't take another one of those," she told him, her voice as wispy as a puff of smoke. "I'll die."

Jordy kissed her hip, then rested his head on her thigh. He looked as content as she felt.

"So I did good?"

"Your retirement plan should be teaching classes in cunnilingus."

"Are you saying I've got a PhD in pussy?"

"Graduated with honors." Annie combed her fingers through his hair, trying to untangle some of the knots she had made. "If you give me twenty minutes to become a functioning human, I'll repay the favor."

"This was just about you, sweetheart." Jordy kissed her stomach then pushed back from the table. "I'm also very late for an interview."

Annie pushed herself up from her reclined position. "An interview?"

"Yeah. I've got…" Jordy trailed off, looking up at the ceiling while he counted things off on his fingers. "Three interviews, a brand call, a conference call with our team trainers because I'm old and they're worried I'll hurt myself unsupervised, and then I'm doing video calls for some children's hospitals. Do you want some oatmeal before I go?"

"But I thought—" Annie cut herself off. Saying that Jordy just played football was like saying all she did was look at birds. It was an ignorant oversimplification. She had vaguely wondered where he had gone the day before, but she had assumed he had been goofing off. It wasn't until he listed it all out that she realized how much he *did* in a day. Any appetite she had faded away. "I made you late?"

"I made myself late." He went to the sink to wash his hands. "Don't worry about it. Some former teammates have a little internet sports show. I do a spot once a week. They'll understand why I'm late."

"You're going to tell the world wide web you're late because you were eating me out?"

"No." Jordy dried his hands on the dish towel draped over the oven handle. "I'm going to tell them that breakfast is the most important meal of the day, and I was really enjoying mine."

He grabbed a bowl from the cabinet, then an instant oatmeal packet from the box he'd left out. Instead of measuring the water with the measuring cup she knew was in the kitchen, he filled the empty packet with water before dumping it into the bowl with the oats. While the microwave ran, Jordy packed up his laptop, then disappeared into his room, reappearing before the beep with a change of clothes in his hands. Those got stuffed into his backpack with his laptop. He fixed her oatmeal the way he ate his, and kissed the top of her head when he put the bowl on the table. The whole thing was over and he was out the door in three minutes.

Annie settled into the chair Jordy had been sitting in, and scooped a bite onto her spoon. It was halfway to her mouth when she remembered something very important.

Her underwear was still in his pocket.

ELEVEN

"Don't say burning to him, it brings up bad memories."

Jordy had to laugh. Darnell and Quinton loved to tease him about his sexual history. The former linemen were still close friends of his, even though they had been out of the league for seven and ten years respectively. Darnell Baggs had been his first left tackle in pro ball, and Jordy would have walked through fire for him. In addition to protecting his ass on the field, the Stanford grad had taken a young, stupid Jordy under his wing and taught him all about finance. Because of Darnell, Jordy had a well-managed portfolio and a healthy bank account. And Quinton Garnett had taught him about the birds and the bees, metaphorically.

"It was one time!" Jordy shouted, pretending to be embarrassed.

They all laughed. This was why Darnell and Quinton had one of the top internet sports talk shows. Their easy banter with each other and their guests kept viewers coming back for more.

"But seriously, man," Darnell said, "the question we got the most this week in emails was fans wanting to know what's up with your contract. Are you staying? Are you going? Are you retiring?"

Jordy plastered his best press conference smile on his face, but it didn't reach his eyes on his screen. He rolled his shoulders back, trying to appear loose and relaxed, even as his legs bounced. "Man, I wish I had a good answer for that. Uh, my agent is working hard with the front office to try and make something happen to keep me in LA, but these things are complicated, ya know?"

Quinton raised an eyebrow a fraction of a centimeter, but it was worse than if he had outright called Jordy out for his PR answer. "What would it take for you to stay?"

"A contract?" Jordy joked, but it was the truth.

"Are you open to a trade? In the past you've said that you wanted to retire with the Phantoms. If they don't extend you, if they let you lapse into free agency, or if they want to trade you, would you opt to retire and leave some of that money sitting on the table? Or would you go play somewhere else?"

Fuck Quinton and his fucking journalism degree.

It wasn't like Jordy hadn't known this question was coming. It was in every interview prep email he had received since February. It had been the topic of every conference call he'd had with Priya and Yvonne, his public relations representative. So why was he weighing giving a variation of the canned response they had rehearsed or speaking the truth?

"I would love to retire with the Phantoms. My heart is in LA with our fans, but there are a lot of moving pieces right now. I feel like I've got a lot of miles left in these tires so nothing is off the table at the moment."

From the corner of his eye, Jordy saw that Graham had stepped into the room. The hotel had excellent Wi-Fi, and he'd offered Jordy a small, unused conference room to use as a workspace. It was a good thing too, because if he'd tried to work at the lighthouse he'd probably have spent every day balls-deep in Annie trying to discover all the ways to make her moan.

"What *is* your retirement plan?" Darnell asked, willing to let the non-answer slide.

"I don't know. If I told you any of the suggestions I've been given lately, I'd end up getting fined."

Darnell laughed. "You can afford it."

"Yeah, but my mom watches this stuff."

Quinton was not as willing to let him coast through the rest of the interview. "How are you feeling about the draft? You know there's a rumor floating around that you skipped town instead of going optional training because you think you're about to get replaced."

"I mean, I feel about the draft the same way I always feel about the draft. It happens at the end of April, and I have no control over it. Trying to guess how the draft is going to go has never worked out well for me."

The year Jordy had been drafted, he had been projected to go in the first half of the first round. The Phantoms didn't select him until the end of the second round. That chip on his shoulder, that burning desire to prove everyone wrong, had powered his career. He was the only quarterback from his draft class still playing.

"And are you in LA? Because that doesn't look like your living room," Darnell said, wiggling his eyebrows conspiratorially.

"It is not my living room, Sherlock. I'm out of town visiting friends. My buddy is getting married soon, so I'm trying to enjoy some time with him."

"Aw, that's cute."

Their conversation wandered back into safe territory where Jordy could talk without having to think too much about what he was saying. Then their producer, whose screen got edited out, made the gesture for them to wrap up Jordy's segment.

After he clicked out of the video call, Jordy stretched his arms above his head. "Am I still a charming asshole?" he asked Graham with a grin.

"I don't know how you do it." Graham shook his head. "I hated giving interviews."

"It's just talking." Jordy shrugged, and put his hands in his sweatshirt pocket. Soft cotton brushed his left hand, and his pulse jumped. Annie's underwear. He had forgotten they were in there. Would they fall out if he took his hand out of his pocket? Would it be weird if he left his hands in his pockets while he talked to Graham?

"It's not just talking. You're..." he waved a hand like he could conjure the words from thin air.

"A bullshit artist?"

"I think there's a little more strategy than that, but yeah." Graham chuckled, taking the seat kitty-corner to Jordy's at the conference table. "You need to teach Sam how you do that."

"I don't think Sam gives a shit anymore." Jordy rubbed the soft cotton of Annie's underwear between his fingers. "He needs a break."

"The only thing I regret about leaving LA is that most of the time I feel like I have no idea what's going on with you guys." He sighed wistfully, lacing his fingers together on top of his head. "Sometimes I miss having you assholes break into my house."

"We didn't break in," Jordy corrected. "We had the gate code." His fingers brushed something damp, and he deserved one of Peter's acting awards for keeping a straight face when he realized it was the crotch of the panties. He shifted in his chair, immensely grateful for the table between them because his dick had risen like a standing ovation. "I can break into your house here if it would make you feel better."

"It won't be hard. I've started to forget to lock the front door."

"Wow, you've really gone full small town."

"Oh yeah. I get pissed off when it takes me more than ten minutes to get to work during tourist season. If I'd gone the same distance in forty minutes in LA, I would've thought I'd missed the rapture."

"This is why I ride a motorcycle. Split the lane."

"I don't know how Priya has gotten the safety clause written out of every one of your contracts." Graham shook his head in disbelief. "How's your contract coming? Any movement since we last talked about it?"

"It's..." Jordy searched for the kind of safe answer that wouldn't make Graham worry. He balled Annie's underwear into a wad in his pocket and concentrated on not letting his legs bounce.

During a day when he would be spewing bullshit left and right, he wanted to tell someone the damn truth. That this was all terrifying and he was worried he wouldn't know who he was when he was done playing football. How he hated that what he wanted was out of his control. That he worried that he only mattered to people when he was in front of them and no one would care about him when he faded from view.

There wasn't a safe and truthful answer.

"Priya is starting to prep me for the worst-case scenarios." The admission tasted like burnt coffee in his mouth. He could swallow it down, but he hated it.

"Do you want to talk about it?"

"No because that makes it real, but yes because you're smarter than me and might have some sage advice."

"You're older than me," Graham reminded him.

"Yeah but no one ever remembers that," Jordy said with a false smile. He sighed, and carefully removed his hands from his pockets so Annie's underwear wouldn't fall out. Was this how Annie felt before she launched into one of her long rambly rants? Like there were too many words in her head and she'd explode if she didn't get them out? "I hate that none of this feels like my choice anymore. Retirement, trade, free agency... If I go, it's not because I want to. I always thought this would end on my terms."

"You think it's going to end?"

"I do." Jordy had never said that out loud before. He hadn't even allowed himself to think it in the kind of concrete way that could make it true. But he had felt it rumbling in the distance like an avalanche for a long while. "It's not like I didn't know this would happen in the next few years. I'll be thirty-eight when the season starts. It's...it's just that football is all I ever wanted to do. There was never a backup plan. I don't know who I am without football."

"You're Jordy Taylor," Graham answered simply.

He rolled his eyes. "Thank you. That was incredibly helpful."

"No, I mean your job doesn't define you." Graham leaned forward, resting his forearms on his thighs. "I know you're not going to believe me, but your whole life is about to start. You don't have to have it all figured out today."

"You had it all figured out when you moved on."

"No, I didn't. I didn't even know if Eloise still wanted me when I left my company. But I knew that my career had made me miserable, and that if I didn't make big changes I was going to lose the best thing I had ever known."

"I don't think I'm unhappy, though," Jordy countered. "I love my job. I'm not ready for it to end. There isn't something better waiting for me. You got Eloise. I might get the contents of my locker handed to me in a box."

And that was the worst of it. That he might not get to say goodbye to the game he loved. That he hadn't appreciated the last time he walked out of the tunnel, the last time he called a play, or the last snap he took. If he had known it was his last game, he would have savored every moment. The smell of the grass, the heat, the weight of his pads, the noise, the adrenaline and anxiety. He would have even enjoyed getting laid out on his ass.

Jordy took out his phone to check the time. There was a text from Annie.

HEAD BIRD NERD

SOS. You have my underwear in your pocket.

He pursed his lips together so he wouldn't smile.

"What is it?" Graham asked, and Jordy slipped his phone back into his pocket.

"Nothing. I have another interview in five minutes."

Graham stood. "Do you want to come over for dinner tonight?"

"I think Annie was planning on cooking." He had no idea if she was planning on cooking, but he very selfishly wanted Annie to himself.

"Still just friends?"

"Still just friends. We both know she's out of my league."

TWELVE

ANNIE HAD BEEN in Crane Cove for over a week, and every time she asked Eloise if there was something she could do to help with the wedding, her cousin told her to relax and enjoy her vacation. Except Annie wasn't relaxing. The only useful activity she had done all week was apply for jobs, and if she wrote one more cover letter, she was going to scream. The only time she relaxed was after Jordy delivered a stupefying orgasm.

The man was magic.

But she'd recognized the vacant, I'm-making-lists-with-subsections look on Eloise's face Thursday night at Cranberry Brothers, so this time Annie was not taking no for an answer. Even though it was a Sunday, Jordy had plans, so her plan was to badger Eloise.

"Are you sure it's not an imposition?"

Annie sighed as heavily and dramatically as she could.

"Eloise. I have nothing better to do. I can drive to Portland to pick up the menus and whatnot from the printer."

At least when Jordy asked her what she did that day, she could say something other than "I applied for jobs."

He had to think she was a loser.

"But you're supposed to be—"

Annie clapped her hand over Eloise's mouth. "If you say relaxing, I'm going to scream."

It was Eloise's turn to sigh. In a very juvenile move, she licked Annie's palm.

"Ew." Annie wiped her hand on her pants.

"Fine." Eloise wrote down a few names on one of her periwinkle sticky notes. The company had stopped producing her favorite color, so Graham special-ordered them for her. "If you want to run errands, you can run errands. Let me give you gas money."

Eloise reached under her desk for her purse. The small manager's office at the hotel didn't have a lot of extra space for storage. When they had renovated the Crane Hotel, Graham and Eloise had decided not to change the office for nostalgia reasons. Annie had a feeling those nostalgia reasons had happened on the desk.

"Shit. I forgot I used the last of my cash at the farmer's market. Graham's probably in the kitchen having his weekly screaming match with Amara." Eloise pushed back from her desk.

"Why is he having a screaming match with your chef?" Annie asked as she followed Eloise out of the office and across the lobby.

"I don't understand it. I think they both need to yell at someone or they'll explode. Vent their frustrations on someone that can take it without getting offended."

"That doesn't sound healthy."

Eloise waved a hand dismissively. "As long as they're not yelling at me, I don't care anymore."

"Did you figure out the RSVP thing?" Annie asked, it popping to the front of her mind at the mention of yelling.

"Yeah. I decided to let Graham be the bad guy—did I tell you about that?"

She searched her memory. "Actually, I think Jordy told me."

"Pillow talk?" Eloise teased, moving her eyebrows suggestively.

"No," Annie said with a laugh, "kitchen talk."

Every night except for Thursday, which was barbeque night at Cranberry Brothers, Annie had made Jordy dinner. The first night she had cut the recipe in half because it was just the two of them, but that had been a mistake. Jordy could *eat*. She had slid her half-eaten plate over to him because he had a forlorn Oliver Twist look on his face. He had finished it and then gone looking for snacks. After that, she made enough for a family of four and barely had enough leftovers for lunch the next day. She liked cooking for Jordy, though. He ate whatever she made without complaint and did the dishes.

"I've been thinking about it. I don't care if you fuck him, as long as you know that he won't stick around. I would hate it if you got hurt."

"I'm not going to get hurt," Annie assured her.

"If you do fuck him though, I want details. Everything I know is hearsay."

Since they were old enough to talk, Annie and Eloise had told each other everything. There had never been anything off-limits. It was a miracle she could still look Graham in the eye after the stories she'd heard. But Annie balked at telling her cousin about what she was doing with Jordy. She couldn't quite put her finger on why, but she wanted to protect him and what they had.

The two of them had fallen into a pattern. In the mornings, he went down on her. If she got up early enough, she could talk him into having sex. Not that it took a lot of convincing, but he had a schedule to keep. Meetings, interviews, workouts. Between eight a.m. and five p.m., she didn't see him. And Annie tried not to listen for the sound of his car, but she did take out her headphones at 4:45 p.m. The minute he walked in the door, she pounced on him. Sometimes he was still sweaty and his lips tasted like salt. She didn't care; she was happy to see him. Then they would fuck.

Annie hadn't gotten up the courage to talk to him about the list she'd made on her phone of the things she wanted to try. It wasn't that she thought Jordy would say no, but she was afraid that he would think she was boring. Handcuffs and blindfolds probably weren't interesting to him. At least if they stuck to the basics, she could pretend that she had the possibility of being creative.

A laugh Annie could have identified with her head underwater filtered through a closed door as they walked past. Her stomach got the top-of-the-rollercoaster butterflies, her face flushed, and when she heard the muffled sound of his voice, her pussy got wet so fast it throbbed.

She had a damn Pavlovian response to his voice.

"Is that Jordy?" Annie asked like she didn't know with scientific certainty it was, stopping a few feet away from the door. Eloise stopped walking, and looked from Annie to the door and back again.

"Yeah. I think that's the room Graham gave him to use for work stuff. I don't know what he does all day."

Annie bit her tongue so she wouldn't rattle off Jordy's schedule.

"I need to ask him if he's seen my binoculars. Meet me in the lobby after you break up the showdown at the OK Corral?"

"Sure. If you need any condoms, there's some in the top left drawer of my desk."

Annie filed that piece of information away for later, and

waited until Eloise turned a corner at the end of the hall before letting herself into the room.

Jordy was seated at the end of a small conference table with his laptop open, his headphones on, and a microphone situated in front of him. He glanced up, and his facial expression didn't change, which wasn't a bad thing because he had been smiling already. Under the table, he held up his index finger to let her know he'd be done in a minute.

"No, I appreciate you having me on today," he said. "It's always great talking with you guys...Yeah, you, too."

There was a six-second pause before Jordy shut his laptop, unplugged his microphone, and hung his headphones around his neck.

"What's up, Doc?" he asked, pushing his chair back from the table.

"I heard your voice," Annie said, needing no prompting beyond him patting his thighs to go straddle his lap, "and I wanted to say hi."

"Hi." Jordy tugged on the end of one of her French braids gently. "How's the job hunt going?"

"I think I'm going to become a cam girl instead." She looped her arms around his neck as he squeezed her ass with both hands. "I have an expert who told me I have excellent tits."

"You know how I know we've been spending too much time together? I don't know if you're talking about your rack or making a bird joke."

"A little of both." Annie wiggled just to see his eyes roll back in his head. "How was your interview?"

"Same as the rest of them. What are you up to today, since you've decided to change career paths?"

"I need to go buy a laptop with a better camera, lights, lingerie..." She felt his dick twitch under her. She grinned, brushing his hair away from his face. "I need to go to Portland to pick up some wedding stuff for Eloise."

Jordy groaned dramatically, his arms going limp and his head falling back. "You cannot get a guy's hopes up like that."

"I wouldn't know what to do anyway."

"I think," he began as he ran his hands up her thighs, his voice dropping to a pitch that made her hot all over, "that you would pretend that you wanted to put on a show for one person. That you wanted to test the limits of their self-control, to see how badly you could tease them before they snapped—"

"My powers of seduction are limited to throwing myself at you."

Jordy chuckled, his hands outlining the curves of her hips. "No complaints here. When are you going to Portland?"

"Now? I don't have anything else to do."

Annie felt his muscles tense under her hands, and a worried furrow formed between his eyes.

"What if," he began slowly, addressing her boobs instead of her, "you waited until tomorrow and we drove up together?"

"Did you need to go to Portland?" Annie asked, not objecting but curious.

"Um, yeah." Jordy cleared his throat. "Did you, maybe possibly, want to go to the zoo tomorrow? With me?"

Annie's heart lost its rhythm. Was this a—?

"And my nieces and nephews," he added. "My mom ratted out my location to my sisters, and they want a break from their kids."

Not a date.

She hated the stinging disappointment, like a sunburn for her feelings. This was why she had insisted they had rules. It was easy to forget that Jordy wasn't forever. He was three weeks of decadent bliss, and then he would move on and never think about her again.

She fixed him with a suspicious glare that had no weight behind it.

"Are you trying to pawn your babysitting duties off on me?"

"No. I want to score super-cool uncle points by bringing a scientist with me." He plucked at the hem of her shirt. "You don't have to go. You can drop me off and run errands. Or go today like you planned. Either way."

"You think bringing me is going to score you super-cool uncle points? You play professional football. I think you maxed out already."

Jordy snorted. "Who even cares about football when they can learn about penguins from an expert?" He frowned. "You do know about penguins, right?"

Annie laughed and kissed his worried wrinkle. "Yes, I know about penguins."

"So do you want to go?"

The way he looked at her was so vulnerable, like if she said no to this simple zoo trip it would break his heart, that all the disappointment she'd had at it not being a date faded into a wisp.

"Of course I want to go."

JORDY NEGLECTED to tell her how early they would be leaving. But it was hard to be mad at a man whose idea of a wakeup call was cunnilingus.

She thought she was having a wonderful dream, so when she woke up, she was disappointed for a second before Jordy's tongue swiped her clit. Apparently he had taken her at her word when she said he could have her whenever he wanted.

"It's time to get up," he murmured, his warm breath sending shivers zipping up and down her body.

"Five more minutes," she groaned.

"You want to go back to sleep?"

"No, five more minutes of this," she said, and patted his head.

She got five more minutes of unhurried worship before he made her get out of bed. The goal was to be there when the zoo opened to avoid the crowds, which meant leaving as the sun was peeking over the horizon.

Annie liked to think she was a good road trip buddy. She connected her phone to the Bluetooth in Jordy's rental car and turned on the road trip playlist she'd made for them. Then she fell asleep before "What's Love Got To Do With It" finished playing.

She woke up when Jordy slowed down getting off the freeway.

"What....aw, shit. I'm sorry." She reached for her warm-ish coffee, which was a lukewarm testament to her travel mug. Her mouth was dry, and her neck was stiff. "I didn't mean to fall asleep."

Jordy reached over and squeezed her thigh. "It's okay. You were sleepy."

"Who am I meeting again?" The plus side to falling asleep was that she hadn't had hours to work herself up into a nervous mess about meeting Jordy's family. That didn't mean her brain wasn't going to try and make up for lost time in the last three minutes.

"Nadine and Aimee are my sisters, and between the two of them, there's seven kids."

"Seven?" Annie's eyebrows shot up.

"Nadine has three, and Aimee has four."

Annie let out a low whistle. She was an only child.

The parking lot was a quarter full. Parents unloaded strollers and helped kids out of cars, then wrestled unruly toddlers into lightweight coats because the temperature had dipped again. She'd brought her raincoat, and she noticed that Jordy had dressed much more nondescript than he usually did. If he wasn't in a T-shirt, he loved a tropical print button-up, so seeing him in a subdued black windbreaker was unsettling.

Jordy parked across from a pair of minivans that were unloading, and Annie's stomach flipped. He got out immediately, but she couldn't seem to make her body move. Those were his sisters and nieces and nephews. It was easy to guess by the loud shrieks of "Uncle Jordy!" that penetrated the car. She watched him get swarmed from the side mirror, the younger kids colliding with each other as they jostled for hug space. A preteen girl with blonde hair the same shade as Jordy's watched from the side, arms folded across her chest. Whatever Jordy said to her made her roll her eyes.

Annie flipped down the visor and examined her reflection. Her hair was a mess from sleeping in the car and she should have worn mascara to look a little more pulled together. When she'd gotten dressed she hadn't been thinking about who she was meeting; she'd still been half asleep.

There wasn't a lot she could do now.

She pulled her hair out of its floppy bun and combed it through with her fingers. It didn't really help. This was how she looked. Why couldn't she be more put together all the time like Eloise? Eloise wouldn't have met Graham's family in the last of her clean clothes with no makeup on and car-nap hair.

"It doesn't matter how you look," she said to her reflection. "It doesn't matter what they think about you. You are not his girlfriend. You are his friend."

A friend that he fucked several times a day.

As a precaution, Annie checked her neck for hickeys.

No spots. She could do this.

The sound of the car door shutting made ten heads turn her

direction. The sound of one of Jordy's sisters backhanding his chest echoed through the parking lot.

"Owww." He rubbed the spot where she had hit him.

"Who is that?" his sister hissed in a stage whisper.

Cold anxiety flooded her body even as Annie felt her face start to burn. Jordy had asked her to come, but should she have said no? Was she intruding on a family moment?

"Is that your girlfriend?" one of the kids asked loudly.

If there had ever been a good time for a sinkhole to appear beneath her feet, this would have been it.

"That's my friend, Dr. Annie. She's a scientist," Jordy told his nephew who had asked if she was his girlfriend.

"Like a doctor that gives shots?" asked another one of the girls, her eyes growing wide with fear.

"Did you seriously bag a doctor?" Jordy's other sister asked.

"Nobody has been bagged," he said, his cheeks growing redder by the second. "And she's not a *doctor* doctor, Mimi."

Annie wished she'd stayed at the lighthouse. All she wanted at that very second was to curl up under her blankets and never come out. But she couldn't, so she slowly walked across the parking lot, hands in her pockets, with a smile pasted onto her face.

"I'm an ornithologist," she told Mimi, the one that was afraid of shots. "I have a doctorate, so I get to write doctor in front of my name. They don't give us prescription pads."

"You bagged someone with a *doctorate?*"

"No one has been bagged!"

The sister with short blonde hair put her hands on Annie's shoulders and looked her in the eyes. "Blink twice if you're being held against your will."

Annie blinked twice slowly.

"How did you meet?" asked his other sister, who was balancing a chubby baby on her hip.

"She tried to kill me with a knife."

His sisters exchanged a look.

"Yeah, that tracks."

"Sounds about right."

"Nadine." Jordy pointed to the one with short hair. "And Aimee." He pointed to the one with the baby. "They'll be leaving soon."

"We could stay," Nadine offered, and Aimee nodded rapidly.

"If you need help, we can cancel our massages."

"And deprive you of a morning off?" Jordy shook his head. "Never."

"But it's all seven kids," Nadine reasoned.

"Yeah, don't think I didn't notice that you asked me to come on a day they don't have school." Jordy picked up a cloth contraption from the back of one of the minivans and buckled it around his waist. He held out his hands for the baby.

"It was a snow makeup day. Forgot it was on the calendar," Nadine said with feigned innocence, then winked at Annie conspiratorially.

"Okay, so I packed two bottles for her. The formula is already measured. There's warm water in the thermos. Fill to the sharpie line and shake." Aimee picked up a large backpack. "There's also snacks and water bottles for the big kids."

"If you sugar them up, please run them down," Nadine told Annie. "And don't let the twelve-year-old boss you around."

Annie nodded. The click of a buckle caught her attention, and when she looked over at Jordy, her biological instincts almost knocked her over.

The cloth contraption she hadn't recognized immediately was a baby carrier, and Jordy had strapped the chubby little cherub to his chest. He kissed the top of her fuzzy head as she blew spit bubbles into his jacket and Annie's bones nearly liqui-fied from the heat that flooded her body.

Nobody should look that good holding a baby. Nobody. And she shouldn't listen to the evil, horny little voice in the back of her head whispering that she should throw away their condoms and beg him to come inside her so she could have his babies. Sure, she was on birth control, but that was a minor detail.

A small hand slipped into hers. Annie looked down. The little boy who had asked if she was Jordy's girlfriend was looking up at her with big blue eyes. The Taylor genetics were strong.

"Are you going to be my aunt?"

"Umm..."

Nadine snickered. "Tori is going to be so mad she missed this."

"I will pay for your massages if you leave right now and don't tell Tori," Jordy said, terror underscoring his tone.

"Okay, be good for Uncle Jordy and Aunt Annie," Aimee said, waving goodbye to the assembled kids. Nadine whispered something to the oldest kid, the preteen girl, who rolled her eyes, but nodded.

"We'll see you later. Byeee." Nadine climbed into the passenger side of Aimee's van.

"Uncle Jordy," said a little voice, "I have to go potty."

THIRTEEN

"AND WHICH ONE IS THAT ONE?" Ethan pointed at the duck pond again. Annie wasn't sure which duck he was pointing to because the ducks were moving and his finger was not.

"There's pictures, dummy," snapped Kaia, pointing to the sign by the railing. Kaia was twelve and Ethan was ten, and they had reached the ages where it was impossible for them to get along. Kaia was annoyed by everything her little brother did, and Ethan had the audacity to breathe. At least that was how Jordy had explained it to her.

"That's a northern shoveler," Annie answered, squeezing his hand. Ethan held her right hand, and Hugo, Aimee's four-year old boy that had declared his need for a bathroom before they left the parking lot, held her left. Nolan, Aimee's six-year-old who was very interested in her relationship with Jordy, was pouting because Uncle Jordy had made him rotate out with his little brother when they got to the waterfowl. "You can tell because his beak looks like a shovel."

"How do you know it's a boy?"

"Because of his feathers. The males have green feathers on

their heads and white-and-brown bodies," Annie explained, picking her words carefully to keep them age-appropriate. "And the females are just brown."

"That doesn't make any sense," complained Olive, one of the eight-year-old girls. There were two of them, and one belonged to Nadine and the other to Aimee, but Annie couldn't remember who went where. All she knew was that Olive and Ida reminded her of her and Eloise. "Shouldn't the girl have the pretty feathers?"

"Well, scientists think the most likely explanation for females having dull coloring is because it protects them from predators. If they blend in, they're less likely to get eaten. And the males have bright feathers because they want to impress the females."

"Why do they want to do that?" asked Ida.

"So they can have babies."

A sardonic smile spread across Kaia's face. "Uncle Jordy, is that why you wear such bright shirts?"

"Who wants to see cougars?" Jordy asked loudly, and Annie's small posse abandoned her, crashing through the door that kept the ducks in their enclosure. "Don't run! Kaia, go make sure they don't get eaten."

He waited until they were alone, except for Briar, the baby, who was using Jordy's jacket zipper as a chew toy, and sighed heavily. "I'm sorry. I know they're a lot."

"They're kids. They're curious. The world is big and new, and they want to know everything. I can relate." She smiled at him. "Do you have any questions about the ducks?"

"Yeah." Jordy checked over his shoulder to confirm they were alone. He leaned down, and for a breathless moment, Annie thought he was going to kiss her. Instead, he asked, "How do ducks fuck?"

"Jordan. Little ears." Annie cupped her hands over Briar's

ears. "I don't think your sister would be happy if her first word was 'fuck'."

"I can tell her she's saying 'duck'." Jordy grinned at her. "You avoiding the question, Doc?"

"I'll tell you on the way home. But do me a favor and promise me you'll never look up duck penises."

"Why?" They walked out of the ducks area and toward where the six kids were crowded around the glass of the cougar enclosure.

"Because it's an evolutionary arms race gone horribly wrong."

"Cats!" Hugo declared, pointing to a pair of cougars that were curled up in front of the glass, unbothered by the children.

"Uncle Jordy." Nolan raised his hand. "I have to go potty."

ANNIE DECIDED she was going to need extra-strength birth control when Briar fell asleep on Jordy's chest.

Despite saying he wanted to impress his nieces and nephews with a scientist—and she was trying her best to be impressive—Annie had assumed that the real reason Jordy wanted her along was to help with the kids. She had expected a helpless bachelor, overrun and unprepared. But by the time they reached the polar bears it was clear that her help was appreciated, but not needed.

"Polar bears are actually classified as marine mammals," Annie told Nolan, who had attached himself to her again, "because so much of their lives depend on the ocean. *Ursus maritimus*. In Latin, maritimus means 'of the sea'. So, bear of the sea."

"Wait." Nolan frowned. "The Little Dipper is called Ursa Minor, and the Big Dipper is Ursa Major."

"He's a space man," Jordy explained with a wink. Annie's insides flipped.

"Oh, you'd like my dad. He's an astrophysicist. Ursa Major and Ursa Minor mean Big Bear and Little Bear."

"So Ursa is bear?"

"Exactly." Annie beamed at Nolan, and a blush spread across his freckled cheeks. "Are you going to be a scientist when you grow up?"

"Maybe. Or a football player."

"Be a scientist. Less head injuries," Jordy told him, ruffling his hair before walking over to Kaia, who was texting.

"Are you having fun?" Annie asked Nolan.

"Yeah, but I wish we got to go to Disneyland. One time, Uncle Jordy took us all to Disneyland, and his friend Peter came. Peter can do *all* the voices. And we had a special guide that walked with us." He squeezed Annie's hand. "You're like our zoo guide. You know everything."

"It is hard to beat Disneyland," she agreed. "Who's cooler, me or Peter?"

He thought hard before saying, "It's a tie."

"Diplomatic. I'll take it."

"Why are polar bears white? Is it to blend in with the snow?"

"Polar bears aren't actually white. Their guard hairs are hollow and transparent, and their undercoat is also colorless. They look white because of how the light reflects. If you were to shave a polar bear, it would be black."

"What does transparent mean?"

"WHO ARE YOU TEXTING?" Jordy grinned as Kaia jumped, and fumbled her phone back into her pocket.

"Mom," she answered flatly.

"Oh yeah? What are you talking about?"

"You." Kaia nodded her head toward Annie, who had the attention of all the small kids but Hugo, who was walking up and down the big concrete steps. "And her. Mom and Aunt Aimee want allll the updates."

Jordy tried to play off the spike in adrenaline with a casual shrug. "What updates? We're friends."

"Tell that to your sisters so they'll stop texting me."

"I did. I told them to their faces."

"Well, their faces didn't believe your face."

"Is that why you're being so surly? Because your mom won't stop texting you?"

"I wanted to stay home, but Mom made me come with the little kids." Kaia rolled her eyes. She was going to strain a muscle if she kept doing that.

"You're twelve," Jordy reminded her.

"Almost thirteen!"

"Oh, I know." Jordy gave an exaggerated shudder and saw a crack of a smile.

There was a bitter sweetness to the kids growing up. His oldest sister Tori's kids were all in high school now. Dash, his oldest nephew, was as tall as he was, and Jordy didn't think he would ever get used to the fact that the newborn baby he'd once held could now look him in the eye. Kaia was at an awkward age. Last year at Disneyland she had been a wide-eyed kid excited to meet the princesses. In a span of months, she had outgrown many of her childhood favorites. And before he knew it, she would change again. It was all too fleeting.

"I don't want to be treated like a little kid anymore," she complained.

"I'll make you a deal." Jordy wrapped an arm around her shoulders. "You stop acting like a butthead, and I will put in a good word with your mom."

"Ugh. Deal."

"THAT'S AN AFRICAN RED-BILLED HORNBILL. Does it look familiar?"

Their group had found their way into the aviary after watching the elephants meander and making another stop so Olive and Ida could use the bathroom. Annie was crouched down next to Hugo, whose face was scrunched up in deep concentration. Nolan had a hand on her shoulder, but was paying more attention to Annie than the birds she was teaching him about. The boy hung on her every word, admiration and adoration shining on his face. Jordy understood the feeling.

"It's a bird?" Hugo guessed.

"Have you seen *The Lion King*?" A sly grin was forming on Annie's lips. Jordy wanted to taste it. It was hard enough to make it through a day without kissing her when he wasn't with her. Being near her and not able to touch her like he wanted was cruel and unusual torture.

"Uh-huh! Rawr!" Hugo raised his hands like they were claws.

Annie laughed, delighted. "Shhh. You'll scare the birds," she told him gently, hazel eyes sparkling. "Zazu is an African red-billed hornbill."

"That's Zazu?" he shrieked.

So much for volume control.

"Well, I don't know if his name is Zazu, but they might be related." She touched Hugo's neck. "The first two vertebrae—those are the bones in your spine—are fused, so stuck together, so he can hold up his big beak."

Jordy couldn't tell if he was horny or—he didn't know the word. He was always horny when Annie was around, and the way her ass looked in her leggings made him want to worship at the altar of her body. But the normal ache in his balls was mixed with an ache in his chest. Was it possible to be nostalgic for a moment that hadn't happened yet? Because watching her with his nieces and nephews made him wish that these were their kids, that she was teaching their children about polar bears, elephants, and birds. The way she patiently listened while Nolan told a long, winding, rambling story that would end up not having a point, or how she leaned into the hug Hugo gave her, made his heart feel too big for his chest.

"I'm so fucked," he mumbled.

"What did you say?" Ida asked, and he jumped. The two girls, closer than sisters and co-conspirators, had snuck up next to him.

"Flocked. Flocks. Flocks of birds." Jordy stumbled through the revision.

Olive and Ida didn't look convinced, but they had the smirks of kids who could be bribed into forgetting.

"We're hungry, Uncle Jordy," Ida said, and he could hear the scheme coming. "Can we get elephant ears?"

"DID YOU KNOW," Jordy said in a low voice near Annie's ear, "that a flock of flamingos is called a flamboyance?"

The six kids that could walk were glued to the railing watching the pink flamingos groom themselves. Briar was still conked out on his chest, her small mouth parted. Jordy knew an opportunity when he saw one.

Annie shivered, and their noses brushed when she turned her head to look at him. "Did you read that on the sign?"

"No. A sexy bird nerd told me that."

"Oh? What else did she tell you?"

"That hummingbirds build their nests with spiderwebs."

Jordy had been laboring under the impression that the best

thing was to make Annie laugh. He'd been wrong. It was watching a light pink blush spread across her cheeks as she melted.

"You were listening."

"Iron-billed wooflespoof," he said, and pressed a featherlight kiss to her lips before walking toward the kids. A drive-by kiss. Because if he let himself linger, he wouldn't stop lingering, and then Kaia would make his life hell by telling his sisters.

Jordy knew that he had nothing figured out post-football. When he told Graham there was no backup plan, he wasn't being dramatic. Before Annie, he couldn't conceive of a life without football. But as they had been watching the giraffes—or, more accurately, she had been watching the giraffes and he had been watching her—Jordy had been able to fathom that there was more to life than football. That there was a possibility he could be happy not spending six months of the year trying not to get knocked on his ass while he located a moving target and threw a ball at it.

The feeling of peace had wrapped around him like a warm blanket and he enjoyed it for the five seconds it lasted. Because when Annie smiled at him, he remembered that he had nothing figured out and nothing to offer her outside of sex. Her career was just starting, and his was waning. How was he supposed to look her in the eye—someone with all the potential in the world —and ask her to take a chance on him when he didn't know what kind of future he could offer her? Sure, he could provide financially, but could she be proud of him in front of her friends and colleagues?

Jordy still wanted to play football if he could, but getting his post-football life sorted was important too. The way he saw it, he had roughly two weeks to get his shit together in one way or another so he could ask Annie out on a date with the confidence of knowing where his life was headed.

"Who wants to ride the carousel?" he asked, knowing it was the only way to lure the kids up the big hill at the end of the African rainforest section.

The screaming chorus of "Me!" hurt his ears.

"WERE THEY HORRIBLE MONSTERS?" Aimee asked as Jordy handed off a cooing, smiling, freshly-changed-into-a-brand-new-outfit-because-she-had-blown-out-her-diaper Briar. He and Annie were trauma-bonded from changing her in the family bathroom. That much poop should not come out of a person so small and cute.

"Rotten. Every one of them."

"I see we're in new clothes. Did someone have a poopy?"

"I think Briar had an exorcism." Jordy held up his thumb and forefinger and squeezed the air between them. "She was *that* close to hitting her hair."

"How was Kaia?" Nadine asked as she counted heads to make sure Jordy hadn't lost anyone.

"She warmed up to the idea," Jordy answered. "Might have happened sooner if someone wasn't texting her the whole time."

His sisters had the nerve to act innocent.

"I needed updates." Nadine caught Ethan before he could poke Ida again. She didn't even look. Her hand shot out, grabbed him by the shoulder, and pulled him to her to be used as a human shield. "Moms worry."

"Uh-huh. Did you get any good dirt?"

Aimee grinned wide. "You looked like a cartoon character with big ol' heart eyes in every photo."

"What photos?"

Aimee dug her phone out of her pocket to show Jordy the group chat they had set up with Kaia. Sure enough, in between a lot of *Little Mermaid* gifs of the crab singing "Kiss The Girl," were a few candid photos. In almost every one, Annie was looking somewhere else, and Jordy was looking at her. Cartoon heart eyes was an accurate description.

"Send me that one," he requested, pointing to the one photo where they were smiling at each other, instead of him watching her like a lovesick puppy. Jordy wanted proof that, on some level, he could make her happy. Hell, he might print it and use it as motivation.

"Umm...I don't know how to use the car seat," Annie called from the other side of Aimee's minivan. Nolan had wanted Annie to buckle him, which was ludicrous because he was in a booster seat and could easily buckle himself, and that had made Hugo want Annie to buckle him too.

"I'll help her," Jordy told his sisters.

"Show off," Nadine stage-whispered behind his back.

Annie had gotten the buckles connected, but the straps were loose. Jordy reached around her and fished the harness tail out from under the adjustment button and pulled. Annie sagged against him.

"I have a PhD. This is embarrassing."

"It's in biology. This is engineering." The urge to hug her was overwhelming, so he put his hands in his pockets.

"Were you an engineering major?" Annie asked hopefully.

"God, no." Jordy shook his head. "Do I seem smart enough to be an engineer?"

"Yes," she answered matter-of-factly.

Jordy had a lot of self-deprecating jokes at the ready when it came to the topic of him and school, but he was wholly unprepared for Annie to disagree with him. There wasn't a good comeback to the unshakeable belief in her eyes.

"It wasn't engineering."

"What was it?"

"I want to see if you can guess, because no one ever gets it."

Annie narrowed her eyes. "I'm going to get it. I'm an incredible guesser."

He hit the close button on Hugo's side of the van and the door slid shut. "Is that how you got through your PhD?"

"Shhh. Don't tell anyone." She tapped her chin. "Kinesiology?"

"I can't even spell kinesiology." Jordy put a hand on her lower back and guided her to the back of the minivan.

"Thanks for watching the kids." Nadine wrapped her arms around him and hugged him tight. "Come visit more, okay? We live on the same coast now."

Despite growing up all over the Midwest, the Taylor kids had scattered to the coasts as adults. Slowly but surely, they all seemed to be migrating west. First Aimee, then Jordy, and Nadine had recently gotten a good job in the Portland area. Jordy gave it three years on the outside before his parents gave up tornado warnings and blizzards to be closer to the bulk of their grandchildren.

"Be careful what you wish for. I might be asking to live above your garage next week."

"You're going to be okay, champ." She squeezed him again, then stepped aside so Aimee could hug him.

"If you screw things up with the cute doctor, I'm going to be so mad at you," she whispered in his ear. "Drive safe."

FOURTEEN

"GEOLOGY?"

Jordy chuckled. Annie had been peppering in guesses about his major since they left the zoo. They would be having a normal conversation, or listening to one of her many playlists, and she would spout off a field of study, like surprising him would startle the answer out of him.

"No. But I have been told I've got rocks for brains."

She huffed.

"It's killing you, isn't it?"

"Yes! I've said everything but—you were a general studies major, weren't you?"

He grinned. "Yeah, that's the official major listed on my degree."

"What's the unofficial major? What did you generally study?"

"Besides girls, beer, and football?"

"You mean women's studies, fermentation science, and... sports management? I lost steam there." Annie popped a big spoonful of ice cream into her mouth, and then sucked on the spoon. It was a miracle she hadn't caused an accident yet, because she was too smart to not know what stuff like that did to him.

When they had stopped to pick up the paper products from the printer, Annie had spied an ice cream parlor down the street. He had been tasked with getting her ice cream for the drive back to Crane Cove while she ran a covert errand for Eloise. The mystery contents of the matte black shopping bag stuffed with pale pink tissue paper were driving him nuts.

"I'll tell you where I landed if you tell me what's in the bag."

"Mmm...you first. I need to make sure this is worth breaking the sacred bond between bride and bridesmaid."

Jordy set the cruise control as traffic eased around them. Between the drive to Portland, carrying Briar for hours, and then more time in the car running errands, his back and hips ached.

"I ended up taking a lot of classes in the art department. What's in the bag?"

"No, no, no. You don't get to vaguely say 'art department' and move on." Annie turned down the music. "Why art? What did you enjoy? Are you still doing it?"

"Then the bag?" Jordy held out his pinky and waited for Annie to hook hers with his before starting. "I ended up in the art department because of a girl, and stayed because I actually really liked it. Photography was my favorite, followed by life drawing."

Life drawing had proved to be incredibly useful for his sex life. Asking to take pictures of girls? Sometimes came off creepy. But if he casually mentioned he was taking drawing classes, suddenly everyone wanted to be the Rose to his Jack, and would he please draw them like one of his French girls?

"If you liked it, why weren't you an art major?" Annie asked again, scraping the bottom of her ice cream dish.

"The whole portfolio process freaked me out. And my football schedule made it hard to do some of the classes I would have needed to take." He left out how his coach used to ask him how his finger-painting classes were going and if macaroni necklace design was a prerequisite or capstone class.

"Do you still do it? Take photos and draw?"

"I, um..." Jordy tried to find a way to explain himself. "I don't really draw anymore. I doodle sometimes. As for the, uh, photos...um..."

"You've elevated dick pics to a fine art?" Annie ventured, and when he glanced at her, she was fighting off a grin.

"There have been some portraits."

"You should do penis pop art," she suggested. "Brightly colored dicks hanging in galleries around the world."

Jordy rolled his eyes. "So, what's in the bag, Doc?"

"Lingerie. Eloise ordered some things from a boutique and asked me to pick them up."

"Did you pick anything up for yourself?" He tried to keep the hopeful desperation out of his voice, but he was more than casually interested in her answer.

"Jordy, I was in the store for ten minutes."

The crash of disappointment was swift and severe. Annie didn't need lingerie to be sexy, but the visual would have kept him warm for the rest of his life.

"Can I ask you a question?" Annie asked, putting her empty ice cream cup on the dash. She twisted her thick brown hair into a bun that was going to escape her scrunchie in ten minutes or less.

"Shoot."

"Why were your sisters so surprised to see me? You've

brought friends to outings with your nieces and nephews before."

The heat from the blush spreading across his face was going to boil his brain. "You're prettier than Peter."

"We both know that isn't true. Peter isn't human. He's an angel that stumbled down from heaven and thought humans were fascinating so he stayed."

"Gee, you know how to make a guy feel great about himself."

"Well, I've never sucked Peter off in the woods, so..."

"If I'd known birding was so much fun, I would have gone years ago." He winked at her, soaking in the buzz he got from making her blush and cover face with her hands while she laughed. "Nah, I just don't bring women around. The last time my sisters saw me with a girl was when they all came home to embarrass me on prom night. I didn't think it would be such a big deal."

"Because I'm just a friend?"

"Because you're you." *Too damn good for me.*

Annie drew her knees up to her chest. "Can I ask you another question? This one is kind of personal."

"Shoot."

"Why *are* you still single? You're a nice, funny, attractive guy who's great with kids and has a job. I've been on the apps. You are the white whale." She adjusted her bun. "Do you *want* to be single?"

Jordy groaned. "My mom has been asking me that question every week since I turned thirty." He checked over his shoulder before changing lanes again. "It's easier for me to be single. No one gets hurt that way."

"What do you mean?"

"I have an incredibly demanding job. It's a lot of time and a lot of time away from home. It puts even the best relationships to the test." He sighed. He hated that he didn't have to think hard to come up with examples. "My first two years of professional ball, I sat behind a guy named Robin Carro. He was a fucking asshole, but a great quarterback. My second year, his marriage fell apart. Wrecked his game, ended his career."

"But that doesn't happen with everyone," Annie pointed out.

"No, but if I want to be fully focused on my career I can't have those kinds of distractions. If I want to stay late, I can stay late. No one at home to get mad at me for it."

"Don't you get lonely?"

"It's not hard to find sex, Annie."

"Says you." She pulled the sleeves of her sweatshirt over her hands. "I guess it makes me sad that you come home after a long, hard day and no one's there for you."

"Don't be sad for me. I'm fine."

Before she had tried to stab him in the shower, Jordy would have believed what he had said. He was fine. He wasn't lonely. He didn't need anyone but his friends in his life. But then Annie had destroyed a shower curtain and kneed him in the balls, and nine days later he was rethinking his entire future. The only time Jordy watched a clock was during a game, but he found himself obsessively checking his watch in the afternoon so that he could be at the lighthouse at five on the nose. He spent his whole day looking forward to the moment when Annie would jump into his arms, smother him with kisses, and after he fucked her good, comb her fingers through his hair and ask about his day.

The last bit was a clear violation of the "no more than ten minutes of post-coital cuddling" part of their arrangement. It always lasted longer than ten minutes. But Annie never pushed him away, and he decided if she wanted to break her own rules, he wasn't going to stop her.

"I'm scared to live on my own," Annie admitted, resting her cheek on her knees.

"You don't live by yourself?"

"No. Jake and I still live together."

Jordy's hands tightened around the steering wheel until his knuckles turned white. "Why? You broke up."

"It was easier. Moving is expensive, and our apartment is great. We were on opposite schedules for a bit so we didn't really see each other."

It was a good thing they were driving, because if Jordy could have used his phone, he would have done something impulsive and idiotic, like buying her apartment building so she wouldn't have to live with her ex.

A sickening thought settled over him like a cold winter fog.

"Would you get back together with him?"

The silence that followed was crushing, but not as painful as Annie's quiet "I don't know."

"How do you not know?"

"Because," she began, her voice getting quieter, "we were together for a long time. I thought I was going to marry him. And sometimes, when I have too much time to think, I wonder if I overreacted and blew it all up for no good reason."

"What happened?"

THAT WAS THE MILLION-DOLLAR QUESTION.

"I don't know when it ended for him. We both stopped trying, but it happened so slowly, I didn't notice."

For a long time, she and Jake had been ships passing in the night. At some point, they had dropped off each other's radars entirely. When he had night rotations, the only sign of life she had from him was missing leftovers from the fridge and dirty

Tupperware in the sink. The last year of their relationship, they were both so busy that Annie would look up from writing her dissertation because she realized she hadn't kissed Jake in two weeks.

"When did it end for you?" Jordy asked.

"Halloween. I had just defended my dissertation, and I wanted to celebrate. We were at a party with a bunch of his doctor friends and other people I didn't know. Jake kept forgetting that I didn't know anyone, so I had to introduce myself. One guy said 'I'm Dr. Anders Underhill,' and so I said 'I'm Dr. Annie Price.' Then he asked me what my specialty was, and Jake jumped in to explain that I wasn't a *doctor* doctor."

It had been the lowest moment of her life. Annie had understood that Jake couldn't take the day off to come watch her defend her dissertation, or that the flowers he brought home to celebrate had been left over from a patient's room—the "Get well soon, Grandma" card had given that away. But she thought he was proud of her. She thought he would be proposing soon, since she was done with school. She had turned down a prestigious summer research opportunity because they might be moving for his job.

"After the party, Jake told me not to introduce myself as Dr. Price because it was confusing for people, especially because he was a doctor. And that was basically what ended things between us."

It had taken her two more weeks to work up the courage and to find the time to actually break up with Jake. The words had eaten away at her like carrion-feeding birds on a carcass.

On the other side of the car, Jordy was silent. Annie was afraid to look at him. He was probably judging her for breaking up with her boyfriend of almost ten years because he'd had the audacity to clarify that she wasn't a *medical* doctor. But when she looked over, because the suspense was killing her, he was gripping the steering wheel so tight the veins on his forearms were sticking out.

He wasn't judging her. He was fuming.

"Annie. I need you to give me one good reason not to turn this car around, drive to Seattle, and punch him in the face."

"You'd be arrested for assault."

"I'm going to need a better reason."

"He's not worth it."

"But you are."

"Jordy, I'm not—"

"Don't. Start." He pulled down roughly on the brim of his baseball cap and growled. "You—Annie, you deserve...I don't know. The world isn't enough. The moon and the stars aren't enough. I don't know what you deserve, but it wasn't *that*."

Annie picked at a thread that was coming loose on the sleeve of her sweatshirt. "I don't think he meant to make me feel bad."

"I don't give a flying fuck what he meant to do. You. Did. Not. Overreact. You are a doctor—Oh, fuck." All the tension rushed out of his shoulders, and his head fell back against the headrest. "I did it too. This morning in the parking lot."

"Yeah, you did."

"Fuck," he whispered. A large, warm hand cupped her thigh. "Sweetheart, I—"

"I'm not mad at you. I'm not. It hurt for a second because of the memory attached, but I know you were trying to comfort Olive."

"I don't want to hurt you. Ever." Jordy's hand rooted around until it found hers buried in her sleeve, and then he laced their fingers together and brought her knuckles to his lips. "I'm sorry."

Annie didn't know what it said about the last few years of her life that a scrap of tenderness and an apology made her want to cry, but a painful lump formed in her throat and her eyes grew damp.

"I am still waiting on that one good reason. The next exit is in two miles." He pointed to the sign without letting go of her hand.

"Because if you break your hand on his face, you can't do that thing I like."

"Fine. But I'm doing that thing until you beg me to stop."

"Oh no," Annie deadpanned. "Not that. Anything but that."

The tension in the car dissipated as they shared a laugh. Her fingers remained laced with his, their joined hands resting on his thigh. There was no way to play it off like he had forgotten either, because his thumb was softly stroking the back of her hand, rubbing her like she was his lucky rabbit's foot.

She could be brave. Asking for what she wanted with Jordy always worked out for her.

"So, um, remember last week when I texted you during wine night," she began, shifting in her seat, "and I might have mentioned a list?"

A smirk quirked the corner of his mouth. "You're finally ready to talk about the list?"

"Yes. I am." Annie fumbled for her phone. The measly two percent battery left did not bode well for their driving jams. She swiped for her notes app. "These might seem really boring to you, but I've never had the chance to branch out."

Jordy frowned. "Weren't you in a long-term relationship?"

"Our sex life was..." Annie searched for a diplomatic phrasing. "Less than?"

"I can't decide if I want to punch him more or less now." He squeezed her hand. "What's on the list, sweetheart?"

"Please don't judge me for how boring this is." She filled her lungs with a deep, calming breath. "Handcuffs. Blindfold. Sex in a semi-public spot—"

"We already did that one," Jordy interrupted.

"I think you're thinking of someone else." Which was a little insulting, but understandable.

"You blew me in the woods with a group of senior citizens nearby."

"Oh, yeah. I forgot about that."

"You forgot?" Jordy was incredulous. "That was one of the best moments of my life, and you *forgot?*"

"I meant more like..." Annie trailed off as she felt a hot blush start in her chest and work its way up her neck and across her face. "Um...well, sometimes Graham and Eloise fuck in their office at the hotel."

"That is not the only spot they fuck in that hotel." Jordy changed lanes to get around a semi-truck. "What else is on the list?"

"Um, we pretend we don't know each other and you pick me up at a bar." Annie scanned the list again. Wine Drunk Annie had a hard time spelling. "Spanking? I hope I meant spanking because sparking sounds terrifying..."

"Nothing has to be scary. There's nothing wrong with trying something and deciding you don't like it. I did electro play one time, and it wasn't for me. You might hate being handcuffed."

"Actually," Annie began, stretching the word out on its vowels. Her heart rate had gone from fast to supersonic, and she swallowed in a vain attempt to get moisture back in her mouth. "I was thinking you'd be the one in handcuffs."

Silence.

Right at the moment Annie couldn't take the quiet anymore—which was 3.5 seconds after she'd divulged her fantasy—Jordy blinked rapidly and let out a long, exaggerated breath.

"We shouldn't have had this conversation on the road," he said. "I think I blacked out for a second there."

"You don't like it?"

"No, I like it too much." He untangled their hands, then pressed her palm against the rigid, pulsing length of his cock. Even through his pants he felt hot. Annie gently squeezed his erection, and Jordy made a sound that was somewhere between a whimper and a moan. "If you keep doing that, we're going to end up in the ditch."

"So, is that a yes to handcuffs?"

"You could ask me to dress like a chicken and cluck while I fuck you, and I'd probably say yes."

Annie laughed, her head falling onto his shoulder while her own shook.

"What does it say about our relationship that I'm hard as hell in your hand and you're laughing at me?" Jordy asked, and planted a kiss on top of her head.

Her laughter tapered off, and she sighed happily. "That you make me happy." She squeezed his cock again, and smiled when he shuddered.

"Were you talking to me or my dick?"

"Both?" Annie playfully nipped his shoulder and unlocked her phone to continue with the list. "Is the chicken thing on the table?"

"Cluck, cluck."

Her phone went dark. "My phone died. How good are you at navigating by stars?"

"The sun hasn't set yet," Jordy pointed out, and handed her his phone. "Some navigator you are."

"You keep me around for my DJ skills, not my directional ability." Annie typed o-o-o-o as a joke, and his phone unlocked. "Jordan. I was kidding when I asked if your password was o-o-o-o. Is your password 'password'?"

Jordy had the decency to blush. "It's not anymore."

The temptation to snoop and read his unread text messages was real. Who did he talk to? What did he talk about? Did he talk about her?

Annie started the map route to Eloise's house instead, then opened his music app. All of her assumptions about his musical tastes were shattered when she opened his first playlist.

"Why is your warm-up mix mostly Jenna Fox?" she asked. "I didn't peg you as a fan."

"Because she makes fucking catchy music. And she's a friend. Well"—he paused, choosing his next words carefully—"she's Sam's friend. We've hung out a lot. Not the way you're thinking. Don't really want to get involved in all of that."

"Are the engagements real, or is that for press? Is she a friend of Sam's or a *friend* of Sam's?"

"Just a friend. They came up in the industry together. And the engagements are very real."

Jenna Fox fascinated Annie. She'd found fame as a teenager as a member of Sweet Destiny, a girl group that had come out of a TV singing competition, and then launched a successful solo career a few years later. Eloise and Annie had spent a lot of weekend sleepovers trying to learn the choreography from her music videos and performances. Jenna also had three engagements to Annie's zero.

"Was Sam's engagement real?"

Sam had been engaged for almost a year to a member of Sweet Destiny before their relationship and the band had broken up in a spectacularly public fashion.

Jordy sighed. "Unfortunately. I didn't know him then. I wish I had, because someone should have told him twenty was too young."

A text appeared at the top of Jordy's phone.

KERI

Not as good as the ones you take. Miss you.

"Who's Keri?" Annie asked, curious but hesitant to expand the preview.

"Someone I slept with once. Why?"

"Because she misses you and is sending you photos."

Jordy's eyebrows raised so high Annie was worried they would get lost in his hairline.

"I didn't ask for those and don't open them," he told her, reaching for his phone.

"What if the pictures are of her dog?" she teased, locking the phone before handing it over.

"More like a kitty photo," he grumbled, lifting his hips momentarily to shove his phone deep inside his pocket, like he could bury the device where no one would ever find it again.

"Does she have a cat....Oh. That kind of kitty."

An idea began to form in Annie's brain, becoming clearer by the second, like a lens sliding into focus.

"Do you like those kinds of photos?" she ventured.

"I told you I didn't ask for it. Women send me photos. They don't mean anything."

The desperate, pleading edge in his voice made her heart twist. She reached across the car and raked her fingers through his hair, letting her nails graze his scalp the way he liked.

"Jordy, I'm not mad," she assured him, trying to make her voice as soothing as possible. "We're not together, and this all happened before I showed up. I was just asking if you like getting photos like that."

He leaned against her palm. "I don't know."

"If I sent them, would you like them?"

"If you sent them, I'd have a hard time not using them as my wallpaper."

The fact that Jordy Taylor, who was very obviously not having any shortage of nudes, wanted to save her hypothetical nudes made Annie want to preen. "Why wouldn't you?"

"Because you deserve better than being another girl on my phone."

"What if it was on the list? What if being a girl on your phone that you look at when you masturbate was on my list?"

"Roxanne." Her name was a heavy sigh. "You are the only thing I'm going to be thinking about for a long, long time."

FIFTEEN

JORDY RELUCTANTLY DROPPED Annie off at Eloise's house. He had bargained his way into helping her carrying the boxes of stationery and the lingerie bag up onto the porch, and then had trapped her against one of the porch columns to try and win her over to his position.

"Tell her you can't do wine night," he said, rubbing his persistent erection against her hip like a cat trying to scratch an itch, "and we can go back to the lighthouse and check at least three things off your list."

Annie felt bad for him. She was aching in all the same ways he was, but if she gave in, there was a good to definite chance she would never find the courage to do what she wanted to do again. If they hadn't been running late, she would have let him pull over at a truck stop so they could relieve some tension. Not that they would have fit in the backseat; they were both too tall.

"Do you have a chicken suit at the lighthouse?"

He groaned, pressing his nose into the curve where her shoulder met her neck. "Me and my big mouth."

"I have to go inside," she reminded him, and he sighed dramatically. "You can pick me up in two hours."

"You know what they say about erections that last more than four hours, right?" he mumbled against her neck, the drag of his lips sending sharp pulses of pleasure between her legs.

"Don't worry. I'll take care of you."

Annie pressed what was supposed to be a quick kiss to his lips. But Jordy wasn't interested in quick kisses. If he had to suffer, so did she, and he punished her with a kiss that left her chasing his mouth for more when he pulled away. It was a good thing she'd bought new underwear, because the ones she was wearing were trash now.

"Go inside before I fuck you over the railing," he told her, and Annie puckered her lips for one more kiss. Jordy obliged, his tongue slipping back into her mouth like it belonged there.

"Get a room," someone catcalled from the porch steps, and Annie and Jordy jumped apart. Mallory Morgan grinned at them as she ascended the porch. The petite blonde had a bottle of wine in one hand, and a Cranberry Festival canvas tote over her shoulder. She looked between them, and Annie wanted to die from embarrassment on the spot. A bolt of lightning would have been excellent, but it was a gorgeous night with only cotton candy clouds in the sunset sky.

Mallory waved her finger in the space between them. "I like this." She looked up at Jordy. "Sybil let you live when she found out?"

"No one knows." Jordy raked his hands through his hair. "Though she did remind me she owns garden shears last week."

"We're hooking up," Annie clarified. "Nobody else needs to be involved."

"Wasn't offering. Tempting, but I think I'd get squished between you giants."

Jordy looked how Annie felt: ready to be vaporized into oblivion by any obliging god.

"What I meant was—"

Mallory cut her off. "I know what you meant. I was teasing." Her focus shifted to the boxes by the door. "Is that Graham's idea of a home security system? Box barricade?"

"It's wedding stuff. Programs, menus..."

Mallory let out a low whistle. "How many people are coming to this thing?"

"A lot. The seating chart is intense."

"Color-coded and cross-referenced?"

"Oh yeah." Eloise's seating chart was an organizer's wet dream. "The binder has back-ups, too. Plans A-H."

"That's our girl." Mallory assessed the boxes again. "I hope Graham ordered enough booze."

"Eloise did some calculations, and he over-ordered based on that."

The front door opened and Connor cast a shadow across the porch. "I thought I heard—Mal?" His voice went up, and his eyes widened. "What are you doing here?"

"I've been gone since Christmas, and that's how you say hi? I know your mama raised you better than that." Mallory clicked her tongue in reproach, then held up the wine bottle. "It's wine night. I have wine."

"But how did you know to come here?"

"Well." Mallory stepped over the boxes blocking the door-way. "No one was at my house, and if I guessed wrong with Eloise's house, yours is across the street." She pressed the bottle into his chest. "It's from Spain. You're welcome."

Connor took the bottle, and Mallory took the opportunity to stretch up on her toes and honk his nose. He rolled his eyes, and she beamed at him before disappearing into the house. Connor looked down at the boxes.

"I'll get some help," he said to Jordy, and he shouted for Graham as he headed for the back of the house.

"That was close," Annie said when everyone was gone. She

picked up the lingerie bag. "If Graham is here, are you sticking around?"

"Might as well." Jordy sighed, trying to adjust himself through his pants. "Maybe this will finally kill my boner."

Annie held up the bag. "I'm going to take this up to Eloise's room—" Jordy's eyebrows shot up hopefully. "Down, boy."

Graham's voice floated out the door from down the hall. "Yeah, no, I heard him. I'm going...yeah, I can get the mail." A moment later, Graham appeared in the doorway, still wearing his blue dress shirt and gray slacks. "Sorry, I just got home from work." He picked up a box. "Thanks for picking these up for us. I heard you went to the zoo with the rug rats? How are they?"

Jordy bent over, and Annie snuck a stare at his ass, thanking her lucky stars that Graham and Eloise had been less than their normally organized selves for long enough to place her in his path.

"They're huge. Time is a thief, man."

He lifted a box, and she got lightheaded watching his biceps and forearms flex.

"I'm going to run this up to your room," Annie quickly told Graham, and squeezed past him before taking the stairs two at a time to the second floor.

Graham and Eloise's bedroom was the last door on the right. As she shut the door behind her, it occurred to Annie that she hadn't figured out how she was going to pull this off. Too much time spent telling Jordy every fantasy she had ever thought about and not enough time figuring out logistics.

She put the black bag on the floor of Eloise's side of the closet and dug around in the tissue paper for a moment. Lace and silk tickled her fingers, and then she found it, the small package wrapped in its own tissue paper.

It had been an impulse purchase. She had been standing near the register, waiting for the saleswoman to come back with

Eloise's order when she saw the set hanging on a rack, the only one of its kind left. When it had turned out to be her size, she decided it was fate.

Annie buried the bag behind the skirts of some of Eloise's longer dresses, then scurried across the hall to the upstairs bathroom and locked herself inside. She yanked off her sweatshirt and T-shirt at the same time, letting them fall into a heap on the floor. Next she wiggled out of her sports bra, adding it to the pile. The red lines from the band and straps couldn't be helped by anything but time, so she hoped Jordy would be too distracted to notice.

With a deep, calming breath, Annie slipped her thumb under the branded sticker holding the tissue paper closed, and broke the seal. Fine green mesh embroidered with a florist's shop's worth of multi-colored flowers revealed itself as the tissue paper unfolded. There hadn't been time to try it on in the store, so she hoped it really did fit. Women's sizing was so fucking obnoxious.

It wasn't itchy like she had expected it to be. Annie hadn't bought anything like this...ever. The last time she bought lingerie was for her five-year anniversary with Jake. That silk nightie wasn't half as gorgeous as the bra from the set. She admired her reflection as she adjusted her boobs in the cups for maximum cleavage. It made her feel like a nymph, born from the wildflowers in spring. The embroidery on the underwear would absolutely show through her leggings though. Which was fine. She could wear it later.

Annie pulled the waist of her leggings up where it belonged over her belly button, which was slimming. No wonder all the fitness influencers did it. The illusion worked. She shook out her hair and fluffed it, trying both sides in an extreme part until she found the way that made it look the fullest.

Was the lighting too harsh?

They had stopped at a gas station on the way back and the cheap car charger she'd bought had given her battery a little life. Her hand shook as she opened the camera app.

Was this a selfie photo or a mirror photo?

Don't think. Just do it.

Annie fired off a couple of quick shots, twisting her body to achieve different angles. Modeling was harder than it looked. There were one, maybe two, photos she was remotely happy with, but she couldn't spend forever in the bathroom directing her own boudoir shoot. Selecting Jordy's message thread filled her with anxious butterflies, and she double-checked it was his phone number before attaching the photo, tapping out a message, and hitting send.

The little clock under the message, indicating it was sending, mocked her. Fucking Crane Cove and their ridiculous cell-phone service.

Annie pulled her top layers back on, then shoved her sports bra and fancy underwear deep into her purse. The embroidered flowers rubbed against her nipples and she wished she had given Jordy some secret signal to follow her up to the bathroom. This counted as a semi-public place. The odds of getting caught were uncomfortably high.

The message finally sent, and she dropped her phone in her purse so she wouldn't stare at it until he messaged her back. *If* he messaged her back.

Dear god, what had she done?

"HOW ARE you feeling about the draft on Friday?" Graham asked as they placed the last of the boxes in the formal dining room, which had been transformed into wedding central. There were mock centerpieces on the table and a poster board on an easel with a seating chart and a key to show what all the colors meant.

"I have zero interviews scheduled this week specifically so I don't have to talk about that." Jordy stretched, and enjoyed how Graham winced when his back cracked.

"Well, if you're interested, there's a community baseball game Friday night. It's a pickup league, so whoever shows up gets to play."

Jordy frowned. "Isn't a large portion of the population here elderly?"

"The seniors have their own league. It's fun. Might take your mind off things." Graham grinned at him. "Unless you'd rather play in the senior league. They're done by four for dinner."

Graham jumped away as Jordy half-heartedly swatted at him, and laughed. Playing baseball hadn't been on Jordy's agenda for Friday night. The plan had been to convince Annie to play with his balls, which were so tender he was shocked he wasn't limping. That woman was a menace, and he adored her.

"We'll see." Jordy heard laughter coming from the living room. "So what happens at wine night?"

"They drink wine and whine about the week."

He frowned. "But it's Monday."

"And that is enough of the week to whine about." Graham pointed to the ceiling as he unbuttoned his shirt sleeves. "I'm going to go change if you want to grab a drink."

"Yeah, sure, I guess?" Not like he had anything better to do. Might as well kill time until Annie took pity on him. "Where are we going?"

"Cranberry Brothers? Backyard? I don't care."

"Is Backyard another bar?" He hadn't heard of that one, and it wasn't like Crane Cove had a thriving nightlife scene.

"No. I mean *the* backyard." Graham pointed to the back of

the house. "The one outside. With the fence. Connor and the twins helped me build a firepit." He paused, then amended, "They built the firepit. I paid for it and supervised."

"You change and grab us some drinks. I'll build a fire." Jordy took two steps into the hall, then asked, "You have wood, right? This isn't going to be a repeat of the camping trip?"

"Oh, fuck off."

To get to the backyard, Jordy had to pass by the living room. The group of five was seated around the room on the assorted couches and chairs. Annie happened to look over her shoulder at the right time, and when their eyes met, she blushed and quickly looked away. Mallory and Connor were locked in a heated debate about the baseball game on Friday night. Mallory had risen onto her knees to try and gain a height advantage over Connor, which would be easily lost if he did the same. Eloise looked too tired to care that red wine might get spilled on her carpet. And Sybil was glaring at him.

A cold shiver ran down his spine, and Jordy hightailed it to the backyard.

Jordy had a strong, crackling fire going by the time Graham came outside, a rocks glass in each hand. He passed one off to Jordy and settled into the Adirondack chair next to his with a heavy sigh.

"What did you make?"

Before becoming a CEO and then a hotelier, Graham had been a bartender. Whenever they got together, Graham had been in charge of making the drinks because he didn't have to stop and look up the recipes.

"Whiskey, ginger ale, and lime juice. I'm too tired to make anything fancy." Graham swallowed almost half the glass in one drink. "I need this wedding to be over before my wife loses her goddamn mind."

"She's not your wife until next weekend," Jordy reminded him.

"Close enough. I'm rounding up. And I like saying it. My wife. Feels good in the mouth."

Smug bastard.

In his pocket, Jordy's phone buzzed. He dug it out, anxious to see if it was Priya with an update.

HEAD BIRD NERD

Would this make a good wallpaper?

He opened the message as he took a sip of his drink, and choked so hard that ginger ale and whiskey almost came out his nose.

Annie had sent him a topless photo. Almost topless. Close enough to topless that he was still trying to look at the picture with watery eyes and a burning nose. She was wearing a sheer green bra with fiddly flower embroidery covering the best bits, and the same teasing smile she got when she was about to do something he would really, really like. When and how and—

Annie's blush as he walked past jumped to the top of his mind.

She had taken the picture here. That bra was possibly on her body at that very moment.

There was no way he was going to make it two hours. There was serious doubt he was going to make it ten minutes.

"I, uh, have to go," Jordy said, getting up and trying to find a spot to put down his drink.

"Go? You just got here."

"I've got a thing I need to do," he said, and pushed his drink into Graham's hand.

That thing was Annie, and he would do her on the side of the road if she pushed him any further. As fast as he could without running, Jordy walked into the house and to the living room.

"Annie, we need to go," he said. She tilted her head back to look at him, half a glass of wine in her hand.

"Go?" Her voice was echoed by four more.

Jordy nodded. "I have an early thing, so I need to go back. Get some sleep. You know."

After that picture, she had better know what he was talking about.

"What early thing?" Sybil's voice was as smooth as the edge of a butcher's knife.

"An interview. East coast market. Super early time for the morning slot." Was he speaking real words? He didn't know. But if Annie didn't get up by the time he counted to three in his head, he was going to pick her up, toss her over his shoulder, and carry her out to the car like a sack of sexy potatoes.

"I can drive her back," Sybil offered.

Annie finally got the hint. "No, it's fine. I don't want you to go out of your way." She downed the rest of her wine and put the empty glass on the side table.

"It's not far," Connor pointed out, and Mallory took a drink to cover up her snort.

"Jordy's already going," Annie said, and exaggerated a yawn. "I'm tired, anyway. We had a long day."

"Drive safe," Mallory said, cutting Sybil off before she could offer to take Annie back to the lighthouse again.

Annie grabbed her purse, gave her cousin a hug, and then moved with a purpose out of the house.

"Did you get my text?" she asked innocently once they'd cleared the porch steps.

"Oh, I got it." He put a hand on the small of her back to propel her quicker down the walkway.

"Because you didn't respond."

"I'm going to respond." He yanked open her door. "In."

Annie hesitated, her forehead wrinkling into deep worry lines. "Did I do something wrong?"

"No," he said, trying to keep his voice firm. "Now get in the car before I put you in the car."

Annie dropped into the passenger seat.

"Good girl."

Being bossed around was on her list. Lower, but it was there. And while domming wasn't his favorite thing to do—he was always afraid he would go too far or not far enough—this situation was perfect for it.

"I need to show you something," he said after buckling his seatbelt. He took one of her hands, which were demurely folded in her lap, and placed it over the thick ridge his cock was making through his pants. "You did that. And you're going to take care of it."

Annie's eyes widened.

"How do you want me to take care of it?" she asked and squeezed.

How the fuck was he supposed to think when she did shit like that? How was he supposed to *drive* when she was oh-so-innocently dragging her thumb across the ultra-sensitive head? All his brain function centered on Annie's hand. He was already rolling through stop signs like he was home in California, barely pausing before going ten miles over the speed limit through town.

"Do you still have the bra on?" His voice was ragged, like he'd spent a week screaming plays over the roar of a sold-out stadium. Annie nodded. "Show me."

She pulled her shirt and sweatshirt up the moment they cleared the last stop sign in town. It was a miscalculation on his part, because he wanted to stare when he needed to drive, but it got her hand off of him so he didn't bust in his pants.

"Did you like doing that? Teasing me? Seeing how far you could push me until I snapped?"

Her answer was a breathy whisper. "Yes."

"You wanted to get spanked, right? Because I'm going to make sure you can't sit without knowing exactly where each one of my fingers was on your ass."

He heard her breath hitch over the drone of the engine as they climbed the hill.

"Do you know why I'm going to slap your ass red?"

"Because I sent you a picture?"

"No. Because you pushed me too far, sweetheart. I was already going to fuck you hard when we got home, but now..." Jordy turned down the driveway, and parked next to her car. He caught her chin in his hand so she had no choice but to look at him. "Now I'm going to fuck you so hard you're never going to forget I was there. Is anything on your list fair game?"

"Yes," she squeaked, wiggling in her seat, already trying to crawl across the center console to get at him. He held her face firm.

"If something goes too far, or feels weird, say flamingo." He let go and pointed to the door. "Get out of the car. Wait for me."

In sports, mental game was important as physical game. Jordy had to get his head into this particular game so it wasn't over before it began.

Condom. He needed a condom. The overwhelming need to be bare inside of her, to fill her up and stay inside of her as long as he could so nothing slipped out, meant he absolutely needed to wear a condom. Bless the one he kept in his wallet. It occurred to Jordy as he pulled it out that he had never had a condom in his wallet long enough for it to expire.

Annie stood near her car, arms crossed under her chest as she looked out at the ocean, waiting for him like he told her to. The bright moon reflected off her pale skin so she glowed.

Fuck, she was pretty.

"Take off your shirt," he told her, and leaned against her car, hoping he looked casually interested instead of ravenous.

"Here?" Annie reached for the hem of her sweatshirt anyway.

"Yeah, here. You gonna ask questions, or are you gonna do what you're told?"

Bulky cotton landed on the ground with a soft *thud*. That bra had to be stitched together with black magic, because it somehow made her boobs look almost as good as they did fully naked. There wasn't anything to it, either. No special padding or magic effects. Just her and some fancy stitching. Annie was a goddess, and he wished he had his camera.

"Hands on the hood, Roxanne."

He waited until her hands were where he wanted them before he approached. One little touch from her, and he would be toast.

Jordy dropped the condom next to her left hand, then he brushed her hair away from the right side of her neck, so while she was looking at the condom, her neck was more exposed to him. The way she shivered as he trailed kisses down to her shoulder would be burned into his memory.

"Don't move those hands. If you move them, I'll stop," he told her as he hooked his fingers into the waistband of her leggings. "Do you want me to stop?"

"No." Annie pushed her ass toward him.

Screw slow seduction. He could mess with her anticipation another time. He pushed her leggings and underwear down around her thighs, and smoothed his hands over her ass. His mouth watered.

Smack.

The first slap made her jump, but Annie kept her hands on

the hood. Jordy rubbed the spot, placing a tender kiss under her ear.

"Have you had enough?"

Annie shook her head.

"I'm going to make good on my promise," he warned her, kneading her ass. "Every finger, remember?"

"Fuck, I want your fingers," she moaned, tilting her head back to look at him with pleading eyes. "I feel so empty."

The entirety of his self-control needed to be measured using a microscope. Any other time, he would have caved instantly and given her exactly what she wanted. But he was supposed to be the one in control.

Smack.

"You'll take what I give you."

Smack.

With every slap, her ass jiggled, and Jordy became addicted to the reverb. He waited until her body stilled before rubbing away any hurt, kissing her shoulder or her neck as he did so. Her fingers curled a few times, but ever the overachiever, Annie kept her hands on the hood. After twenty whacks—ten to each cheek—he gave in and slid his fingers between her legs.

She was soaked.

"Oh, fuck," Annie whined as he explored without penetrating. Every time she tried to catch his fingers and impale herself on them, Jordy moved his hand away. "Please, please, please. I can't—fuck, I can't take it anymore."

When he picked up the condom, her body went slack with relief, and she lay on the hood, raised up on her tiptoes so her pussy glimmered in the moonlight, presented in case he forgot how needy she was.

Jordy tugged off his shirt and dropped it in front of her. "Lay on that," he told her, then pushed his pants down around his ankles. As Annie arranged his shirt, he rolled the condom down his length, hissing at the contact. He'd played with her too long. This was going to take less time than microwave popcorn.

"Good girl," he praised as he notched the tip of his cock against her opening. "You're so ready for me, aren't you?"

Annie rocked back against him, and his cock slid a quarter of the way with little resistance. He pushed forward the rest of the way to give the illusion that penetration had been his idea.

"Hot" and "tight" became the only two words his brain understood.

Jordy gripped Annie's hips and began to fuck her mercilessly. With every stroke, she cried out into the crook of her arm, trying to bury the sound so it wouldn't travel across the water. There wasn't much he could do about the sound of their bodies slapping together.

"Fuck, you feel too good," he grunted through gritted teeth, digging his fingers into the fleshy part of her hips. There was no way he was going to make it through the next minute. If he made it thirty more seconds, he deserved an award, presented on television to raucous applause.

Annie clenched tightly around him, shrieking into her forearm. Jordy felt like he got punched in the gut as he came so hard he saw stars. His body shook as relief cascaded over him like standing under a waterfall. All the pressure that had been building and building and building through the day was gone, leaving only tingling bliss.

His abs were going to hurt in the morning.

"Holy fuck," Annie groaned beneath him. "Every time I think you can't top yourself...fuck."

Jordy moved her hair off her neck again, and he kissed the soft skin on the back of her neck several times, before sealing his mouth in an "O" and sucking. Annie gasped, her pussy clenching around his sensitive cock, and Jordy's knees shook.

"What was that for?" she asked, her voice dazed and dreamy.

"Mine," he said against her skin.

And it was true. She was his. But, more accurately, he was hers. She owned him, body, mind, and soul. He needed to figure out his life so he could hand her the keys to his house, because he didn't know how he was going to live without her.

Post-nut clarity could be a real bitch.

SIXTEEN

"LEO, I need a big strawberry milkshake, extra whipped cream and cherries on top, sprinkles if you have them, and—" Annie skimmed the menu. "I don't know. Whatever has the most calories and a dangerous amount of sodium."

Buff Santa looked ready to inquire after her cardiovascular health, but then the bell over the door jingled, and he abandoned her for whoever had arrived.

Queens was surprisingly busy for a Thursday, so Annie was perched on top of a pink stool at the counter, watching the line cooks work their magic on the lunch rush. The cute tweed blazer she had borrowed from Eloise fit funny, and the black square neck dress underneath felt too hot and heavy.

Would she have to dress like this every day if she got the teaching position she had just interviewed for?

Seemed a moot point since she had blown the interview so badly that she was trying to eat a month's worth of feelings in one sitting.

She had applied to the position back in February, and when tax season came and went without hearing anything, Annie had given up on it. So, when the call from the small liberal arts school in Maine came Tuesday morning, she'd been shocked. Dropped her spoon in her cereal bowl and made a mess shocked. It wasn't a big biology department, but it was the first one that had called, so she jumped at the interview. Even if she wasn't sure she wanted to move to Maine anymore.

When Annie had started applying to jobs—any job—relocating across the country had seemed like the dream scenario. Fresh start, closer to the bulk of the family, even if her favorite member stayed on the west coast. But when she had been updating her job application spreadsheet, she noticed that for the last week, she had been concentrating on jobs in California. Particularly southern California.

The entire interview, she kept thinking that Maine was a long way from Los Angeles. That was probably why she had flubbed it. Teaching philosophies? Never heard of them. What was her dissertation on? No clue, but something about birds. What did she think she could bring to the department? Donuts.

That interview was going to be the main feature on the insomniac movie screen in her mind at two a.m.

A strawberry milkshake, piled high with whipped cream, ladened with a jar's worth of cherries, and smothered in confetti-colored sprinkles, was placed in front of her.

"Thanks, Leo," she said, stabbing it with her straw.

Someone plopped down on the stool next to her.

"Wow. That is an entire kid's birthday party right there."

Annie didn't even bother turning her head. She tilted it to the side so she could keep drinking her shake, which was made with really good ice cream, the kind that actually could fix all of life's problems. The woman sitting next to her was about her age, with faded teal and bubblegum pink hair, the kind of unicorn combination Annie had always wanted but had been too afraid of bleaching her hair to try, pulled back into a bun. She wore a baggy sweatshirt from a cruise line with the neck cut out so it slid off one shoulder, leggings, and had the kind of posture Annie would have killed for.

"I'm eating my feelings," Annie mumbled around her straw.

"What kind of feelings require a carton of liquified ice cream?" she asked, and quickly added, "Not judging, just asking. Let me know if you want me to shut up and mind my own."

"No, it's fine," Annie told her, rearranging her cherries to make a smiley face. The impulse to open up about her conflicting feelings was strong, and who better to listen objectively than a stranger? "I blew an interview for a job I don't even know if I want, but it was the first place to call me, and I've been applying for months. And I'm worried that I subconsciously sabotaged myself because I don't know if I want to move anymore."

"Oof. Been there. Sort of. The whole unemployed thing." The stranger waved her hand when she talked, like she was conducting an orchestra. The movement was so graceful it was hypnotic. "Why don't you want to move?"

"Because..." Annie hesitated. Telling the woman sitting next to her suspicions about why she didn't want to move back east made those suspicions truths. And being honest with a stranger meant she had to be honest with herself about what had shifted. "There's a guy. And he lives in California. Which is the opposite of Maine. And I don't really know what's going on between us, but if I move to Maine, or South Carolina, or fucking Florida, I'll never find out. And maybe I want to find out?"

The woman let out a long, low whistle. "Wowww." She shook her head, and pointed to one of Annie's cherries. "Can I have that?"

Annie plucked it from the whipped cream by its stem and handed it to her.

"Thanks." She separated it from its stem with her teeth,

chewed, then said, "Is it a bad career move for you to not take the job in Maine?"

"Not necessarily."

"Are there ample career opportunities in California?" She held up her hand. "Wait. Let me rephrase that: do you think you can get a job in California?"

"I don't know." Annie sighed. "I already gave up a really great opportunity because of my ex, and I'm freaked I'm going to make the same mistake again."

"How long have you known this guy?"

"Uh...if we're counting from the first time we kissed, four months. If we're counting from the first time we actually had a conversation, almost two weeks?"

"Wowww." Her eyes widened. "That is not a lot of time to be making that kind of decision. My two cents? Don't move for a guy. Don't *not* move because of a guy. Fuck following guys, or waiting around for them to figure their lives out before you figure your life out. Because chasing someone else's dream is how you end up tits-deep in debt teaching tap to toddlers. Obviously based on a real example."

"Got some experience?" Annie asked, using the end of her straw to spoon whipped cream into her mouth. Bless Leo and his house-made whip.

"Heaps. I'm a chronically bad picker with terrible decision-making skills." She sighed. "I was supposed to be a Rockette. But my boyfriend at the time wanted to move to Nashville to be a country music star so... that's what we did. Because my stupid ass thought we were going to get married and—I'm sorry. I talk a lot."

"No, no, it's fine. Normally I'm the one that talks too much." Annie offered her another cherry. "I'm Annie."

"Lacey." She popped the cherry off its stem. "So what's so

great about this guy that you want to plan your life around him after two weeks? Is the sex really that good?"

"The sex is *really* that good."

"Well, damn." Lacey grinned at her. "Does he have a job? Health insurance? A retirement plan? These are the things I always forget about when I'm getting my back blown out."

"Currently employed. I think they have health insurance? I don't think he has a 401k, but he's got money." She paused, then added, "His job is kind of an issue."

"Why?" Lacey leaned forward and dropped her voice, whispering, "Does he do porn?"

Annie laughed and shook her head. "No. He could, but no."

"So what's the issue?"

"If he's still doing his job, he doesn't want to date because dating is a distraction."

"Is he a SEAL?"

"No, an athlete."

"Ah. Part of the holy trinity of fuckboys." When Annie frowned, Lacey clarified, crossing herself like a nun at mass as she went down the list. "Actors, musicians, and professional athletes."

"Experience?"

"Musicians are my weakness. None of mine had money, though. They were all 'pre-successful'." Lacey did air quotes. "I've lived in New York, Nashville, Chicago, and Los Angeles. I've seen a lot. Talked to a lot of crying girls in club bathrooms. Don't be one of those girls. Do what's right for you. He can afford the plane ticket."

Leo dropped a paper bag on the counter in front of Lacey. "Gavin was supposed to take the lunch I packed him this morning."

Lacey shrugged. "He forgot it." She slid her arm through the handles and hopped off her stool with a graceful bounce.

"You've been together for thirty years. This shouldn't surprise you."

"You're supposed to remind him."

"And miss out on free lunch? Never." Lacey wrapped an arm around Annie's shoulders and gave her a tight squeeze. "It was nice to meet you, Annie. If you ever want to hang out, I'm around and have no social life."

Lacey blew a kiss at Leo and left the diner. He shook his head and rubbed the back of his neck.

"Those two are trying to kill me," he told no one in particular.

Annie was served a thick double cheeseburger with ooey-gooey American cheese and tater tots so fresh out of the fryer they were still steaming. Leo brought her a side of ranch, ketchup, and buffalo sauce, then very pointedly pretended not to notice her mix them together.

There was something magical about salt, fat, sugar, and carbs that helped her think. Because Lacey had a very good point. She couldn't plan her life around the possibility of Jordy working out. If there was ever a time in her life to be unabashedly selfish with her plans, this was it. But the horrible, needling sense that she needed to be looking at jobs in southern California wouldn't leave her alone. That Jordy was something special and she was a fucking idiot if she didn't set herself up for success there.

The glaring unknown was his future. Because he had been clear that he didn't see himself being able to juggle a serious relationship and playing football. Their road trip conversation about relationships had been enlightening and disheartening. Jordy still wanted to play football, and Annie wanted that for him. If it was only for another year, she didn't mind waiting around for him. Longer than that, she wasn't sure because she didn't want to waste another ten years on a man that wasn't ready to fully commit.

Annie wiped her salty, greasy fingers on her napkin. If nothing else, she was going to enjoy the next week. She owed herself that.

BARBECUE NIGHT at Cranberry Brothers was the busiest night of their week. To hear Eloise, Graham, Sybil, and Connor complain about it, it was always packed. It was a backhanded "We're so happy Chase and Cole are doing well, but…"

Annie's job, as the unemployed loser in the group—her words, not theirs—was to arrive early and stake claim to a table big enough to hold the group. Because it had been an unusually warm day, leading into an unusually warm weekend, the twins had opened up the patio a week early. That was where Annie set up shop: two picnic tables shoved together on the back patio, three bowls of popcorn spread down the middle in a line, and a beer that was rapidly changing from cold to room temperature in her hand.

People kept glancing at her, sitting by herself at her gigantic table, like Jesus at the Last Supper minus the apostles. Annie checked her phone. She'd texted Jordy after lunch but hadn't heard much back.

JORDY

Not coming back to the house. See you at CBB

K

Where are you?

Annie started to type that she was on the back patio at the

brewery, when a big, cold hand pressed against her bare back, right between her shoulder blades. She jumped, barely keeping her beer from sloshing out.

"There you are," Jordy said, placing his beer on the table, then straddling the bench next to her. "I was looking for you inside."

Relief flooded Annie, all the tension and stress of the day washed away in the instant she saw him. She wanted to curl up in his lap, bury her face in his neck, and take deep breaths until his scent replaced her oxygen. He would smell good too. Jordy's hair was still damp at the roots and tips, so he'd recently gotten out of the shower.

"Mallory didn't tell you I was out here?" Annie asked.

"She did. Eventually. Watched me wander around like an idiot, go upstairs... I like this dress."

Annie had borrowed more of Eloise's clothes after her interview. The blue cotton sundress was simple, and the summer-like day had made her grab it. It had large wooden buttons down the front, and delicate straps that were tied into bows at the tops of her shoulders. Jordy touched one of the bow tails, rolling the string between his fingers, and Annie blushed.

She reached out and ran the flat of her hand down his chest. "I like this shirt."

It was the same shirt he'd been wearing the night they'd met. *Agapornis fischeri, Myiopsitta monachus, Ara macao.* Fisher's lovebird. Monk parakeet. Red macaw. A riot of color proclaiming universal love and devotion.

"Oh yeah?" He looked down, pulling out the hem to give her a better look. "You know I was wearing this—"

"The night we met. I remember." She skimmed her fingers over a green wing. "Lovebirds."

The evening air grew warmer between them, heavy with something Annie couldn't quite put her finger on. It wasn't lust; she was intimately familiar with that feeling. Another L word whispered its name in her ear, but she wasn't ready to hear it. It was too soon, too much, and there was too little figured out to be thinking that.

The abrupt notes and finishing trills of the song sparrows that lived in the shrubs filled the silence.

Jordy cleared his throat and took a sip of his beer. "How was your interview?"

Annie groaned. "Horrible."

"I doubt that. They probably loved you." He dragged his fingers up and down her spine, and Annie grew wet as her brain served up all the other times he'd done that. "I'm sure you did great."

"They asked me what I thought I could bring to the department, and I said donuts."

Jordy laughed, then tried to tamp it down when he realized she hadn't been trying to make a joke.

"That was funny," he promised her, squeezing her shoulder. Intentionally or not, he pressed his thumb into the hickey he'd given her Monday night. "Everyone likes a sense of humor, right? And who doesn't like donuts?"

"It's not what they meant." She hung her head. "The last time I screwed up an interview this badly, I still had braces."

"Which job was this?" Jordy pulled a bowl of popcorn closer and took a few pieces out, tossing each one into his mouth.

"The teaching position in Maine."

"No lobst-ah for you." His accent was terrible, but it made her smile. He smiled back. "It's one job, sweetheart. You're going to get other interviews. Would it make you feel better if I told you my very first pass as a professional quarterback went straight into the grass?"

"A little bit." She brought her thumb and forefinger together and squinted at him through the space between her fingers.

"You got the first-pass jitters out of the way." He looked around, head swiveling like an owl, then leaned in and asked, "Want to check an item off your list and have a quickie in the bathroom? I bet I can make you feel better in five minutes or less."

Annie shoved him with no force at all. "We already checked semi-public off the list."

Jordy shook his head. "Nah. I was thinking about it in the shower. That was super public. Completely out in the open. Semi-public is sneaking into that bathroom, locking the door, and trying to finish before anyone gets suspicious. Then there's getting out without getting caught. Very risky. Very sexy."

"The last time you thought about me in the shower, I came at you with a knife."

"Oh, sweetheart. That was not the last time I thought about you in the shower."

There was going to be a puddle on the bench when she stood up if he kept talking.

"You have to trust the process." Graham's voice came from the door.

"I am trusting the process. The process isn't working," Eloise bit back, frustration rolling off her in palpable waves. She plastered a big smile on her face and walked over to the table, her heels clicking against the concrete.

They were both still dressed for work, though Graham had rolled his shirt sleeves up to his elbows. Eloise sat at the end of the bench on Annie's other side, forcing Graham to either sit next to Jordy or on the other side of the table. He chose the other side of the table.

"What's wrong?" Annie asked, accepting Eloise's hug.

"We're taking dance lessons," Graham explained, "and someone is frustrated that we're not professional dancers yet."

"I know we started late but I thought we would be further along by now. I'm still stepping on his toes, and I don't think we could find a beat with a GPS." Eloise laid her cheek on Annie's shoulder. "Did you put on sunscreen? You feel warm."

"Some?" That was a lie. Forgetting to wear sunscreen the first few nice days of the year was a persistent Pacific Northwest problem. Annie's annual sunburns usually happened in April or May.

Eloise sat up and began to examine her back. "You're a little pink," she said, moving Annie's hair off her shoulder. Undoubtedly, she caught sight of the hickey, because Eloise quickly put her hair back where it had been, covering the mark. "This dress looks really cute on you."

Oh yeah. She'd seen it.

"Thank you. It felt weather appropriate." Annie squeezed Eloise's hand. "You seem stressed. How can I help?"

"You can crash our dance lessons if you want. It would be nice to not be the only one Gavin is criticizing."

Graham sighed. "He's not criticiz— Okay, I'm wrong. Never mind." He held up his hands in defeat.

Hell hath no fury like a bride the week before her wedding.

"We can be clodhoppers together," Annie promised.

Eloise frowned. Annie could see the list forming in her head, and the growing hesitation about sharing the list.

"Eloise," Annie tried to make her voice as soothing as possible, "you're supposed to ask for help when you need it. Remember? Don't make me throw you under the bus with Sybil."

"That's what I've been telling her," Graham mumbled into his beer.

Eloise's shoulders drooped. "It's all the small stuff now.

Putting welcome bags together. Updating the check-in spreadsheet so I know *when* to put the welcome bags in the rooms."

"Don't you have staff that can do that?"

"I don't want to put them out. It's my wedding and my responsibility." Eloise put her head back on Annie's shoulder. "And now Mom is saying we need wedding week activities so people won't be bored. Half of these people haven't been to the west coast. There's the Pacific Ocean. Look at it." She groaned. "So I have to plan that now."

Jordy and Graham shared a look. *Sandra strikes again.*

"Dump some of that on my plate. Jordy and I can make an assembly line and stuff welcome bags. And you forget that I am a data entry queen. If you set up the formulas, I'll input the information."

Eloise hugged her tightly. "This is why you're my favorite."

"I'm right here," Graham reminded her.

"She's known me longer," Annie said.

Graham raised an eyebrow. "It's kind of hard to beat birth."

"Sounds like a personal problem." Sybil dropped onto the bench next to Graham, making him jump and almost spill his beer.

"You need a bell. Or ominous theme music." He shuddered.

"Like *Jaws*. Duh-*duh*, duh-*duh*," Jordy sang. Annie bit back a laugh as Sybil glared.

"Aren't you supposed to be playing with balls?"

"Don't take the bait, Jordy." Connor sat down next to Sybil. "She's been picking fights all week."

"I am not." She pulled the popcorn bowl away from him as he reached for it, and pushed it towards Graham. "When are the rest of your idiot friends getting here?"

Graham arched his eyebrows. "Why are you so hostile?"

"It's a day ending in 'y'." Sybil turned her attention to Eloise.

"Sam's coming this weekend. Peter said he would be here Thursday, but his assistant said Friday so...one of those days. Maybe sooner." Eloise frowned at Graham. "Did you remind Dempsey about his tux?"

"Sam is in charge of bringing the tuxes from the tailor. If he doesn't bring them, I will personally put him back on an airplane, economy middle seat across from the bathroom to go get them."

Eloise relaxed, either Graham's firm, assuring tone or his freakishly well-thought-out retribution soothing her nerves.

Sybil drummed her fingers on the side of her pint glass. "Thursday or Friday? Isn't that cutting it a little close?"

Graham brushed off her comment with a single shouldered shrug. "He'll make it."

"Like he made it to your engagement party?"

Eloise tensed again.

"I don't understand your problem with Peter. You haven't even met the guy." Graham moved the pilfered popcorn bowl out from under her hand. "This is why you weren't invited to the group chat."

"The same group chat that lasted two weeks?" Connor asked.

"The planning and execution of the group chat was not my finest moment, okay?" Graham moved the other popcorn bowl away from Sybil, so he had a comical collection at the far end of the picnic table.

Sybil glared at him. "You're hogging the popcorn."

"Do you promise to be nice?"

"I will be civil."

Graham grabbed a handful of popcorn and deposited it on the table in front of her.

Annie's phone buzzed in her pocket. Bless a dress that had pockets.

Surreptitiously she checked it under the table.

JORDY

Bathroom?

SEVENTEEN

JORDY REGRETTED ASKING to join Connor on his morning run. High school English teachers weren't supposed to have thighs carved from granite or the stamina and speed of an ostrich. After Mallory warned him that Connor was a marathoner, Annie had told him that an ostrich could finish a marathon in under an hour. There had been more to the bird facts lecture, like something about how ostriches had twice the amount of elastic energy in their tendons than humans, but the sun had been setting and the light was so perfect he wished he had his camera to capture the way she glowed.

As they turned down the lighthouse driveway, it occurred to Jordy that Connor had run to the lighthouse to meet him, and was going to run home before school.

Annie's car was gone, and the disappointment hurt more than his side ache. She had been singing off-key in the shower when he was getting ready to leave, and if Connor wasn't one of those very on-time people, he would have joined her in the shower. The bathroom at Cranberry Brothers had proved they could have fun in five minutes or less.

The half-lidded bliss on Annie's face as he pumped into her from behind, his hand over her mouth, reminding her over and over that they needed to be quiet, was something else he wished he could have captured on camera because the memory would never be as good as the real thing.

Jordy stopped at the door, leaning over as he put his hands on top of his head, his chest heaving with the effort to breathe properly. The last time he had run that fast, it was because he was being chased down a football field by a pack of heavy men that wanted to tackle him.

Connor had the nerve to be breathing heavily but steadily. Asshole.

"So, are you going to be at the baseball game tonight?"

"That depends on if I make it through the next five minutes," Jordy gasped. "I don't know if I'll be able to walk later. Are you even human?"

"Got a lot of pent-up energy." Connor paced back and forth, his hands on his hips. "Baseball?"

"We'll see."

Connor checked his smart watch, probably admiring how his heart could pump jet fuel. "I have to get going, but I'll bring an extra glove to the field tonight for you."

As he jogged off, Jordy shouted after him, "Show-off! I'm supposed to be the professional athlete here!"

Connor just waved.

Jordy stripped off his sweaty shirt as soon as he crossed the threshold, tossing it in the general direction of the washing machine. Putting his dirty clothes directly into the washing machine was a weird habit he had developed after he started living by himself, but it worked for him. Once the machine was full, he could start the load right away, and he never had the overflowing basket problem. Annie had an overflowing basket problem.

He should go check her room for dirty clothes.

The sound of his phone buzzing on his nightstand sent him in the opposite direction.

Priya.

Careful not to move his phone too far away from the spot where it had service, Jordy sat down on the floor to answer the call.

"Hey, what's up?" he panted.

"I know it's early, but did I interrupt something?"

He tugged out his ponytail holder and leaned his head back against the mattress. "No. I just finished a run." The fact that it was early and Priya was calling hit him like a runaway ostrich. "Is something wrong?"

The brief pause on the other end of the call aged him six years.

"I don't know. Are you sitting down?"

"Yeah." He sank lower.

"The team has been talking to some quarterbacks from this draft class. I don't know if they'll take anyone because they're number twenty-four and this is just an okay year for QBs but... Jordy, we need to revisit our options."

"I don't want to move to Miami."

Unless Annie went to Miami. Then he would move to Miami before the ink was dry on a trade.

"I have a call with them at nine. I need some direction, Jordy."

Jordy ran his fingers through his sweaty hair and regretted the decision instantly. He wiped his damp hand off on his shorts.

Was the answer supposed to fall out of the sky and hit him on the head? What did he want from the rest of his career? Was he ready for it to be over so he could enter the next part of his life? Or did he want one more run at a ring?

He did want one more run at it. But if he picked football, did that mean giving up Annie? If he got down on his knees and begged her to give him a real chance tomorrow, they would barely get any time before he started work again. Could he be the partner she deserved when he needed to give his job one hundred and ten percent?

If he got one more year, would she wait for him?

"I want to try and stay in LA. That hasn't changed."

"Okay. I'll see what they're looking to do. Are you watching the draft tonight?"

"Uh, no. I'm going to a baseball game." He didn't think he could watch his team potentially draft his replacement in real time.

"Do you want me to call if they draft a QB?" Priya asked, the sound of her keyboard filling the silence.

"Yeah, sure. Have a good day, Priya. Good luck with the call." He hung up and banged his head against the mattress several times.

Jordy felt like he was going to throw up, and not from the run. Every person should get to use a genuine crystal ball once in their life to see into their future so they knew for certain if a decision was the right one. Jordy wanted his go at the crystal ball right then and there.

Should he have given Priya the greenlight to talk about trades? Or was telling her to keep pressing forward with the current plan the right call? If, and more particularly when, the Phantoms drafted a quarterback was the best way for him to know where he stood at this point. If it was in the first round, then the writing was on the wall. After that or not at all, he had a fighting chance.

He groaned as he pushed himself off the ground. Maybe he needed to book himself a massage at the hotel. Or use the chilly

Pacific Ocean as a massive cold tub. He definitely needed to stop running with Connor.

Jordy tossed his phone on the bed, and it hit something. A box of colored pencils and a sketchpad. There was a note taped to the pencils.

I got these yesterday and forgot to give them to you. Retirement plan? XO, Annie

---

THE CRANE COVE High School baseball field looked exactly like the one Jordy had played on when he was in high school twenty years ago. And not in the "all baseball fields look the same" way, but in the "I could crumble one of the dugout bricks with my fingers" way.

"There you are," Jordy said when he found Annie sitting on one of the bleacher steps. Her thick brown ponytail had been pulled through the hole in the back of her ball cap, and he was torn about whether to pull her ponytail or push down the brim of her hat. Instead, he sat down next to her and bumped her shoulder with his. "Where were you today?"

She sighed, looking at him sidelong. "Don't take this the wrong way, but you're very distracting."

"I'm going to take that the right way." Jordy leaned back, propping his elbows on the bench behind them, and stretching his legs out in front of him. "What was I distracting you from?"

"Helping Eloise with wedding stuff. I camped out in her office until she relented and gave me a list of chores." Annie held up her left index finger. It was wrapped in a unicorn Band-Aid. "I got a papercut and had to steal this from Kiki's stash."

"See, I would've thought Kiki's would have vampires on them."

"I save those for October." Kiki daintily lowered herself down next to him. The assistant manager of the Crane Hotel knew how to leave an impression. Dressed from head to toe in black, she could have been packaged and sold as Sports Goth Barbie. The gigantic black sunhat and the small umbrella shielded her from the sun, like the long sleeves and leggings under her T-shirt and shorts weren't enough.

"I have some 'I Want To Suck Your Blood' stickers leftover from the blood drive, if you want," Kiki offered. "What's your blood type? You have great veins."

"A negative," Jordy answered. "Only time I've gotten that kind of grade."

"I'm B positive," Annie said, leaning across Jordy's lap to better talk to Kiki. She wrapped her hand around his leg and tucked her fingers into the bend of his knee.

"Only time I had a better GPA than you, too," he joked, trying to think about anything that would keep the blood in his brain.

Kiki twirled her umbrella. "What was your GPA?"

"A big ol' 'Oh No'."

Annie sat up straight, and before Jordy could wonder why, Mallory stopped in front of their group with Connor on her heels, a clipboard that said Coach McMahon on the back in her hands. Connor must have come straight from track practice because he had a whistle hanging around his neck and a faint sheen of sweat on his forehead.

Mallory pointed the end of her pen at Jordy. "Did you ever play baseball?"

"Uh. Little league through high school."

"Were you any good?"

Connor scrubbed his face with the heel of his hand. "The man's a goddamn professional athlete, Mal."

The pint-sized blonde was undeterred. "Answer the question."

Small, aggressive women terrified him. "Uh, yeah? I was the varsity catcher?"

Mallory nodded, wrote something down, and showed it to Connor, who didn't need any help looking over her shoulder.

"I mean, it's a choice," he said, shrugging.

"Annie, what about you? Sports?"

"I ran track in seventh grade?" Annie offered, her fingertips digging into the soft underside of his knee. "I was a Mathlete. My team sports were Science Olympiad and Knowledge Bowl. Sorry?"

Mallory made a note. "We're going to talk about bar trivia later, Doc."

"That's what I call you," Jordy grumbled under his breath as Mallory and Connor walked away. He looked at Kiki, who was still twirling her umbrella. "What are they doing?"

"Scouting report," she said. "They take the baseball games very seriously."

"Are they captains?"

"Co-captains. Unofficial town ordinance states that Mallory and Connor have to be on the same team because they're too competitive. It's safer for everyone if they're on the same side."

"I'm having flashbacks to PE," Annie joked, but her grip on his leg tightened again.

Jordy looped an arm around her shoulders. "You'll be great."

A sharp whistle pierced the air. Connor tugged his whistle —still looped around his neck—out of Mallory's hand.

"Hey!" Mallory shouted. "Shut up!"

About thirty adults had gathered around the bleachers, and a collective twenty-nine heads turned toward the sound. Kiki looked up at the sky.

"Think it'll rain?"

Connor shook his head. "Usual rules apply. You can pick overhand or underhand pitch, but you're stuck with what you pick for the duration of the inning. Tie goes to runner. The ump is God—"

"And we got an ump that looks like a God! Thanks for volunteering, Leo!" Mallory pointed to where Leo was standing next to the stands and lead the group in a round of applause.

Connor put his hands on his hips and glared down at Mallory. "You're making this hard," he told her, and she shrugged. He rolled his eyes and resumed his booming shout. "Your entire lineup has to bat, and everyone has to play defense at least once. No bench riders."

"Schoolyard pick-'em. No take backs, no trades," Mallory added, giving the other team's captains a long, hard stare. Jordy didn't recognize them.

"Are the twins coming?" Annie asked Kiki. "This seems like the kind of thing they'd be into."

"They usually don't make Friday games. And Sybil won't be here because she's serving a six-game suspension for nailing Mitch Appleton in the balls." Kiki collapsed her umbrella. "She claims it was an accident, but he deserved it."

Jordy pulled his knees together.

There was a quick game of rock, paper, scissors to determine picking order. Mallory won.

"Jordy!" she and Connor called at the same time.

"I finally got picked first in a draft," he joked, and took his phone out of his pocket. The draft that mattered would be starting any minute.

He turned off his phone.

"Can you put this in your purse?" He held it out to Annie. She took it, and tucked it in with her stuff.

The first few rounds of selections went fast. This was a close community where everyone knew everything about everyone. The more obvious athletes went first, and as that pool narrowed, Mallory and Connor's list came into play. They crossed off names when they were called, and had a brief conference before every pick. The bleachers began to thin out, and Jordy watched Annie try to make herself smaller and smaller as the minutes ticked by.

He stepped over to Connor, turned his back to the bleachers, and hissed, "Why haven't you picked Annie? She's just sitting there."

"She's a low-priority pick," Connor said, tapping the clipboard. Mallory called out a name that wasn't Annie's.

"I'm about to be a high-priority pain in your ass."

The shorter captain from the other team waved his finger at the bleachers. "Uh...you, in the purple. Next to Kiki."

Annie looked at Kiki, then down at her shirt. Purple. Another University of Washington T-shirt. She wandered over to her team.

"Trade someone for her," Jordy growled.

"No trades," Connor reminded him. "Schoolyard pick-'em is hard enough without this turning into a White Elephant. Joel!"

And so it went, with Kiki being their team's last selection.

"It's not personal," Mallory told him as they walked to the dugout. "It's baseball."

It sure as hell felt personal.

Connor held out a big red gear bag. "Catcher," he told Jordy.

"Don't I get a say?"

"No," the co-captains answered in unison.

Assignments were doled out for the first inning. Jordy had no idea when they had found the time to create a roster and a batting lineup, but there it was, hanging on the nail in the dugout.

"Um, Mr. Taylor, sir?"

Jordy turned around, still adjusting his protective gear, and found himself eyeball to eyeball with a kid whose ability to legally vote was seriously in question. Could he even drive?

"Yes?"

Nervous laughter filled the air. "Wow, um, it's, uh, very nice to meet you, sir. I'm, uh—" He wiped his sweaty palm on his shorts and held it out. "I'm Clifford. Cliff. I am a really big fan and I can't believe I'm meeting you. I've been watching you on TV since—"

Jordy cut him off. "How old are you?"

"Nineteen, sir."

He could feel his bones crumbling into dust. "I can do the math. Please don't confirm the numbers for me." He shook Cliff's hand. "I'll get you an autograph or something after the game, okay?"

Jordy hadn't gotten into a catcher's stance in a very long time. It was inevitable that his knees and hips were going to hate him in the morning, so he hoped that Connor pitched as good as he ran so the innings would be short. Maybe he could tag in that Cliff kid...

A few practice pitches, and Connor signaled he was ready. They hadn't worked out any signs, so Jordy was going to have to guess what was coming at him. Odds were it was going to be a fastball special all night long. The first batter stepped up to the plate, tapped the end of his bat three times against home plate, and assumed a stance that looked like it belonged in a cartoon about baseball. It would work, but it was inefficient as hell. His high school coach would have beat him with the bat if he'd stood like that.

The first pitch was fast and so far on the inside of the box that the batter jumped as he swung.

"Strike one," Leo called.

The batter turned to argue, and Mallory shouted from short-stop, "No arguing with the ump, Mitch!"

Was this the same Mitch Sybil had hit to earn her suspension? If so, Jordy had to question if Connor hadn't thrown it close on purpose. The guy did have a very punchable face.

After a second strike, Mitch tipped a foul ball that Connor worked way harder than he needed to to catch, and the batter was out. Jordy still didn't know who the guy was, but the smug satisfaction that he was out was contagious.

Connor's pitches lost the killer instinct after that, and he didn't get so close to any of the other batters. His underhand pitches were less controlled, and Jordy had to chase them to catch them.

Kiki caught a ball that was almost a homerun to end the inning. She had spent most of the inning making a crown from the flowering clover in the outfield, so it had caught Jordy off guard to see her run and jump for the ball heading for the fence. Her sun hat flopped as she jogged in.

The other team placed Annie in the outfield, and Jordy was thankful none of the balls went towards her. She looked so determined and so terrified at the same time. He wanted to run out there and protect her from pop flies.

The fun thing about community baseball games was watching players who came out just for fun jumping up and down when they finally made it on base. It became obvious to Jordy by the end of the second inning that Crane Cove didn't have enough people who took the game seriously to create a competitive league, but those that did take it seriously bit their tongues to keep it friendly.

Connor only pitched the first inning, then moved to third base. He was replaced by a girl who looked barely old enough to drive. She could definitely pitch, though.

Halfway through the top of the fifth, Annie came up to bat

for a second time. Her first at bat had gone quickly, but that was because she'd swung and missed three pitches. The grim determination on her face made his stomach clench. Something was wrong.

The first pitch was low, and she chased it. Strike one.

The second pitch was dead center, but she only chipped it, and it skittered foul.

As she lined up for her third pitch, Jordy saw her jaw tighten, her chin wobble, and the corners of her mouth quiver.

Fucking hell.

He jumped up. "Time!"

Jordy took off his glove and tucked it under his arm, but left his catcher's mask on because it was the only thing keeping him from kissing away all the frustration, embarrassment, and sadness he could see so plainly on her face.

"Hey." He kept his voice low so only she—and maybe Leo—could hear. "What's wrong? Why are you upset?"

"I suck," Annie whispered back, her voice cracking on the vowels. "This is just the latest in a string of things I'm horrible at lately."

If she'd been looking for the quickest way to break his heart, this was it.

"You do not suck. Ty Cobb, best batter there ever was, only hit about three and a half of every ten balls thrown to him. You got a chunk out of that last one."

Annie sniffled. "You're just being nice so I won't cry."

"I don't want you to cry, but that's not why I'm being nice." Jordy wrapped his hand around the back of her neck and pressed his forehead—or more accurately the top of his catcher's mask—against hers. "I believe in you. You don't quit when something is hard. If you did, you wouldn't have a PhD. You are Doctor Roxanne Motherfucking Price. You can do anything you put your mind to. And that"—he tapped her temple—"is a great mind."

"You mean it?"

"Every word."

Annie took a deep, shaky breath. "Woooo...Okay, shake it off. Shake it off." She wiggled her whole body like someone dropped an ice cube down the back of her shirt.

"Let's fix your stance."

"What's wrong with my stance?" Annie asked as Jordy rearranged her hands on the handle. "I hold the bat and swing at the ball. Isn't that it?"

"This is about fifty percent of why you're not hitting," he explained, tapping the insides of her feet with the tip of his toe until she moved them far enough apart that he was happy. "The other half," he continued, angling her hips, "is that you have no patience and swing at everything that gets thrown at you."

"That feels like a metaphor for my life...Everyone is staring at us."

From the direction of third base, Mallory shouted, "You're not supposed to be helping her! She's on the other team!"

Jordy ignored her, pushing Annie's back elbow up and her front elbow down. "How does that feel?"

"Weird."

"Yeah, well, you said that about—"

"Jordan. Public," she hissed, her cheeks turning a brilliant shade of pink. He grinned at her, loving watching the negative tension slowly disappear from her face.

"When you swing, make sure you follow all the way through. Don't stop once you make contact."

"You're really sweet," she told him, and he wanted to melt like butter on a hot sidewalk.

"Nah." Jordy forced his hand back into his glove. "You ready to hit this out of the park?"

ANNIE DID NOT HIT it out of the park. But she did get on base, and when the game was over, with Jordy's team winning 8-5, he took her out for ice cream.

Crane Cone was overflowing with sweaty, vaguely dirty adults. The teens working called Connor "Mr. McMahon," which made Mallory snort-laugh. In response, Connor pushed the brim of her hat down so she couldn't see. Jordy had to dig in Annie's purse for his wallet, and the amount of random crap in there was fascinating. Old receipts, loose tampons, a rock...

"Why do you have a rock in here?" he asked.

"Nolan gave it to me at the zoo."

His obituary flashed before his eyes. *Jordy Taylor died in an ice cream parlor after he found that the woman of his dreams was carrying around a rock his nephew gave her. Autopsy reports confirm his heart expanded too fast and burst.*

"Shouldn't the loser pay?" Annie asked when he finally extracted his wallet from the bottom of the black hole she called a purse.

Jordy handed the cashier a twenty, waved off the change, and took their cones.

"No." He handed her her waffle cone. "My dad used to take me out for ice cream after every game to celebrate something I did right. You had a base hit."

"I only made it to first," she pointed out as they exited the crowded shop onto the equally crowded sidewalk.

Jordy grinned at her. "Want to make it to first again?"

"I was hoping for third." She took a long, slow lick of her Blackberry Bramble, and the blood rushed to his cock so fast his vision blurred.

"You're bad," he admonished, and Annie frowned. It was on

the tip of his tongue to apologize when she rooted around in her purse and pulled out her phone.

"Eloise is calling." She swiped to answer and put the phone to her ear. "Hello?...Yeah, I'm with him. Why?...Sure. I'll put him on." Annie held out her phone. Jordy took it, careful to keep it in the same spot so it wouldn't lose service.

"Eloise?"

"Sam called looking for you because you're not answering your phone."

"I was at the baseball game." His heart rate skyrocketed. "Is something wrong with Sam?"

Sam was, by his own admission, the world's most boring rock star. He didn't drink, smoke, or do drugs. His vices were kitchen supply stores, specialty markets, and yarn stores. But that didn't mean Jordy didn't get a panicked chill every time he had more than two missed calls from his best friend. What was so wrong that Sam was searching for him?

"No." Eloise drew out the word, and then he heard the shuffle of the phone being passed off.

"Where are you?" Graham asked, his voice in the no-man's-land between frustrated and panicked.

"Uh, Crane Cone. Why?"

"Because your phone is going straight to voicemail and Sam thinks you jumped off a cliff."

"I turned it off before the game started," Jordy explained. "Why is Sam worried about—"

It was like trying to figure out why his camera wasn't working only to realize he'd left the lens cap on. The draft. Something must have happened if Sam was calling and calling. Jordy's stomach clenched and his cotton candy-flavored ice cream cone felt like a hundred-pound weight in his hand.

"I'll call him," he finished, and handed Annie back her phone.

Jordy found his phone in her purse, then wandered down the sidewalk away from the crowd, turning it on and continuing to walk until the avalanche of texts and voicemails began to roll in. Priya, his teammates, friends, all wanting to know how he was doing. Six voicemails from Sam. The timestamp told him the first had come during the first hour of the draft.

Then the news alerts popped up.

Phantoms Trade Up, Take QB Nelson Sims In First Round.

He needed to sit down.

For months Jordy had wondered how he would feel during this exact scenario. Anger, sadness, even relief, were emotions he was prepared for. But numbness? The empty void of nothing was more painful than having both of his collarbones snapped at the same time. Because he wanted to feel *something*. He could deal with *something*. Years of mental skills coaching could be used on *something*. But nothing? There wasn't a fix for nothing.

SAM I AM

Answer. Your. Fucking. Phone.

I'm fine.

He wasn't.

Annie wrapped her an arm around his middle and rested her head on his chest.

"Let's go home," she said softly.

They dropped their ice cream into a nearby trash can and wandered back to Annie's car. Jordy felt like he was in a dense fog, unable to see more than a foot in front of him. The beep of her doors unlocking might as well have been a mile away. She had to remind him to buckle his seatbelt.

Nothingness consumed him, chewed at the edges of his mind, spat him out, and started again. He let Annie guide him into the lighthouse, dimly aware of her starting the shower.

With robotic movements, he stripped off his clothes, fully on autopilot. Her hand, which always felt so small in his, curled around his fingers and tugged him under the water. In Jordy's experience, women liked to scald themselves in the shower, and growing up with three older sisters, he got used to lukewarm showers. But the lava water felt good. Almost as good as Annie's nails scratching his scalp as she worked shampoo into his hair. He dropped his head for her, let her rinse and repeat with conditioner, gently working out any tangles she found.

Then she was handing him a towel, scrunching out the wetness from her hair, and then his when he didn't do it, and she led him back to his room, handing him clothes before putting on a T-shirt of his and a pair of his boxer briefs. Normally he would have found that sexy as hell, but the scared, sad look in those beautiful hazel eyes told him she was too afraid to leave him to put on her own clothes.

Did he look that bad?

Jordy lay down on the bed. The little lighthouse that had been too cold for the last two weeks was too hot, and Annie opened the window to let the cool ocean breeze in. The gentle sound of the ocean meeting the coastline filled the room.

Annie stood by the bed, glancing between him and the door, the worried crease in her forehead deep.

"Stay?"

His voice creaked like a hinge rusted by the salt air, but the request was all she needed. Annie drew the knitted throw blanket over them and nestled herself against his body. A featherlight kiss tickled his neck. Half of him wanted to roll her onto her back, sink into her welcoming warmth, and find solace in her body. Making her arch and gasp gave him a purpose, and he wanted purpose right now. But the other half, the half that won, had found its safe spot in her arms, simply being held without needing anything else.

Everything else might be shit, but this, this was perfect. This was what mattered. Annie mattered.

Jordy drifted to sleep like that, the smell of salt water and clean hair in his nose, and the sound of waves and synchronized breathing relaxing him.

EIGHTEEN

JORDY WAS A SNUGGLER.

Annie wasn't exactly surprised. He was very affectionate when he was awake, but the degree of snuggling caught her off guard. She woke up with him half on top of her, his leg wedged between hers, his face nestled between her boobs, and his arms tight around her. She had to pee, but she couldn't bring herself to wake him or even try to extract herself from his hold. The hollow look on his face from the night before would haunt her for a long time and if staying half trapped beneath him kept it away, she would do it.

Outside their little open window, the world was waking up. The birds were talking to each other, the ocean was leaving the shore until midday, and the sun was casting its first pale rays. The light caught the sleep-rumpled frizz of Jordy's hair, turning each strand to glittering gold or silver. Gently, Annie combed back the waves that had fallen across his face.

He was so beautiful it hurt.

This was why she had said they shouldn't *sleep* together. Because the intimacy, the vulnerability, was too much to bear. The horrible, terrible truth she couldn't deny in the softness of the morning was that she was falling in love with him. Not just the funny, goofy guy who made her laugh until her stomach hurt and she was scared she was going to pee her pants, but the man who stopped a baseball game because he saw that she was spiraling to a dark place. The man who teased her but never made fun of her, who made her oatmeal and juggled eggs. And the man that spooned her on the sofa while watching Sandra Bullock movies, but also fucked her in a brewery bathroom.

In retrospect, Jake had been easy to get over because she wasn't grieving the loss of his love, but mourning the time, energy, and effort she had poured into something that was never going to pan out. Someone who didn't value and respect her the way he should have. They had been perfect on paper, but lackluster in reality. Jordy was the opposite. They shouldn't work, but they did. Simple, easy, perfect.

There had been a guilt-ridden glimmer of hope when she realized his football career might be over, because then she stood a chance. It might have been a snowball's chance in the Sahara Desert, but the chance was there. If he retired, she could find her courage and ask him out on a date. And then ask him to stay with her forever. What a wonderful world it would be if she went to work every day and came home to him waiting for her.

She hoped she wasn't the only one falling in love.

Jordy's sharp intake of breath scared the shit out of her.

He groaned, arched like a cat being woken from a sun nap, and then rubbed his nose against her sternum.

"Oh, hi," he mumbled into her chest. She could hear his smile.

"Are you talking to me or my boobs?"

"Both?" Another nuzzle. "You're wearing my clothes."

Annie chuckled. "I wear your clothes a lot." Once she'd started, it turned out she couldn't stop.

"I like it," he said, kissing the inner curve of her cleavage through the cotton. The scrape of his teeth made her jump.

"Nuh-uh," she tsked, gripping his hair and pulling his head up a fraction of an inch. "My bridesmaid dress doesn't allow for hickeys there."

"What does your bridesmaid dress look like?" Jordy's pupils dilated, and Annie wondered what his imagination was conjuring. Probably a neckline that went to her belly button and a slit that went to her hip.

She loosened her grip on his hair. "Do you want me to spoil the big reveal?"

"A little." He pressed a kiss to her diaphragm. "Like, is this a good spot?" Another one right above her belly button. "Or here?"

"You'll find out next week," Annie promised, shivering as the blanket followed Jordy's exploration down her body. And then his cotton-muffled kisses found her clit, and she shivered for a different reason. "Whatcha doin', buddy?"

"Trying to find a safe spot," he said innocently before licking her clit again. "I've never been turned on by men's underwear before. I'm having a weird moment right now."

She lifted her hips toward his mouth. They needed to have a talk about his future and their future, but that could happen after she'd had an orgasm or two.

Her bladder had other ideas.

"I have to pee."

"And that's a hard no." Jordy sat back on his heels. "Hurry back."

Annie scrambled out of the bed. The little house was back to its normal brisk temperature, and her skin sprouted goosebumps as she rushed to the bathroom.

After she'd relieved her bladder and given her teeth a cursory brush, Annie paused in the living room. She'd been saving a certain surprise for later, but there was no time like the present.

The brown padded envelope was shoved in the back of her nightstand drawer. Annie grabbed it, tore open the top, and grabbed the cold metal handcuffs from inside. Bless two-day shipping.

"Are you coming back?" Jordy called from across the house.

Annie had a sexy, dramatic reveal planned for the cuffs, but she only got as far as the door lean before she burst out laughing. Jordy was lying stretched out on his side, completely naked, one hand resting jauntily on his hip. And he was grinning. That was what made her laugh. That damn cocky grin.

At the start of every school year, a tent filled with posters popped up on the mall at whatever college she had been attending so students could decorate their rooms. The posters changed every year, but there was one of Burt Reynolds that was always there. He was laying on a bearskin rug, completely naked, the only thing between the world and his penis a strategically angled wrist. That was what Jordy's pose reminded her of, minus the shielding of the goods.

"Miss me?"

"Why?" she wheezed, still laughing, clinging to the door frame for support.

"I was trying to make myself appealing for you." He patted the mattress next to him. "Now get back here so I can pick up where I left off."

Annie dabbed away the tears in her eyes with the collar of his T-shirt and took a few steadying breaths, though the first few dissolved back into snickers.

When she'd calmed herself, she said, "I actually had a slightly different idea."

She held up the handcuffs, letting them dangle between her fingers. Jordy's eyebrows shot up, and his cock twitched.

"I'm listening."

"What if"—Annie sat down on the bed, at peace that there was no way she could be the seductress she wanted to be but it didn't matter because Jordy was going to pounce on her no matter what—"I handcuffed you to the headboard and tortured you until you couldn't take it anymore?"

"Define torture."

"Suck your cock." She flicked open one of the cuffs. "And if you're a really good boy, I'll sit on your face."

Jordy blinked at her, his expression blank. Two weeks ago, that would have freaked her out. Now she knew it meant that she had broken his brain a little bit and the only sound in his head was a dial-up tone.

"Yes."

There was a brief ground rules discussion as Jordy found a comfortable position and Annie threaded the handcuffs through the metal rods that made the headboard: their safe word was still flamingo, there might be some begging she was supposed to ignore, and absolutely no tickling.

Annie straddled his chest to lock the handcuffs around his wrists.

"Do those feel okay?" she asked.

Jordy nodded. "Yeah. Are you going to sit on my face now?"

"I was going to, but now I can't because you asked me to." She slid down his body until her face was level with his neck. He loved it when she kissed his neck. Drove him wild. So, she planted a few open-mouthed kisses and closed-lip pecks up and down his pulse. His breath hitched, and he jerked against the cuffs. "I'm in charge, remember?"

"Fuck," he groaned, relaxing into the mattress. "I hate this already. I want to touch you."

"Are you saying flamingo?"

"No." Jordy sighed dramatically, but turned his head to give her better access to his neck.

Annie denied him, instead trailing kisses down his shoulder, then his chest, pausing to briefly swipe her tongue across his left nipple. That didn't get much of a reaction, so she continued her journey southward. The squirming started up again when she reached his stomach.

"I said no tickling."

"I'm not tickling you. I'm kissing you."

"In a very tickly way."

"I can stop?" she offered, lips hovering over his skin.

"Don't," he begged.

"Good boy."

Annie took her time near his hips and pelvis. She was fascinated by how his pubic hair could be soft and wiry at the same time.

"You have a gray hair down here," she told him, then amended her statement, "Actually, there's a few."

"Roxanne." Jordy sounded like a man pushed past his limit and she hadn't even started. "You are so close to my dick I can feel your breath on it when you talk, and you're looking for grays?"

"Well, I never get a chance to look," she said, curling her fingers around the base, "because usually I'm—" Annie used the flat of her tongue to lick from her fist up the rigid shaft, to the weeping head, where she sealed her lips around the crown and sucked. The sound of Jordy's gasping wheeze made her drunk with power. She released him with a *pop*. "—busy."

"Whatever you want."

Annie had promised him torture, but it was closer to worship. She wanted to bathe every glorious inch of his cock in kisses, little thank-yous for all the pleasure it had brought her over the last few weeks, how it was always so happy to see her.

His small whimpers and moans made her wet, and the guttural groan when she finally took him all the way into her mouth, letting the shaft slide to the back of her throat as far as she dared to take him, made her pussy throb. His body was hers for the taking, but she missed the weight of his hand on the back of her head as she bobbed up and down.

"Ah," he moaned, squirming again. The longer she did this, the more restless he got.

Annie hummed.

Jordy winced, sucking in a sharp breath between his teeth. "Ah...ahh...shit...flamingo. Flamingo. Goddammit."

She pulled off immediately, wiping the trail of spit off her chin. "What's wrong?"

"Shoulder," he told her, grimacing again. "Cramp. Ow. Fuck, I didn't think I was too old for this, but maybe I am."

"In defense of your shoulder, it has been your moneymaker for the last twenty years." Annie crawled up the bed to where Jordy's hands were bound to the bed. "Maybe it's just jealous of all the love your penis gets."

"I tried to hold out," he promised. "I didn't want you to stop."

"Let's get you out and maybe you can sit on your hands while I blow you." Annie searched for the little lever that was supposed to release the cuffs. It wasn't there. "Um...do you know how to unlock these?"

"Push the little lever."

"It's not there."

"What do you mean it's not there?" The rise in pitch was not comforting.

"Don't they come loose if you tighten them more?"

At the same time she squeezed the cuffs tighter, Jordy said, "No."

"Oh shit."

"Key, Annie. Get the key." Jordy sounded calmer than she felt. Her lungs refused to fill and the walls of her chest were closing in with every truncated breath.

She ran across the house to her room and grabbed the bag the handcuffs had been delivered in, and tipped it over. No key fell onto the bed.

Maybe it had fallen out earlier?

Annie dropped to the floor, searching under the bed and the nightstand, trying to guess where a small key could have bounced or skidded if dropped from roughly the height of her chest.

It was nowhere to be found.

"Can you hurry, please?" Jordy shouted from across the house.

"Fuck, fuck, fuck," she hissed, shaking out the quilt and tossing the pillows to the floor.

Still no key.

Her heart was pounding in her throat, and her stomach had fallen out her ass and slithered down to the ocean. It wasn't the draft that was going to end Jordy's career. No. It was her and her stupid handcuff idea. The circulation was going to be cut off to his hands and they were going to need to be amputated and it was all her fault.

"Annie?"

She wanted to hide under the bed and never come out. How was she supposed to face him? But on trembling legs, she forced herself back across the house to stand in the doorway and say with a voice already choked with tears, "I can't find the key."

Jordy closed his eyes and took a deep breath. "Okay. Can you get my phone and call Sam?"

She edged around the bed like he could jump off the bed and hurt her. "Why Sam?"

"Because he's into this kind of stuff, and he might have a solution."

Jordy had a lot of Sams in his phone, but the only one without a last name was a Sam I Am, and Annie could make an educated guess. When the phone began to ring, she put it on speaker and left it on his chest, retreating to the corner of the room.

"Would you come here?" The thinly veiled frustration didn't make her want to move, but she sat on the end of the bed.

The ringing stopped.

"Why...are...you...calling...me...this...early?"

Sam's voice was muffled, like his face was in a pillow.

"I'm having a bit of a, um, situation," Jordy began. "Kind of stuck in some handcuffs."

"The sun is barely up. How are you already stuck in handcuffs?"

"You know I'll try anything once."

There was a sharp intake of breath and some shuffling. His voice became clearer, so he must have rolled over. "Is this how you're dealing with the news? Letting randoms chain you to things?"

Annie looked up at the ceiling, trying to blink back mortified tears. Her cheeks burned like she had fallen asleep in the sun and she wondered exactly how far it was from the edge of the cliff to the water and if there were sharp rocks for her to hit on the way down.

"A little less judgment and a little more helpful, buddy."

The eyeroll could be felt through the phone. "Your first mistake was using handcuffs. Next time, something with Velcro or a buckle, okay?"

"Sam," Jordy growled.

"There's a little lever—"

"There's not a lever," Annie interrupted, her voice cracking.

"What do you mean there's not a lever? There's always a lever or a button. Some kind of fail-safe."

Jordy sighed. "Yeah, there's not. I'm looking at them up close and personal."

"What the fuck kind of equipment are you using?"

"I don't know," she sniffled. "There was wine involved."

"Do you have any bolt cutters?"

"Why would we have bolt cutters?" Jordy asked.

"Why would you use handcuffs without safety measures? I don't know what you're doing up there." Sam grumbled something unintelligible, then said, "Call Chase and Cole. They're with the fire department. They'll get you out, and it won't end up in the news. They'll give you shit, but no press."

"Chase and Cole," Jordy repeated. "When are you coming up?"

"Soon. Did you still want me to grab—"

Jordy cut him off. "Yes."

"Okay. See you later. Love you."

"Love you, too," Jordy said, and then the screen changed when Sam hung up. "Can you find a number for the twins?"

It took twenty minutes to get a hold of the twins. Both of their phones went straight to voicemail, so they called Connor, who gave them the number for the McMahon farmhouse. Bitsy McMahon, mother of giant men, answered, and Jordy made a little small talk before asking to speak to Chase and Cole. Then they had to wait for her to go get them. Jordy looked like he was in agony, but whether it was physical, mental, or both, Annie didn't know. When the twins finally got to the phone, Jordy blurted out the problem: he was handcuffed to the bed and needed them ASAP.

They had the decency not to laugh.

Even with the promise to speed, it was still going to take

them a minimum of twenty minutes to reach the lighthouse. The tide of panic started to rise again.

"I need my underwear," he said.

Annie looked at him. His penis was flaccid, and if it never got hard for her again, she didn't blame it. Or him. Hell, as soon as the twins arrived, she was going to start packing. There were options: the hotel, Eloise's house, Sybil's house, her car.

"Maybe some pants too," he added.

Annie found his clean clothes and grabbed the first pair of underwear from the top, and then his sweatpants from the floor. She dressed him, unable to look him in the eye as she fought off tears. As soon as he was decent, she got off the bed to give him space.

"Sweetheart, you're not going to leave me here, are you?"

"I..." Annie's grip on her emotions slipped, and a single, gasping sob escaped. "I'm sorry."

"Please don't cry," he pleaded. "Please, no. No, no, no. Come here. Come here."

"But I hurt you."

"I'm going to be fine. Really. You crying is going to hurt me more than anything else."

Annie sat down on the edge of the bed, one ass cheek hanging off the side.

"I said come *here*."

Reluctantly, Annie slid closer.

"Roxanne." Jordy wasn't amused. "If I can't feel my arms, the least you could do is sit on my face."

Her eyes practically bugged out of her head, and for a second, she forgot about feeling sad or bad.

"That cannot be what you're thinking about right now."

"It's pretty much always in the back of my mind." He grinned at her, confident and casual for a man chained to a headboard. "I look around every place we go and think 'Is there somewhere I could get Annie naked?'"

A watery laugh escaped, and she wiped her eyes with the collar of the shirt again. "You do not."

"I really do." He inclined his head, inviting her closer. "If you're not going to sit on my face, at least snuggle me so I don't think you're going to abandon me to the wolves."

Annie scooted closer until her knee bumped his hip, then she lay down so her head was resting on his hard stomach. There was a familiar twitch in the crotch of his gray sweatpants.

"Oh, thank god."

"What?"

"I didn't think you were ever going to get hard for me again after this."

The force of Jordy's laughter bounced her head.

"You...you didn't think...Annie, you kneed me in the nuts the first night. If *anything* was going to give my dick pause about rising to the occasion, that would've been it."

The twins arrived twenty-five minutes later with a toolkit and a pair of Cheshire Cat grins.

"Sorry that took so long," Chase said as he crossed the threshold into the little house. "We got a little...tied up."

"He's not tied, he's handcuffed," Cole corrected, twisting his shoulder-length blond curls into a bun at the top of his head. Annie wanted pointers on his technique later because the result was amazing. "It's not a good joke."

"You came up with zero alternatives. No solutions, no complaining." Chase glanced around the interior. "So, where is he?"

"In his room," Annie said, pointing to the open door. "Is he going to be okay?"

"When did you find him?" Cole asked as they crossed in a cluster. The twins made the house feel smaller.

"Find him?"

"Yeah. How long has he been handcuffed?"

"Um, I don't know. An hour? Probably less?" Annie shrugged. Should she have been keeping track of the time?

"Okay, that's not bad," Cole fished a pair of latex gloves out of his pocket. "He'll be fine. No lessons will be learned."

"Good morning, sunshine," Chase crooned when he entered Jordy's room. "Isn't it a little early in the morning for bondage?"

Cole set the tool bag on the bed and pulled out a pair of bolt cutters and a key ring filled with tiny keys.

"Why the hell do you have so many keys?" Jordy asked, craning his neck to get a better look.

"Because old people," Chase began, "get up to some freaky shit, and this is not our first 'help, I'm trapped in handcuffs' call."

"We started collecting spare keys," Cole explained, moving up to the headboard to get a better look at the handcuffs. "Holy shit. These are police-grade. Who were you fucking? Willis?"

Jordy's face flushed, and Annie considered excusing herself to change her identity and skip town.

"Just get me out."

"You cool if I cut these?" Chase asked, lining the bolt cutters up with the chain that linked the handcuffs together. Jordy nodded, and with a grunt and a big bicep flex, Chase snapped the chain in two. Jordy's arms dropped like stones. "So, seriously, who was it?" When Jordy didn't immediately volunteer the information, Chase looked at Annie. "Did you see who it was?"

It was hard to tell what was more mortifying: that Chase and Cole didn't think she could be the one fucking Jordy, or that they were about to find out she was the one fucking Jordy.

"Ummm..."

"She's wearing my clothes, asshole," Jordy growled, rolling his shoulders repeatedly.

The two seconds between the words leaving his mouth and them sinking into the twins' thick skulls passed like a year. Trees lost their leaves and regrew them before Cole finally went, "Ohhhh."

"Hold up." Chase looked between them three times. "You're"—he pointed to Annie—"with—" He pointed to Jordy, then back again. "And Graham's okay with this? Because there's a very strict 'No Annie' moratorium."

Cole raised an eyebrow. "I can't believe you didn't choke on that word." He boosted himself up on the bed and sat crisscross in front of Jordy, inserting the first of many keys into the lock.

Jordy shrugged. "We're consenting adults. It's fine." Then he added, "But don't tell Graham. Or Sybil."

Annie wrapped her arms around her middle. Half of her understood that Jordy was protecting her—and them—from scrutiny. But the other half worried that "consenting adults" meant that he really was only in this for the sex, and once the wedding was over, so were they. He wasn't exactly boldly declaring his feelings for her.

"Yeah, I'd be more scared of Sybil," Cole said, making casual conversation while he tried keys. "Graham will get over it. Sybil will wait until you think she's over it, then strike when you least expect it." Cole had gone through five keys with no luck.

Jordy rested his head back against the metal slats. "Comforting."

Cole tried another key. "Remember when I told you we should label these?"

The twentieth key did the trick. Annie counted. Jordy's wrists were red but not raw, and that only made her feel marginally better. The moment the twins left—after getting a promise they would swing by the brewery later—Jordy opened his arms and Annie crawled into their safe haven. She examined his wrists up close to ensure she agreed with Chase's assessment that he was fine and kissed the red marks that were fading.

Jordy kissed her temple. "Are you okay?"

"Shouldn't I be asking you that?"

"You cried. That scared me." He nuzzled her neck, the brush of his nose sending pleasant tingles down her body. "So are you okay?"

She nodded, threading their fingers together and wrapping his arms around her body. The warmth of him behind her and the weight of his arms on her body was perfect. "If you're okay, I'm okay." She tipped her face up toward his. "Do you still like me?"

"Sweetheart," he squeezed her tightly, "I don't think I'm ever going to stop liking you."

NINETEEN

JORDY SHOULD HAVE KNOWN the invitation to brunch was a trap. But no one turned down the chance to eat at the Crane Hotel. Not when a brunch reservation was possibly the most coveted reservation on the entire Oregon coast, if not the state.

Plus, Graham had promised bottomless mimosas.

That should have been the dead giveaway. Because after he had been sufficiently plied with juice, champagne, and fancy French toast, Jordy found himself in the ballroom learning something called the "foxy" from a man who had clearly based his entire look off Robin Williams in *The Birdcage*.

Jordy wanted to know where he bought his shirts.

"Aren't you supposed to be doing this with your wife?" Jordy asked as he took the follower part of the partnership. He wasn't sure he trusted Graham to walk him backwards.

"She's at the spa with Annie. Her mom gets in tomorrow, and I'm trying to pre-relax her. They'll be here soon."

"And I make a good substitute?"

"Well, the long hair helps."

Jordy stepped on his foot. "Oops."

"We're walking, not trodding, boys," Gavin called from across the ballroom, where he was consulting with his assistant, a tall, slender blond woman with fading pink and blue hair. "Don't trample each other, please."

"Is this what you've been struggling to master?" Jordy asked. The basic step was simple enough. Walk, walk, sway, sway was the basic gist of it.

"There was a waltz. Lots of spinning and dipping. This is the panic alternative."

"You'll be fine," Jordy promised. "I think the whole point is to look all goo-goo-eyed at each other while everyone else eyes the bar." He batted his eyelashes to demonstrate.

"Speaking of bars..." Graham trailed off, letting the pregnant pause do the talking for him.

"This isn't a football wedding. I'll behave."

"Thank you."

"Aww, you guys are so cute," Eloise's voice echoed through the empty ballroom. She and Annie were standing in the door, watching with grins on their faces. Annie had her phone out, and Jordy had a strong suspicion she'd been recording.

"No dip?" Annie heckled as the men broke apart. A pair of heels dangled from her fingertips.

"He's heavy," Graham complained, holding out his hand to his bride. Eloise went to him like she was on a string.

They were a far cry from the stressed-out couple they'd been on Thursday night. Eloise pushed herself up on her tiptoes, and Graham leaned down to meet her in a brief, affectionate kiss. Ease and adoration rolled off them in waves. Whatever they did in the spa must be magic because Eloise looked relaxed enough to melt into the floor.

"Decided to get started without me?" she teased, smoothing Graham's shirt front.

"Yeah, but I always finish with you."

Eloise blushed, and Jordy decided he was done eavesdropping on their conversation. If it was him, things would've taken a sharp turn south, and he didn't need to know what happened in their bedroom.

Annie was sitting by the tall blonde woman, talking as she put on her heels, and he wandered over as casually as he could, like he hadn't missed her since she'd left his bed that morning. Friday night, Jordy hadn't fully appreciated falling asleep next to Annie. Too many emotions. But Saturday night? He'd tucked himself against her like a spoon in a drawer and kissed her shoulders and neck. The little tummy she had was soft under his hand, and he hoped she didn't hate him touching it because he loved it. And inevitably, holding her tummy made him think about her tummy getting bigger and rounder, and was there a casual way to ask the woman you weren't dating if she wanted to get married and have babies?

"What's up, Doc?"

"My bones are jelly, and I'm going to break my ankle in these shoes," Annie answered, holding her hands out. He pulled her to her feet. "Have you met Lacey?"

"No, not really." Jordy didn't want to admit he had already forgotten her name.

"Lacey, this is Jordy. Jordy, this is Lacey. We met at Queens."

Lacey looked him up, down, then up again. "This isn't—"

Annie shook her head quickly, which made Lacey raise a skeptical eyebrow, then she crossed herself like she was in mass before walking over to Gavin.

"This isn't what?" Jordy asked.

"Nothing," Annie deflected. "How was brunch?"

"Ah-mazing, but you could have told me we were doing this."

"And deprive Graham of his dastardly plan?" Annie shook her head. "Never."

He looked down at her feet. "Why are you wearing heels if you're going to break your ankle?"

"Because they're my bridesmaid shoes and I don't want to trip in front of everyone." Annie adjusted her bun. "It's not that I *can't* walk in heels, I just don't do it very often and it feels awkward and unnatural. I don't know how Eloise does this every day of her life."

Jordy pursed his lips, then said, "How about this. If you trip and fall, I'll trip and fall, and it will be way more embarrassing for me because I'm not walking around on stilts."

Annie smiled and he might as well have been made out of helium because he felt so floaty. "It's sweet how willing you are to injure yourself to defend my ego."

"Any time, Doc."

Gavin clapped his hands to get their attention. "Less flirting, more being in position to dance." Jordy instinctively took three big steps back from Annie. "You're getting married in less than a week, and unless you want the junior high shuffle-and-sway, we need to get to work."

Not about him and Annie. Graham and Eloise were flirting. The adrenaline leaked out of his system until he felt like a balloon forgotten under a side table found weeks after the party had ended.

"Should we wait for Sam and Sybil?" Eloise asked as they lined up as an awkward class of two pairs.

"Sam wouldn't know on time if it bit him in the ass," Graham said, "and I don't think Sybil was as receptive to the idea as you thought she was."

Jordy perked up. "Sam's here? When did Sam get here?"

Sam hadn't been forthcoming with his itinerary, but that

was normal. In a former life, he'd probably been a feral housecat.

"Late last night. We're trying to get a dinner together tonight, if the lighthouse contingent is interested."

Annie leaned around him. "The lighthouse accepts."

Gavin began teaching, going over the basic steps again. Jordy was jealous of how easy and graceful he and Lacey made the dance look. It wasn't that he was a bad dancer, but there was a smoothness of movements he was never going to be able to replicate.

Annie was not a good dancer. As soon as the music started, her entire frame collapsed, taking any of the tension he needed to guide her with it.

"Stand up straight, sugar," Gavin told her, putting a hand on her back. "I don't know why you tall girls try and make your-selves smaller when you were born to be magnificent." He moved her head next, so she was looking at Jordy instead of her feet. "Your partner is gorgeous. Get lost in those pretty blue eyes and let him do all the work."

Annie nodded, her cheeks growing redder with every second she maintained eye contact with him. Jordy wondered if she was remembering all the times he had told her to relax and let him do all the work. He sure as shit was.

"Step, step, sway, sway," Jordy reminded her as they moved around the floor.

"Why are you so good at everything you touch?" Annie asked, squeezing the top of his bicep.

"This is physical. You'd kick my ass in a spelling bee." He turned her into a shallow dip. "And as long as you look into my pretty blue eyes..."

Annie tried to hide her laugh and snorted at his impression of Gavin's Southern drawl.

He brought her upright, then a little closer than necessary. "Walk, walk, sway, sway. Walk, walk, sway, sway. Look at us."

It was like her baseball swing. Once Annie relaxed and stopped trying to be perfect, she was good. The more he talked to her, the less she tried to look at their feet, and it flowed. As he turned them, a figure lingering in the doorway caught his eye.

"Sam!"

Annie jumped in his arms, startled by the loudness of his voice. Truthfully, it caught Jordy off guard too, but he'd missed the hell out of his best friend and the volume had erupted like a confetti cannon.

Sam put down a backpack Jordy recognized as one from his house and made his way toward them, his hands in his pockets. The excitement had worn off, and Jordy noticed the tired shadows under his eyes and how his face was drawn into a persistent frown. Sam might've been a cranky son of a bitch on a normal day, but he didn't usually look like it from across a room.

"Hey, buddy." Jordy drew Sam into a bear hug, squeezing until he heard Sam's back crack and he grunted.

"Fuck. Stop trying to kill me," Sam groaned, hugging him back.

"You didn't tell me you got into town."

"I didn't know if you were still messing with handcuffs," Sam answered as Graham walked up behind him.

"Handcuffs?"

Gavin saved him.

"We can dance or we can talk, but either way I'm leaving in forty-five minutes." He tapped his wrist for emphasis.

"Come on, Sam," Lacey said, tying her faded multi-color hair back into a ponytail. "I'll be your partner."

Sam scrutinized her. "Do I know you?"

Her eyebrows raised a fraction of an inch in unamused surprise. "Seriously?"

There was a stare-down. It didn't even last the chorus of the song, but it ended with Lacey rolling her eyes and tightening her ponytail.

"Whatever. Come show me what you've got, music man."

What Sam had was rhythm. Jordy could pick up a step, but Sam could pick up the beat, and while it wasn't as effortless as Gavin and Lacey demonstrating, it looked damn good. Even with Lacey looking over Sam's shoulder and Sam looking at her with a deepening frown their bodies moved like they were meant to do this.

Sybil showed up for the last fifteen minutes, and she looked as tired as Sam did.

"I'm here!" she announced to the ballroom. "There was a bean-splosion."

"What do you think a bean-splosion is?" Annie whispered, a coy grin hiding in the corners of her mouth.

"I don't know. Kind of sounds like..." Jordy tickled the back of her hand with his index finger, pretending he was playing with her clit. Annie choked back a laugh.

Lacey used Sam to show Sybil the basic steps, and then moved out of the way. Sybil showed Sam a small hole in the elbow of her red cardigan instead of assuming her dance position, and he examined it. Jordy was pretty sure he said he could fix it because some of the tension in Sybil's body eased. Not that it made much of a difference.

The song switched, and it took five steps before Gavin hollered, "Sybil Morgan, you are not in charge right now."

Her frustrated growl echoed in the ballroom.

At the end of class, Sybil shrugged off her sweater and handed it to Sam. Gavin put his hands on Graham and Eloise's shoulders and, with a dramatic sigh, said this was a much better idea than the original plan.

"We can always work on the waltz another time," he told

them, "but this is a better choice for your wedding. Don't forget to practice, and we'll do this again in the studio on Tuesday, okay?"

Sybil raised her hand. "Is our attendance required for that?"

Annie looked up at Jordy. "You don't have to go," she said. "I probably should."

"You're better than you think you are," he told her, "but if you want to go, I want to go."

Annie started to lean toward him for a kiss, then stopped, her face flushing. She quickly turned and walked over to Eloise and Sybil, wedging herself into their conversation. Jordy needed to have some conversations soon so he could kiss her anytime he wanted.

Sam sidled up to him, Sybil's sweater draped over his crossed arms. "Why did you need your camera?"

"To take pictures."

Graham put his arm around Sam's shoulders and gave him a squeeze. "Pictures of what?"

"The beautiful scenery," Jordy answered.

THE TABLE STRETCHED the limits of Graham and Eloise's formal dining room. It had been set for twelve, and no one seemed to mind that it was cozy. The plates were mismatched because half of them came from Sybil's house, and Jordy was drinking wine out of a Cranberry Brothers pint glass.

Sam proved that he was incapable of making a casual meal because every inch of the tabletop, and a small side table that had been dragged in from the living room, was filled with food. Crab ravioli with a garlic butter sauce, spring vegetable salad, two roast chickens, a cedar plank-grilled salmon, grilled asparagus, fresh bread from Connor's house, and the promise of straw-berry rhubarb pie and homemade ice cream.

Jordy was sandwiched between Sam and Chase. He would have rather been sitting next to Annie, but he got the next best thing, which was sitting across from her so at least he got to look at her. She was having a deep conversation about crows and ravens with Kiki, and goddamn, there was nothing sexier than watching her talk about birds. Well, maybe a couple of things, but if she had her clothes on, Dr. Roxanne Price was his favorite.

Graham stood up and gently tapped his fork on his glass a few times to get the attention of the room, which was about as successful as fixing a broken lamp with bubblegum.

Eloise rose to her feet next to him, and a hush fell over the room.

"This dinner is something Eloise and I have wanted to do for a long time, and while not everyone could be here tonight, it was important to us to have this time with our family before the relatives arrived." He turned to Annie. "Present company excluded."

Annie raised her glass in his direction. "Thank you."

Graham curled an arm around Eloise's waist. "You all are the family of our hearts, the ones we got to choose. Without you, we wouldn't be standing here, getting ready to get married. I know I wouldn't be the person I am without my friends—" His voice caught as he gestured toward Sam and Jordy with his glass. There was a bowling ball-sized lump forming in Jordy's throat, and he was afraid to look at Sam in case he was close to losing it too. "Your friendship has kept me grounded through the years. Without your constant badgering and mockery, I never would have gotten on that plane to come to Crane Cove, and I would have lost out on the best thing that ever happened to me."

Jordy looked over his shoulder and pretended to cough, but he needed to swipe at his eyes instead.

"I grew up without siblings, but I got my brothers exactly when I needed them." Graham looked at Kiki. "And you are the little sister I always wanted. But if you repeat that at work, I will fire you."

Laughter rippled through the group. Even Jordy knew Graham threatened to fire Kiki at least four times a week, but he would walk over hot, broken glass for her.

"Chase and Cole, you are the little brothers I definitely didn't ask for." Graham cleared his throat a few times, clearly afflicted with the same lump Jordy was. "Fuck. Um, whew, okay. Connor and Sybil, thank you for taking such good care of my wife. Annie, thank you for believing me when I told you I loved your cousin more than anything and for giving me the second chance I didn't deserve."

"You're making us all cry, boss," Kiki said, trying to dab at her eyes with her napkin before her mascara ran.

"Okay, okay. I'm almost done." Graham tipped his glass toward Mallory. "I never know what to say to you, Mal. But I'm grateful for your brutal honesty and unwavering support for all of my bad ideas."

"Yolo," Mallory whooped, raising her glass in salute.

"That's still not a word," Connor insisted from the other end of the table.

"All we wanted to say," Graham continued, "is we love you, and we're grateful for all of you." He raised his glass. "To family."

The table raised their glasses and repeated, "To family."

Jordy took a big gulp of his wine and then the dishes of food got passed around the table. By the time everything settled back into place, his plate looked like he'd knocked over a fancy buffet.

"This was supposed to be served in courses," Sam whispered out of the side of his mouth. "But Graham said no because we'd be eating until midnight."

"Some of us are old and have bedtimes," Jordy whispered back. "Still tastes good all at once."

Sam stabbed a crab ravioli.

Jordy gestured at his plate with his fork. "If I pile all of this onto a piece of bread, will your head explode?"

"I will never speak to you again."

"Don't threaten me with a good time." He popped a ravioli into his mouth. Butter, garlic, and salty crab exploded from the pasta, a square Trojan Horse of food. Jordy moaned. "Goddamn. I don't know how you do it."

"I keep offering to teach you."

Jordy glanced across the table at Annie, then back at Sam. "I might be ready to learn if you can tone it down and teach me *easy* stuff."

"Define easy."

"I'm not making pasta from scratch."

Sam rolled his eyes. "Pasta isn't hard."

"If it wasn't hard, they wouldn't sell the dry stuff at the grocery store."

Sam snorted, hiding his smile behind a sip of his seltzer. "Peter's going to be sad he missed this."

"I'm surprised he didn't video in."

"Time zones," Sam reminded him. "I think he's filming tonight, anyway."

Jordy's phone buzzed in his pocket. He reached to silence it, but the hair on the back of his arms rose, and he pulled it out a fraction instead. *Priya.*

"I'll be right back," he told Sam, and pushed his chair back from the table.

The air was markedly chillier than it had been through the weekend, and Jordy knew he would use that as his excuse to snuggle Annie when they got back to the lighthouse. He walked over to the firepit and answered the call.

"What's up?"

The long, drawn-out sigh felt like a bucket of ice water dumped over his head. This was it. The end of his career.

"I still hate you," Priya said, and a flicker of hope ignited in his chest. A tiny, fragile ember of belief. "One year. Twenty-five million, five of that in incentives. Five million signing bonus."

Relief knocked him over like a wave, and Jordy didn't sit so much as fell into the chair behind him.

"I could have gotten more," she insisted. "If we'd gone somewhere else—"

"I didn't want anywhere else, Priya," Jordy reminded her, running a shaking hand through his hair. The flood of adrenaline might kill him. "I get to spend my last season where I wanted to be on my terms. This is my best-case scenario."

The deal had felt like a long shot when he had called Priya with the idea Saturday afternoon. One more year to get a ring, do or die, and he would be done. One more season to figure out his life so he could make Annie proud.

"Can you come back for a press conference?"

"No. It's wedding week." Plus he didn't want to lose any of his time with Annie. "Get the team together and put out a statement. Use small words so everyone thinks I wrote it. Thank the fans, the front office, coaches, yada yada yada. Send me a copy, and I'll put it on my socials."

"We could've gotten more."

Truly, Priya had gotten more than he thought she would get. He had been ready to accept a lot less to make the deal happen. That was why he wasn't in charge of negotiating his contracts.

"You can dry your tears with your big check. Did you get the kid my number?"

Another heavy sigh. "Yes. You know he can afford an apartment, right? His deal isn't exactly leaving him living out of his car."

The other thing Jordy had done that Priya did not approve of was ask her to get his number to his replacement with the offer to crash with him until the kid found a place to live. Jordy still vividly remembered how overwhelming moving to Los Angeles had been, even with the help of the team. He hadn't known anyone, and his predecessor had made things as hard as he could for him. That wasn't the legacy Jordy wanted to leave.

"Think of it like quarterback summer camp. Or don't think about it at all. He might say no."

"I think he'd be stupid to say no. I'll send over the contract soon."

"Thanks, Priya."

Jordy tucked his phone into his shirt pocket and sagged in the chair, looking up at the sky that was fading from pale to dark blue, dotted with fluffy pink and gold clouds.

The end was in sight. His future was on the horizon. He was so damn relaxed he might as well have been floating in his backyard pool with a margarita in his hand. This was the feeling he had been waiting for when he had been struggling to make his decision. Peace. Certainty. Relief.

"Hey, you okay?"

He twisted in his chair to confirm it was Annie behind him, even though he would have known her voice anywhere.

"Yeah, I am." He held out his arms to her, and she sat in his lap, settling herself against his chest. "I get to keep playing football."

The beat of silence was short but so loud it echoed through the yard.

"Congratulations," Annie said, pressing a kiss to his cheek. The smile on her face was broad but didn't quite reach her eyes. "You must be so happy."

He had been. The experience had lost some of its sparkle. He'd seen Annie get more excited over a perfectly golden grilled cheese. He thought his news would have at least ranked up there, if not above.

"One more year," he told her, "then I'm retiring."

"As long as you're happy." Another smile that was missing its usual Annie sunshine. "We should go inside before they think we're up to something."

They returned to the dinner party separately. Jordy didn't understand why Annie wasn't more excited about his news. Was she only interested in him if he was playing? That couldn't be it. Something had been off before he told her that he was going to retire after the season.

So what was it?

It probably had nothing to do with him. Her world likely didn't revolve around him the same way his had begun to revolve around her. Which was smart. One of them needed to be reasonable about this.

Jordy kept one eye on Annie for the rest of the night. Maybe he was paranoid, but it felt like she was avoiding him. No stolen glances, no trying to include him in jokes or conversation. Annie stuck to her side of the table.

Bedtime was quiet too. No music playing while they brushed their teeth, no silly dancing in the bathroom. No sex, either. He wanted to connect with her, to pull her back to him because he felt unmoored. The consolation was that she put on one of his T-shirts and tucked herself into his bed. Peace settled back over him when she put her head on his chest and closed her eyes.

If only sleep would follow.

TWENTY

ANNIE PRIDED herself on having an endless font of patience. So when she snapped at her Aunt Sandra within an hour of her descending upon Crane Cove, asking her, "Whose wedding is this?", she knew she needed to clear her head.

Her head wanted to be cleared by a grilled cheese and a cup of tomato bisque at Queens.

Out of a mixture of habit and desire, she texted Jordy to let him know where she was, then put her phone face down on the table. There was a good chance he wouldn't even get her text, or he'd see it later when they were together.

Together.

What a fucking loaded word.

Annie stabbed her soup with her spoon. Her mind was split into two halves at war with each other. One side was genuinely happy for Jordy, happy that he got to keep doing what he loved, happy that he got to end his career on his terms. The other side was hurt and angry—and overwhelmingly sad—that he was playing another season because it put her decision-making in limbo.

Lacey slid across the vinyl bench seat on the other side of the booth, pushing her tote bag into the corner.

"Hello, gorgeous," she said in a truly horrendous Barbra Streisand impression. "Why the long face?"

Annie lifted a spoonful of soup, then let it drip back into the bowl. "Do you really want me dumping on you?"

"I live to be dumped on—wait, that sounded wrong." Lacey screwed her face up in mock horror and Annie laughed. "Is it the Father of All Fuckboys?"

"He's not a fuckboy," she said, letting the tip of her spoon scrap the bottom of the bowl as she stirred her soup, "but yeah, it is about Jordy."

Lacey leaned forward, propping her head up on her upturned palms. "What did he do?"

"This makes me sound like an asshole," Annie began, the melancholy settling back into her soul like a cold, damp morning, "but Jordy is going to keep playing football."

"Why does that make you an asshole?" Lacey asked, eyeing her plate with thinly veiled interest.

"Because I should be happy for him. This is what he wanted." Annie pushed the plate toward Lacey. "And I am happy for him, but I'm sad for me because I don't know what to do about the next year until he retires."

Lacey pointed to her pickle, and Annie nodded. She hated pickles anyway. Lacey grabbed the spear and pushed the plate back.

"You do whatever you want. You know where he's going to be." She bit into the pickle and sighed happily. "Leo makes the best fucking pickles. But seriously, don't wait on him. Make your career moves for yourself, not for him. Remember..."

"He can afford the plane ticket." Annie groaned. "Do I keep looking for jobs in California? Do I even bother bringing it up or—"

"Did I not enunciate clearly?" Lacey pointed the end of the pickle at Annie. "You. Do. What's. Right. For. You. Don't let Blondie Blue Eyes be a thought in your head."

"I'm falling in love with him."

"Yeah, well, good dick will do that to you."

Annie twisted the baby hairs at the base of her neck around her index finger. "It's excellent dick, but...it's more than that. He makes me feel seen and valued. I don't want to lose that."

"If he's really all sunshine, rainbows, and Prince Charming, he'll support your decisions and figure it out." The pickle in Lacey's hand flopped around as she talked. "Trust me. I got my degree in relationships from the School of Hard Knocks. Maybe some space and time would be good for you. You've been in this perfect vacation bubble. You can't make decisions in a bubble. Unless you're Glinda the Good Witch, but she made some questionable choices too."

Annie snort-laughed.

"Lacey!" Leo shouted from behind the counter. "I don't do delivery. Come get your lunch."

"That's my cue." Lacey reached across the table and squeezed Annie's forearm. "Do me a favor and be fucking selfish, okay?"

Annie nodded.

Lacey picked up her paper bag from the counter, blew Leo a kiss, and held the door open for Jordy on her way out. Behind his back, she made eye contact with Annie and crossed herself.

"Feeling cheesy, Doc?" Jordy asked as he sat down in the spot Lacey had just vacated.

"Grilled cheese soothes the soul."

"What hurt your soul, sweetheart?"

He was so sweet and sincere in his concern that she wanted to scream. All of it started to bubble to the surface like a backed-up pipe, her fears and frustrations about his career and her career and their future together and if they had a future together or if she had spun these fantasies about them from nothing but wishes and hopes. The words bumped against her teeth, and she clenched her jaw, trying to sort and filter before she spoke.

Her phone began to buzz on the table, and their eyes went to it in sync. Jordy flipped it over. The number on the screen seemed vaguely familiar, but Annie couldn't remember why.

The call ended before she could answer.

"I wonder who it was," Jordy mused, stretching his legs out under the table so their calves touched.

"Probably a bot caller." Annie dipped her grilled cheese in her cooled soup. The phone vibrated twice. New voicemail. "Want to listen?"

"Sure, why not?"

Annie hit the cassette tape icon and wondered how many kids had no idea what an answering machine was, and put it on speaker phone.

"You have one new message," the robot voice announced. "First new message."

"Dr. Price, this is Dr. MacArthur-Wilson. I'm calling in regard to the research position you applied for last fall. A spot opened up on the team for the summer, and I wanted to see if you were still interested and available. It would be a quick turnaround, so please get back to me as soon as possible at..."

Annie's ears were buzzing. There was a phone number at the end of the message, but her brain didn't absorb the numbers. Three weeks ago, she would have called the head of the project back before the message had ended. This was exciting. This was what she wanted. This was simultaneously the best and worst phone call of her life.

"Is that a job?" Jordy asked, his eyes flicking from her phone to her face and back again rapidly.

Annie nodded, still processing the news.

"Are you taking it?"

She took a deep breath, consciously filling her lungs with air because this was one of those times she forgot to take actual breaths.

"I don't know."

He frowned. "What do you mean you don't know? I know it sounds temporary, but if it could become permanent—"

"It's out of the country, Jordy." She flipped her phone over.

"Where?"

"South America. Peru."

"Oh."

That single syllable sounded like he hoped she was going to say Canada or Mexico. Somewhere out of the country that wasn't that far. Not a different continent.

"And it's just for the summer?" he asked.

She nodded, looking out the window. A hummingbird fluttered and flitted at the bright pink window box flowers Leo had put out.

"You have to take it," he said. "If you want it, you have to take it."

"It's not that simple..." Annie hid behind her hands.

"What's complicated about it?" Jordy tapped the side of her foot with his, and when she looked at him, his face was so earnest it made her chest ache. "What are you worried about?"

"Everything," she admitted, her voice small. "What if this is the wrong choice? What if there's another job that's long term that I can't take because I went to Peru for the summer? What if I get there and I'm horrible and ruin my reputation? Not that I have much of a reputation to ruin, but I'd rather not destroy it my first year post-grad. What if I'm great but the project is a bust and I wasted a summer of my life? Because a lot of science is 'well, fuck, that didn't work out like we thought it was going to.'"

Jordy put his hands palms up in the middle of the table in invitation, and she put hers in his. The size of his hands still astonished her. Annie wasn't a small woman, but Jordy made her feel dainty.

"As a non-science person," he said, squeezing her hands, "that is not comforting."

Some of the tension eased from her shoulders, and she chuckled. "I won't tell you how many great discoveries have been accidents then."

"Thank you." He squeezed her hands again. "Do you want my opinion?"

"Yes, please."

"Take the research trip. If nothing happens, you're only a couple of months behind. But I would hate to have you miss out on something amazing."

Annie looked down at their joined hands, eyes following his thumbs as they stroked the backs of her hands. It was hypnotizing. "What if I miss out on something amazing here?"

"Everything here will still be here when you get back."

"TAKE MY MONEY!" Jordy insisted.

"No! It's too much. This isn't coffee, Jordan. It's a three-hundred-dollar backpack."

"Roxanne. Do you know what my signing bonus is for this contract?"

Annie narrowed her eyes suspiciously. "No?"

"Five million dollars. Let me buy the fucking backpack."

"You win." Annie pushed her laptop towards him. "I wear size nines if you want to go wild and buy me new hiking boots too."

Monday night Wine and Whining had been canceled

because Eloise's parents were in town—though Eloise probably needed a giant glass of wine more than ever. Jordy had taken advantage of her free night by supplying her with a bottle of wine and he had made dinner. Or tried. The spaghetti noodles were slightly overcooked and the sauce was a little salty, but he had insisted she sit on the couch and shop for her trip while he did everything.

"Which one of these tabs has your student loans?"

"Don't you dare. There aren't enough blow jobs in the world to pay you back for that."

"How many blow jobs does a backpack and boots buy me?"

"Hmm..." Annie tapped her chin. "Three?"

"Three?" Jordy repeated incredulously. "How good do you think you are?"

"I don't know. Something about how you say 'Oh fuck, that's so good' on loop."

"You're getting cocky," he chastised, curling a strong hand around the back of her neck and pulling her gently toward him for a consuming kiss. She had one hand in his hair and one trying to find its way into his grey sweatpants when she dimly heard her phone buzzing on her nightstand.

"I need to get that," she said against his mouth, grinning when his grip tightened.

"No, you don't."

"But I do," she insisted, putting her hand on his chest. Jordy released her neck with a heavy, overly dramatic sigh. "When I come back maybe I'll start paying off that backpack."

"Hurry."

He playfully swatted her ass as she passed him. The sting made more than her left cheek tingle. The night on the hood of the car was something they agreed they didn't want to do all the time—it took a lot out of both of them to maintain that kind of dynamic—but she wondered if he would be up for it one more time before she left for the summer.

"Your shopping cart wants me to add socks," Jordy called after her. "Do you have a headlamp?"

"Yes," she shouted back, grabbing her phone right before the last ring. "Hey. How's it going?"

"It's going fine," Jake answered. "Why do you need your passport? Trying to flee the country?"

"Yes. I finally snapped and killed my Aunt Sandra."

"Someone should have warned her about the side effects of having a stick up your ass sideways."

"You and Maddy were supposed to rock, paper, scissors over that one," Annie reminded him, sitting on her bed.

"I defer to Harvard Medical School on proctology matters."

She laughed. After the last year, she had kind of forgotten that Jake could be funny.

"Did you find my passport?" she asked, tracing the top stitching on the quilt.

"I did. You still haven't told me why you need it though."

"That research program I wanted to do over the summer had a last-minute opening, and they offered it to me."

"No way!" Even if they hadn't dated for almost a decade, Annie could have heard Jake's broad smile through the phone. "That's great! I'm so proud of you."

Was this her ex's way of telegraphing that he had been kidnapped and held against his will? Because the words "I'm proud of you" had never once passed his lips the first time she had gotten accepted into the research program.

"Jake, are you being held hostage?"

"No. I'm just happy for you."

"You do remember this is the same program you asked me to turn down, right?"

The silence lasted so long Annie thought she had accidentally moved out of cellphone range. Finally, Jake sighed.

"I owe you an apology. For the last few years—hell, our entire relationship—I wasn't a great partner to you, and you really deserved better. I've had a lot of time to think lately, and I feel really bad about how things went, especially last year. I'm sorry for everything I did and didn't do when we were together."

Someone could have pushed her over with a downy chick feather.

"Um..." Annie glanced at the door, and wished she'd shut it. This was a weird conversation for Jordy to overhear. "Thank you? I appreciate your apology... But you know we're not getting back together, right?"

"No—I mean yes, no, I understand. I don't think we should get back together either." There was a nervous laugh before he added, "I just really thought you deserved an apology."

"Thanks." She meant it this time. "How are things going?"

"Good, actually. Do you have time to talk about the apartment?"

"What's wrong with the apartment?"

"Nothing," he said quickly. "But while we're on the topic of 'Isn't It Funny How Life Works Out', I'm uh, staying in Seattle."

The absurdity of their situation fell on her like an anvil in a classic cartoon. The irony that if she had taken the position in the fall anyway, nothing in their lives would have changed. They wouldn't have moved. It would be Jake instead of Jordy sharing her bed at night, and she wouldn't have had any idea what she was missing.

She laughed until her belly hurt and she was wheezing instead of breathing.

"Oh...whew....okay, okay." Annie wiped her tears with the heel of her hand. What about the apartment?"

"I didn't know what your plans were for when our lease is up. And if you're going to Peru for the summer..." Jake trailed off. On his end, the microwave beeped. "I want to keep it, personally. It's easy to get to the hospital, and if you're moving, I can find another roommate. But I don't want to leave you high and dry."

"That's very sweet of you." It was shockingly considerate, and Annie felt like there was something he wasn't telling her. "Um, I don't know what my plan is yet, but can I pack what I'm not taking to Peru and store it there? I'm definitely moving out, but I just don't know when or where."

"Yeah. No rush. Should I go around with sticky notes trying to figure out what belongs to who?"

Annie glanced at the door again. In her wildest dream, Jordy asked her to move to LA after she got back from Peru and live at his house until she figured out her career. She didn't need anything but her clothes in that scenario. Hell, she didn't even need clothes. Jordy would buy her a new wardrobe if she mentioned she needed socks.

It was suspiciously quiet in the living room.

"No. I'll buy new stuff so I don't have to move anything."

New stuff. New life. Onward and upward.

"Really? Wow. I have been stressing about this conversation for a week." Another nervous laugh. "So, how do you want me to get your passport to you?"

"I need a picture of it right now," she told him. "I'll be back next week to pack my stuff, and then I'll be out of your hair until September. Oh, and I'm probably going to have some stuff delivered soon, so can you make sure to check for packages?"

"Yeah, totally. I'll take a picture of this and see you next week. Say hi to Graham and Eloise for me."

Annie was not going to do that. Jake didn't need to know how close he'd come to having Graham and Sybil show up in the middle of the night to dole out some vigilante justice after their breakup. Those two were way too protective of her.

"Will do. Have a good week."

She plugged her phone back in. There was no way of knowing how long the picture would take to come through, so she'd deal with it before bed. Maybe after Jordy went to sleep so she wouldn't spend an extra fifteen minutes convincing him that yes, the program would be reimbursing her plane ticket, and no, he couldn't pay for it because she didn't want to explain to her new supervisor why *the* Jordy Taylor had slapped down his credit card for her.

The living room was empty, her laptop open on the coffee table. Jordy wasn't in his room, and the bathroom door was open. Annie frowned, turning in a slow circle. Where had he gone?

She found him outside, standing on the grassy precipice of the cliff. The sun was setting, the sky a wash of golds, pinks, and purples, and Annie stood still for a moment to take him in against the backdrop, to carve this view into her memory. Because he was beautiful, inside and out.

They were only guaranteed until the end of the week. After that, he would go back to Los Angeles, and she would go to Peru for the summer. Anything could happen between May and September, but for the next six days, Annie was going to bask in their happy bubble as much as she could.

Jordy lifted his camera to the horizon and took a few pictures, the click of the shutter getting lost in the sound of the waves kissing the rocks below. Annie wrapped her arms around his solid middle and rested her head in the spot between his shoulder blades.

"Testing out a retirement plan?" she asked, kissing his back.

"Trying to remember how to do this," he answered, resting the camera against his hip and threading the fingers of his free hand into hers. "How's the ex?"

"He's fine. Staying in Seattle, apparently." Annie boosted herself on her tiptoes and dropped her chin onto his shoulder. "Did you spend all your money on outdoor gear?"

"No, but I did get myself locked out of your student loan portal." Jordy pressed a lingering kiss to her temple. "Remember how I said you couldn't be a girl in my phone?"

"I do remember. Have you changed your mind and want my tits as your home screen?"

"Tempting, but I was thinking you could be the girl in my camera."

"What's that supposed to mean?" Annie asked, her voice a breathless whisper because her lungs had decided to pack it in for the night. Who needed oxygen, anyway?

Jordy looked down at his camera, "I don't know. It sounded better in my head." He sighed, the worried crease growing deep between his eyes.

"How did it sound in your head?"

"Like you deserve to be treated like art and not some girl that I fucked once."

Annie was used to having all of her words hit her at the same time, but not her emotions. Love, joy, nervousness, confusion, and terror clamored for her attention, screaming to be acknowledged and released. She didn't know where to start the sorting process or which one to give priority to, so she stayed silent and hid her face in his shoulder.

How was she supposed to leave him at the end of the week?

TWENTY-ONE

JORDY COULD FEEL Sybil's glare burning into the back of his skull from across the coffee shop, but Annie wanted an afternoon coffee and he didn't know how to say no to her. He didn't *want* to say no to her. About anything. Whatever it took to make her smile, he would do it, even if that meant braving Sybil in the light of day to secure a chocolate muffin and a cinnamon latte in a porcelain cup that couldn't leave Stardust.

"How's the Wonka Factory?" Annie teased, pointing her fork at his iced coffee in a plastic cup that could have walked out the door. Sybil had asked him if he funded his dentist's boat when he ordered it.

"She was stingy with the caramel." Jordy took a sip. He liked his coffee sweet enough that he couldn't taste the coffee.

"You could send it back," Annie suggested, and he wanted to kiss the sly grin off her lips.

"See, I think you like me, and then you say things that would get me murdered." He shook his head in mock disapproval. "Shameful, really. After I bought you shoes too."

And a lot of other things. It was probably for the best he would be a thousand miles away when she saw all the boxes.

The bell over the door jingled, and something over his shoulder caught Annie's attention.

"Mom?" Her voice jumped an octave, and she pushed out from the table so quickly that the small table caught him in the diaphragm and knocked the wind out of him.

"Oh, damn." The older woman laughed as Annie hugged her tightly, rocking side to side as they embraced. Annie's mom had chin-length brown hair threaded liberally with gray, deep smile lines, and a rock-solid slender figure at odds with Annie's soft curves. She had to do marathons, or triathlons, or beat up bad guys on the weekends. "We were trying to surprise you."

"I am surprised!" Annie hugged her tighter. "Where's Dad?"

"Parking the car and complaining about the drive from Portland." Her mom wiggled out of the hug and held Annie at arm's length. "Let me look at you." She looked her up and down, and then cupped her cheeks in her hands. "How do you get prettier every time I see you?"

Jordy relaxed, lowering himself back into his chair. After meeting Eloise's mom Sandra, he'd been worried that conversation was going to go a different way.

A man wearing a maroon sweater entered Stardust, and judging by Annie's excited squeal, that was her dad.

"There's my girl," he said as they hugged. "Your cousin picked a stupid place to live."

"Oh, stop, Hugh," Annie's mom said, gently swatting his shoulder. "He's all bent out of shape because of the drive."

"I am bent out of shape. Five hours on a plane, and then that drive? Oof." He stretched dramatically, oozing dad humor.

Annie grinned and scratched the gray beard on his face. "When did you decide to grow this?"

An exaggerated eye roll from her mom. "Your Uncle Dave bet him he couldn't, so he *had* to prove him wrong."

"I think it looks distinguished. I'm leaning into my tweed jacket phase."

Jordy recognized the exact moment Annie remembered he was in the room. It was the crack about not growing facial hair. The lightbulb above her head could have lit up Times Square.

"Where are you sitting?" her dad asked, still trying to stretch his lower back. "I could use a cup of coffee."

Annie looked from her parents, to Jordy, and back again. She couldn't pretend they weren't sitting together. Her purse was under their table.

"Um, over here." She pointed to their table, and Jordy instinctively rose to his feet.

His palms were sweaty, and he scrubbed them on his pants. Meeting the parents wasn't something he did, and he wanted Annie's parents to like him more than he wanted a championship ring.

Be cool. Be calm. Don't say anything stupid.

When they got close, Jordy stuck out his hand in the direction of Annie's dad.

"Hi, I'm Jordan."

He kept his eyes focused on Annie's parents and tried to act like he didn't see her looking at him like he had just introduced himself as Mr. Banana Pants.

Annie's dad's gray eyebrows rose. "Jordan who?"

"Jordan Taylor, sir." His hand felt heavy hanging in the air.

"Jordy," Annie emphasized his name, "is a friend of Graham's, Dad. Jordy, this is my dad Hugh and my mom Wendy."

Hugh finally took Jordy's hand and shook it. There was an art to a good handshake: firm enough to say "Yes, I can and will protect your daughter with my body," but not so firm that any bones got broken. A handshake could make or break a first impression. There was a flash of respect, so quick that if Jordy hadn't specifically been watching for it he would have missed it, and then the men released their grips.

"Nice to meet you, Jordan," Wendy said, offering her hand. In for a penny, in for a pound. Jordy took her hand and shook it the same way he shook Hugh's, and allowed himself to breathe again when the corner of her mouth quirked. "You're a friend of Graham's?"

"Yes, ma'am."

"Are you in tech, too?"

"No, ma'am."

"What do you do?" Wendy asked, adjusting her small leather handbag on her arm.

"I am a professional athlete, ma'am."

Annie put a hand between his shoulder blades. "He's the quarterback for the Los Angeles Phantoms, Mom. He plays professional football."

Wendy's facial expression didn't shift. "And how long have you been doing that?"

"Strictly professionally? Fifteen years. But I started peewee tackle when I was eight."

Wendy regarded him critically. "What's your opinion on CTE?"

This was why Jordy had tried to skirt around his actual career. Wendy had the sharp gaze of a woman who had more information in her pinky toe than he had in his entire body, and he never felt prepared enough to speak on neuro questions when he wasn't so nervous he was sweating through his shirt.

"I don't have an opinion, ma'am. It's science. I've had two confirmed concussions. I understand my risks, the signs and symptoms of degeneration. There's a whole team of smart people that monitor us. I've seen improvements in how we handle things but know we still have a long way to go as a sport."

Hugh crossed his arms. "Sounds like you've had this conversation before."

Jordy nodded. "And I never think I'm the person that should be talking about it."

Wendy opened her mouth, and Annie cut her off with a strangled "Mom" through her teeth.

"What were your plans for the day?" Jordy asked, grateful for the chance to change the subject.

"I want to look around," Wendy said, looking pointedly at her husband. "He wants to sit and do nothing."

Hugh put up his hands defensively. "It's not sitting around. I just don't want to watch you sort through other people's crap and call it antiquing. We don't live here, Wendy. We have to fly it home."

"He's no fun," Wendy said to Annie, and repeated to Jordy, "He's no fun."

"I mean, I don't mind having no fun, if we wanted to split up," Jordy offered. "There's a brewery across the street if you're interested, Hugh. Then maybe we could circle back up for dinner?"

"You don't have to do that," Annie said at the same time her dad said, "That sounds like a great idea."

"Didn't you want coffee?" Annie asked, but it was said as a hint.

Wendy picked up on it and looped her arm through her husband's. "Yes, we did."

"Tell the redhead you're my parents," Annie told them, and the moment her parents were at the counter and out of earshot, she turned on Jordy. "You do not have to hang out with my dad."

Frost began to rapidly form in his stomach. "Do you not want me to hang out with him?"

Annie's posture softened, and Jordy relaxed too, his insides thawing. "It's not that. I just don't want you to feel obligated to entertain him. He's great, but he can be a lot and—"

"I want to, sweetheart." He gave her what he hoped was a reassuring grin. "Besides, how else am I supposed to get embarrassing stories about you if I don't go straight to the source?"

DINNER at the hotel was spectacular. Annie didn't know who Jordy had talked to or what he had said, but a prix-fixe menu had been arranged for their table so they didn't need to order and the wine kept coming until her parents were good and sloshed. Her mom's neck was red and her dad's cheeks were rosy, and they were both laughing about something that wasn't that funny.

"Oh god, I'm going to pee if I'm not careful. Where's the bathroom in this place?" her mom asked, putting her napkin on the table and looking around.

"I'll show you," Jordy volunteered, pushing back from the table. He hadn't even finished his first glass of wine yet. If there was a definition for "best behavior" in the dictionary, Jordy's picture would have been there.

When they were gone, Annie's dad sighed contentedly and sat back in his chair, hands folded over his stomach.

"I like him, Birdie," he said with a soft smile. "I like him a lot."

A blush burned her cheeks until she was positive she was as red as both her parents combined.

"Dad..."

"Even if he is a bit older than I would have expected," Hugh carried on, oblivious to her wanting to hide under the table. "And even if he did beat me at chess. Twice."

Annie's eyes widened. "He did what?"

"He beat me at chess. Twice. The first time I underestimated him, but the second time I was ready. And he beat me." Hugh drained his wine glass, chasing the last few drops of red with his tongue. "I think he threw the third game so I wouldn't feel bad about myself."

Annie was too stunned to speak. She had grown up playing games with her parents. There weren't any other kids in her house to play with, so her parents were her playmates. They'd taught her to play chess before she could read. Beating her dad once in a series of games was a major accomplishment. But twice? She'd never done that before.

"He asked about Jake," Hugh said casually.

Annie picked at the remnants of her dessert with her fork, pretending not to be interested, even though her heart was supersonic. "What about Jake?"

"If we liked him and how we felt about the two of you breaking up." Hugh eyed her dessert enviously, and Annie slid it toward him.

"What did you tell him?" After their initial meeting, Annie had never asked her parents how they felt about Jake. She'd been happy—or at least content—so she hadn't sought out external validation.

"We never disliked Jake because we trusted you to make good decisions. But the last few years it was very hard to like him. We weren't sad to see him go, but it was hard to know you were hurting." Hugh sectioned the remaining dessert into even portions. "All we've ever wanted for you was for you to find someone who loved you and understood how special you are, Birdie. This one does."

Wendy flopped back down into her seat. "Eloise's attention to detail is incredible. Those bathrooms are amazing." She looked around. "Where's Jordan?"

"Jordy. He goes by Jordy," Annie corrected. "No one calls him Jordan. I think you both scare the shit out of him."

Her parents giggled. Actually giggled. They were delighted by the prospect that Jordy feared them.

Jordy sat back down, his hand resting on the back of Annie's chair. "Did I miss something funny?"

"Bad pirate joke," Hugh told him, winking conspicuously at Annie.

Wendy checked her watch and then elbowed her husband, making him miss his mouth with his fork. "Look at the time. It's midnight back home. We need to get to bed."

"Well, find the waiter so I can settle up," Hugh told her, trying to dab chocolate out of his sweater.

"I already took care of it," Jordy said, too casually for someone who had easily dropped three hundred dollars on dinner. Her parents had ordered expensive bottles of wine, nowhere near the same tax bracket as her "whatever is on sale" section of the grocery store.

"Jordan," her parents gasped, and immediately began talking over each other about how he shouldn't have done that, how if they knew he was going to do that they wouldn't have ordered the third bottle of wine, how they were happy to pay at least half...

"It's fine. You can get the next one," he told them, in the tone of voice Annie recognized as "you will absolutely not be getting the next one." He'd used it on her before.

They hugged her parents at the elevator, her mom mouthing "Oh my god" over Jordy's shoulder, and her dad thumped him solidly on the back. Even if things didn't work out between them, her parents might try to adopt Jordy.

"You didn't have to do that," Annie said as she buckled her seatbelt.

"Which part?" The engine roared to life and classic rock

blasted through the speakers. Jordy turned it down. "Sorry. Your dad likes it loud."

"All of it. Dinner, hanging out with my dad, nearly making my mom pee her pants because you're so...you." The crush of emotions overwhelmed her again, and a lump began to form in her throat while her heart felt so full it threatened to burst. "They love you, by the way. I think my dad would follow you into the pits of hell because you beat him at chess."

"The feeling is mutual. Your parents are a lot of fun."

Holding Jordy's hand as he drove was so natural that Annie had stopped noticing she did it. He put the car into drive, then left his hand near the cupholders, and she took it. Every time they drove anywhere, this had become their routine. It struck her as he navigated the curve in the hill that led to the lighthouse that she only had three more days of holding his hand while he drove. Thursday. Friday. Saturday. Then on Sunday he would drive to Portland to catch a flight and Annie would drive back to Seattle, both empty handed.

"You're really quiet," Jordy noted as he flipped on the lights in the small house that had come to feel like their little home. "Are you okay?"

"I—" Annie's chin quivered and she knew if she tried to speak, she would lose her tenuous grasp on her composure. Tears flooded her eyes, and she looked up at the ceiling, trying to blink them back.

"Sweetheart." Jordy put his hands on her hips. "What's wrong?"

She swallowed several times, trying to clear the lump in her throat so she could speak.

"I can't—" It came out as a squeak. The words were there. How the hell was she supposed to get them out?

"Can't do what?" Jordy rested his forehead against hers, his whole heart in his voice. "Don't tell me you can't do this."

"I can't." Annie shut her eyes, losing her battle with a few warm tears that slipped down her cheeks. "Not when I'm leaving. I—" She swallowed. "I don't want to talk about us yet. I can't because I won't leave if—and if you change your mind while I'm gone...I'd rather not know for sure." She could survive not knowing for sure how he felt about her. But if he felt the same way about her that she felt about him? She'd lock them in the lighthouse and throw the key out the window. She would give up anything to stay with him. Lacey's voice echoed in her head. That she needed to put herself first for once. "And I need a little time to be selfish."

"Is the summer long enough for you to be selfish?" he whispered.

"I don't know." She sniffled. "It might be."

"I can wait." Jordy sighed. "As long as you come back, I can wait."

Annie cupped his face, his days-long stubble barely tickling her palms, and kissed him. Words were hard, but showing him that she loved him was easier. Jordy either understood where this was headed or needed the closeness and connection as badly as she did, because he slipped his tongue into her mouth and slid his hands down to her ass and squeezed. They moaned.

Clothing was discarded haphazardly as they stumbled toward a bedroom. Which bedroom didn't matter. His silk tropical print shirt landed on the floor, followed by her top, then her bra, his belt, their shoes...Annie had her fingers on the button to his pants when he ran into a door frame.

"Ow," he said against her mouth.

Annie opened her eyes, and in her periphery was her bed, unmade from the morning. She'd woken up with Jordy's hard cock stabbing her left ass cheek, and then she'd made him hold onto the headboard to finish what they'd tried—and failed—to do with the handcuffs. They'd been playful and teasing, and hearing him beg never got old. That bed was filled with memories, and Annie hated herself for ever trying to hold herself back from him. They could have made more. She could have woken up with the warmth of his body against hers every morning and fallen asleep with the weight of his arms around her every night. In hindsight, they'd been inevitable.

The next three days were going to be unbearably chaotic. Relatives, rehearsals, silly events that were all going to steal her last bits of time with him. So her touches transformed from desperate, needy hunger, to tender reverence as she tried to make it all count. The strength in his shoulders, chest, and arms. The strong, rapid beat of his pulse. The softness of his skin.

His lips were her favorite. Every time he kissed her, she felt like the most perfect, wonderful thing that had ever existed. She kissed him again, endlessly grateful that he had flagrantly abused the loophole in her "no kissing" rule.

The sheets and quilt were cool on her skin when she fell back onto the bed. She arched her back to push her pants off, keeping her eyes on Jordy as he finished stripping down.

Fuck, he was beautiful.

Jordy took out a condom and her vibrator from the nightstand, then settled in next to her, taking a long look at her body. He dragged his knuckles down her side, tracing her peaks and valleys like he was going to make a map of her from memory.

"How do you want to do this?" he asked, palming her hip to bring her close.

"Slowly," she answered.

"Do you want the vibrator?"

Annie shook her head no. "I'm not in a hurry, and I just...I just want to be present."

This wasn't about an orgasm and this wasn't a race to the finish. She didn't even know if she could get into the right headspace to *have* an orgasm. Too many thoughts and emotions bouncing around. That didn't mean Jordy wouldn't be determined to make her feel as good as he could. He slid one, then two fingers inside of her, so familiar with her body that he knew exactly how to touch her to make her blood crackle. She gasped against his mouth when he withdrew his fingers and used her wetness to rub her clit in slow, medium pressure circles.

"I want you inside of me," she told him, and grabbed his wrist when he tried to reinsert his fingers. "Not those."

"Are you sure you're ready?" he asked, like he didn't know exactly how wet she was.

"Yes. I need you."

Jordy rolled onto his back and reached for the condom, and if she hadn't already been wet, she would've been by now. Her brain and her body were in agreement that Jordy rolling a condom down his hard cock meant good things were coming and they needed to be prepared. The way his wrist moved made her mouth water.

Annie let her legs fall open, an unspoken invitation, and Jordy settled himself exactly where he belonged. The first thrust, the initial stretch, was her favorite. This time was slow, as requested, and he eased in with little resistance. The shudder that rippled through his body set off a small tremor in hers.

Jordy cupped her face with one hand, using the other for balance. "How are you so perfect?"

"I'm not," she protested weakly, moaning as he slid in and out of her like they had forever and not a handful of days left.

"Yeah, you are." And then he kissed her so she couldn't argue with him.

Annie got lost in the gentle roll of Jordy's hips. There were small, murmured praises, like prayers against her lips, as he told her how wonderful she was, how brilliant, how funny, how sweet, how brave. It made her heart hurt, and she never wanted it to end.

Their hands found each other, and their fingers interlocked, palm against palm, somewhere around the top of her head. Jordy pressed his forehead against hers, and their noses brushed.

"This feels too good," he admitted, and bit his bottom lip. "Fuck, you feel too good."

"I'm going to miss this. Us." Tears welled in Annie's eyes again, and one slid free and into her ear.

"Me too, sweetheart," Jordy said, his voice clogged with emotion.

They continued, foreheads together, eyes closed, hands clasped, until Jordy's breaths got shorter and rougher.

"It's okay," she soothed. "Come for me."

His mouth crushed against hers and pleasure shot through her body as his thrusts got quicker and rougher. She was on the verge of asking him not to stop when he grunted and tensed. Inside, his cock pulsed and Annie squeezed her inner walls to feel it better, and Jordy made a sound like he'd choked on his tongue.

"I love how that feels," she told him. Annie was usually too busy coming her brains out to really feel him finish. Another giant shudder wracked his body.

"Fucking hell...you can't tell me that while you're gripping me." He shook his head, his muscles twitching again as he pulled out. "I'm going to get ideas."

Annie had given herself some ideas too, but those were best kept to herself until the fall.

"Are you sure you don't want me to use the vibrator?" Jordy asked, stroking her hair.

"I'm fine," Annie reassured him. "I needed that more than I needed an orgasm."

They cleaned up, brushed their teeth while dancing to Jenna Fox, and for a few minutes everything felt normal again.

Like they could continue this perfect vacation from reality infinitely. But when they got back into bed, sleep evaded them. Normally, Jordy dropped off immediately in that annoying way he had where Annie knew he wasn't reviewing every mortifying interaction he'd ever had in high definition, or worrying about the next day. She waited for the arm draped over her to become heavy and his breathing to change into a soft snore, but it didn't. Eventually her eyelids got too heavy, and they pulled her toward sleep.

The last thing she heard, quiet against her hair, was "I don't want you to go."

TWENTY-TWO

"SO THERE ISN'T a maid of honor?"

"No."

"And there isn't a best man?"

"No."

The wedding coordinator's left eye twitched. Helen—at least Jordy thought her name was Helen, it could've been Ellen—plastered a tight smile on her face. "So, how do we want to pair up the bridal party, then?"

Jordy scooted closer to Annie, and their shoulders bumped because she had scooted closer to him too. They'd gravitated toward each other like kids hearing the words "group project."

"Umm..." Eloise surveyed the small group. It was Sybil, Eloise's sister Maddy, and Annie on the bride's side, and Jordy, Sam, and Mallory standing in for Peter, whose bad luck streak with airplanes continued. He was at least stateside by now. "Annie with Jordy, Sam with Maddy, and Sybil with Peter."

Sybil raised her hand. "I would like a different partner."

"Sybil," Graham ground out through clenched teeth, "you are walking up the aisle, you are walking down the aisle. You aren't marrying him, so stick with your damn partner so we can eat."

"I don't mind shuffling," Maddy volunteered. Eloise's younger sister was a head taller than her sister and looked like she survived off coffee and protein bars. She was a doctor—a *medical* doctor, Annie had specified—and their baby brother, Henry, was in law school.

"Everyone is staying where Eloise assigned them," Graham barked.

"What order do you want the bridal party standing for the ceremony?" the coordinator asked.

"Do you want Peter next to you?" Eloise asked Graham. "Since he was your first wife."

Graham pinched the bridge of his nose, but Jordy could see the smile he was fighting. Eloise grinned, clearly proud of herself for breaking Graham out of his stressed grump.

"Okay, so Peter, um...Sam and Jordy, can you figure it out?" Eloise asked.

"I don't care, do you care?" Sam said, putting his hands in his pockets.

"I don't care. Do we do it by height?" Jordy rubbed the back of his neck. "Or is it weird to go brunette, blond, blond, brunette? Do we stagger it more? Brunette, blond, brunette, blond?"

"Oh my god." Sybil grabbed Sam by his elbow and moved him behind Mallory. "Peter. Sam. Jordy." She pointed to Mallory like she was actually Peter. "Because he's going to cry, and someone is going to have to discreetly hand him tissues."

Jordy put his hands on his hips. "Are you saying I can't be discreet?"

And then Sybil fixed him with a stare so sharp and pointed that popped the little bubble of delusion he had been living in: there was absolutely nothing discreet about him and

Annie. Astronauts on the International Space Station—which he had some cool facts about to share with his nephew, thanks to Hugh—could probably see that he was madly in love with her.

"Right." Jordy stepped back into his place.

Helen lined the women up, giving pointers on how to stand to give the photographer the best angles. "Okay, now that we've got that figured out, everyone to the back of the room."

"Shouldn't Maddy be at the front?" Sandra asked as they gathered in the hallway to practice walking down the aisle. "She's the sister of the bride—"

Maddy cut her mom off. "Mom. You are the only person who cares about this. Stop."

"Sandy, it's fine," her husband soothed, rubbing a hand between her shoulder blades.

Sam leaned over and whispered in Jordy's ear, "I know it's wrong to drug people, but do you think it would help if we slipped half an Ativan in her drink?"

"Would half do anything?" Jordy muttered back.

"First we have our officiant." Helen gestured for Connor to walk down the aisle that the hotel staff had set up that afternoon. "Then the groom's parents."

Graham made a low rumble in the back of his throat. Peter had introduced Graham's mom to an Italian model-slash-movie star at a party a few years back, and they'd gotten married two summers ago in a small ceremony in Italy. Graham liked Giuseppe because he made his mom happy, but it ground his gears whenever anyone called him his stepdad. Giuseppe had only recently turned forty.

"Then the mother of the bride and the brother of the bride."

Henry offered his arm to his mother. Sandra looked up at him and sighed, her eyes lingering on his hair. It was thick, dark, and at the worst part of shaggy if he was trying to grow it out. Jordy hated that stage. "You were supposed to get a haircut."

"I can take him in the morning, Sandra," Graham offered, his eyes darting to Jordy's hair.

This mollified his almost-mother-in-law and Henry didn't object, so down the aisle they went.

"Now Graham. Good—slow down a little, honey! Now you two." Helen pointed to Annie and Jordy. "When you get to the front, fan out to your sides. The others will fill in. Remember your marks?"

Jordy nodded and offered his arm to Annie. She looked beautiful in a dress she'd stolen from Eloise's closet, a flowy, long-sleeved thing with a deep V neckline and blue and purple watercolor flowers all over. The little bit of makeup she'd put on threw him for a loop because Annie didn't usually wear any, and he was fascinated by the length of her lashes with mascara on them.

"Walk," Annie said under her breath.

Right. They were supposed to be doing something.

The walk was shorter than he wanted it to be, and then he parted ways from Annie, trying to remember where his mark was. It wasn't his first wedding, and he always hated being point man for the entire line. At least this one was only three people. Jordy had once been in a wedding with twelve groomsmen. That rehearsal had gone on forever.

Maddy and Sam came next, then Mallory and Sybil. Mallory was taking exaggerated steps like she was ice skating, and Sybil looked tense enough to snap in half if someone tapped her on the shoulder.

"Now everyone will rise," Helen announced from the back of the room. "Connor, it does help if you make a motion with your hands so people get the hint."

Then Eloise and her dad were in the doorway. Eloise's smile

was bright and wide, her eyes glued on Graham. Her dad, Dave, was blinking rapidly, fighting back tears. Jordy's dad had been a mess at each of his sisters' weddings. Would Hugh cry on Annie's wedding day?

Connor opened his binder when Eloise got to the end of the aisle. "So we're skipping the presentation of the bride, correct?"

"Yes," Eloise and Graham said at the same time.

Connor nodded and made a note. "Okay, so I will make some opening remarks, maybe work in a reading...Are we still nixing any unity stuff?"

"We're getting married. Isn't that unity enough?" Graham frowned.

"Just making sure." Connor made another note. "Then you'll exchange your vows. At that point, I'll ask Mal—Peter for the rings. We'll do the ring vows. Then the kiss, and you're almost legally married."

Graham had been staring deeply into Eloise's eyes and did a double take. "Almost?"

"You have to sign your paperwork," Connor reminded him, tapping his shoulder with the binder.

"That's the twenty-minute escape clause," Sybil said. "It never happened if you don't sign it and turn it in."

Eloise squeezed Graham's hands. "I promise not to let her kidnap me before we sign the paperwork."

After they'd been released for dinner, Sam grabbed Jordy.

"Come with me. I need to get Sybil's sweater from my car."

"Afraid Bigfoot is going to grab you?" he teased, falling into step with his best friend.

"No," Sam said putting his hands in his pockets as they walked toward the lobby, "I feel like we've barely seen each other since I got here. I thought you were going to be more...I don't know, distraught about football ending."

"I'm fine, Sam. It was my choice."

"But since when? A month ago you were desperate to stay. Friday night I was legitimately worried—" Sam didn't finish his thought, but Jordy could imagine the horrible things he'd been worried about, and he hated that Sam had thought those things. "What changed?"

Jordy looked down at his feet. "A lot."

"That's not an answer, Jordy."

"I know, but I don't know if you'd understand."

"Try me."

"I'm ready to move on with my life," Jordy explained. "I—I fell in love."

It was the first time he had said it out loud. He had thought about it a lot over the last few days, but he hadn't said the words.

"With who?" Sam asked, stopping under the chandelier in the lobby. "You haven't mentioned anyone, and you tell me everything. You tell me when you get new shirts." He gestured to the loud tropical print Jordy was wearing. "This is not news. It's a crime, but it's not news."

Jordy took him by his elbow and marched him outside. The clouds had moved back in during the afternoon and a drizzle had started. The sidewalk glowed where the lights hit it, and raindrops made ripples in the small puddles.

"It's Annie, okay? I'm in love with Annie."

Sam stared at him, unblinking, until a raindrop landed on his nose. "No, you're not."

Jordy's core tensed, and he narrowed his eyes. "How would you know?"

"Because it's been three weeks and you're searching for meaning so you attached it to Annie."

"Graham fell in love with Eloise in the same amount of time."

"Graham is an adult."

"I'm older than he is."

"You know what I mean." Sam sighed, raking his hands through his hair. "Graham's always had his shit together. And he and Eloise were running a business together when they started dating. That's a pressure cooker. Of course he was sure. They'd been through shit. You're having a fling."

Jordy clenched his jaw, biting down on words he knew he would regret later.

"You don't know what you're talking about."

"If you still feel like this in three months—hell, three weeks—I'll eat my words, okay?" Sam shook his head and unlocked his car, taking the red cardigan from a bag in the backseat. "But this isn't going to last."

"What the fuck do you know? You got hurt once forever ago and—"

A car door slammed down at the end of the row, and Peter's voice rang out. "Did I miss it?"

"Yes," Jordy called back, still glaring at Sam. He dropped his voice to a harsh whisper and leveled a finger at him so there was no mistaking who he was talking to. "Fuck you."

Jordy met Peter on the sidewalk and hugged him tightly. Peter gave the best hugs. Good pressure and body contact. They healed the soul and made the world more bearable.

"How was your flight?"

"Flights," Peter corrected, releasing Jordy. "I think it would have been quicker to go by boat." Peter peered around Jordy at Sam, who was standing by his car, arms folded tightly against his chest, squishing the sweater against his body. "Get over here."

Reluctantly, Sam shuffled over, making a point to avoid Jordy. Peter pulled him into a bone-crushing hug that Sam half-heartedly returned, and when they separated, Peter plucked the cardigan from his hands.

"Did you make this?" he asked, turning it over in his hands.

"No, I did a repair on the elbow," Sam said, showing Peter the spot. Jordy couldn't tell there had ever been any damage. He bit his tongue to keep from praising Sam's handiwork.

"I had a sweater like this, a long time ago," Peter said, handing it back to Sam. "I gave it to someone—well, she took it. I wonder what happened to it." He fingered the knit around the collar. "Could you make me one like this?"

"Yeah, sure."

The raindrops had been steadily growing in size and a fat one barely missed Jordy's eyeball. Peter grabbed his suitcase, and the three of them walked quickly to the lobby. Once inside, Jordy shook out his hair like a dog, pushing it back out of his face.

Graham rounded the corner into the lobby, murder on his face. "Where the fu—Peter!"

"Graham Cracker!"

They collided near the middle of the lobby, and it was a small miracle they didn't wind up on the floor with concussions. Peter and Graham hugged each other like drowning men. Jordy couldn't remember exactly how long it had been since they'd seen each other, but it had easily been months.

"You're fucking late," Graham said, his voice tight with emotion.

"I know, I'm sorry. But I made it."

Graham let Peter go, stepping back and casually wiping his eyes. "Are you hungry? We just started dinner."

"Starved," Peter said, and pointed at his suitcase. "What do I do with this?"

"Just leave it with the desk. Or bring it to the dining room. Who cares?" Graham took it from him and wheeled it to the manager's office, pushed it inside, and pulled the door shut. "There. Come on. Amara made these honey-glazed roasted carrots that are so good you'll want to marry one."

The rehearsal dinner had been set up in the bar, close friends and family milling around and filling plates at the buffet. Mallory had transitioned from stand-in groomsman to bartender, cocktail shaker working overtime, while Ian, the bar manager, poured beers and glasses of wine like his life depended on it.

Jordy wanted a drink. Several drinks. Sam was wandering around the room, Sybil's sweater in hand, but there was a distinct lack of cranky redhead in the room. Jordy sat down at the bar next to Henry. Mallory poured a purple drink into a chilled highball glass, garnished it with an orange peel and a tiny purple flower, then handed it to Maddy before turning her attention to Henry.

"And what do you want?"

"A martini. Can you make it extra dirty?" Insinuation dripped from the word "dirty."

Jordy didn't know Mallory very well, but he knew her well enough to recognize the mischievous glint in her eyes that did not bode well for Henry at all.

"You want it *extra* dirty?" she purred, pouring gin and vermouth into the shaker.

"So dirty."

The exact moment Henry realized he'd made a terrible mistake almost made Jordy feel better. Henry's eyes grew wider and wider in horror as Mallory began to pour—and kept pouring —olive brine into the shaker while maintaining eye contact. Half the container went into the shaker before she slapped the other end on and shook it hard. It was hard not to laugh. The resulting drink was so cloudy Jordy couldn't see the olive garnish she dropped inside.

Sheepishly, Henry picked up his martini, took a wincing sip, toasted Mallory, then skulked off to a corner.

Mallory rinsed the shaker several times before acknowledging Jordy's presence. She smiled brightly. "Champagne?"

"Uh, French 75. Not dirty. At all."

Mallory snorted and made his drink. "Do you want to get something for Annie?"

"Good idea," he said, and then waited for Mallory to get started. She stared at him.

"What does she want?"

Jordy had no idea. His first thought was sangria, but was that what she would *want?* His stomach clenched. Knowing someone's drink order was basic, intimate knowledge. Graham had known Eloise's drink the first time he brought her to LA. He'd made her a Vesper before Peter had even finished listing off the drinks in the house. Was Sam right? Had he made sweeping, drastic changes to his life for a person he barely knew?

"Jordy, it's a drink. Pick something," Mallory said.

"I don't know." He searched his memories, turning over every interaction involving food or alcohol, mixing that information with what he knew about her personality. An idea tickled his brain. "This is going to sound weird," he began, "but tequila —either the silver or blanco—pineapple juice, and lime."

"That's not weird. It's delicious." Mallory made the drink, put it in a pretty crystal glass, and garnished it with a lime.

Annie had found Peter, and they were talking in the excited, animated way that made them both so endearing. It was like releasing a pair of puppies into a pen together.

"Here," Jordy said, handing Annie the glass. "You looked thirsty."

"What is it?" she asked, sniffing it.

"Pineapple juice, tequila, and lime."

Her smile untied all the knots his stomach had twisted itself into. "How'd you know?"

"Lucky guess."

But it wasn't really a lucky guess. He knew her, and he felt like she knew him too. Time didn't matter because they got each other in a way he had only experienced with a select few people. Everything else he didn't know was details, and he had the rest of his life to learn those.

TWENTY-THREE

"ANNIE, I can't find my vows." Eloise dumped her purse onto the chair in the bridal suite, pushing the contents around. Four different lipsticks. No vows.

"Calm down," Annie soothed, handing Eloise two tissues for her underarms because the nervous sweats had started. "You have copies. I know you have copies. Where are the copies?"

"Um...wedding binder."

"And where is the wedding binder?" Annie asked, using one of the programs the photographer had snatched to use for photos to fan Eloise, who was waving her hands in front of her face for air.

"Umm....umm...office? Probably the office. That was where I told Helen to stash her stuff." Eloise raised her hands to run her hands through her hair, and an entire room of women shouted "STOP" at once.

Eloise looked perfect. Her off-the-shoulder gown was form-fitting with no embellishments. It was elegant, sexy, and truly timeless, just like Eloise. When they'd gone dress shopping, the brief had been "give Graham a cardiac event." It had been pretty in the store, but tailored to her body, with her hair and makeup done, Annie wanted to find the McMahons to place bets on whether or not Graham would die on the spot.

"I will go find your vows," Annie promised. "Relax. Breathe. This town isn't big enough for you to have actually lost them."

Eloise nodded, closing her eyes as she put a hand on her chest and breathed in and out slowly and deeply.

Sure enough, the wedding binder was in the office, and an extra copy of both Graham and Eloise's vows were in envelopes in the section neatly marked "Vows." Annie took out both envelopes, because she wasn't sure if Graham's vows were in the "Graham" envelope or if Eloise's vows *to* Graham were in that envelope. Better safe than running down the hallway at the last minute.

The hotel staff and the extra catering staff Eloise and Graham had hired for the day were wheeling carts filled with small tables through the lobby to set up the cocktail hour in the courtyard. A large white tent had been erected that morning because the weather couldn't decide if it wanted to cooperate or not. The ceremony would take place in the ballroom, then guests would exit into the courtyard, and the staff would flip the room for the reception in an hour.

Annie was under the chandelier when there was a sharp whistle from the grand staircase. She stopped, turned, and forgot everything she'd ever known, including how to breathe.

Jordy jogged down the stairs, two at a time, in a classic black tux that enhanced everything that was wonderful about his form. The joys of bespoke clothing. She was so lost in his chest, shoulders, and legs that he was almost to her before she noticed something very different about him.

"You cut your hair!" She hadn't meant to shout, but Jordy's shoulder-length hair was gone. There was enough left on top that she could run her fingers through it or get a good grip when he was working his magic between her thighs, but he definitely didn't need to steal her scrunchies anymore.

He blushed, and ran a hand through it, and his fingers kept going, searching for the phantom length. "Yeah. Uh, we took Henry to get a haircut, and I thought why not? Do you like it? Was it a bad idea?"

Annie brushed her fingers around the freshly cut ends of his hair. "I do like it. It's just different." The short sides were soft and prickly at the same time and tickled her fingertips. "Wow... Hi, let me start over. You are stunning, Jordan. I was so distracted by how amazing you look in that tux that I didn't even notice you cut your hair until you were basically on top of me."

His blush deepened, and he dropped his head, trying to hide his shy, bashful smile. "Yeah?"

"You're—" There wasn't a word for how heart-stoppingly gorgeous he was. "You really look amazing. Wow. All around wow." She twirled her index finger slowly. "Do a spin for me."

Jordy obliged, turning slowly, and Annie hoped blessings were heaped upon whoever had made him pants. They deserved a Nobel Prize.

"Hot damn."

"Stop." Jordy was scarlet from the tips of his ears to his tie. The protest was so flimsy that a puff of air would have destroyed it.

"Never." Annie pushed herself up on her tiptoes and gave him a quick kiss that lingered because neither of them pulled away. "Mmm...what are you doing downstairs?"

"I was sent to get the vows because Graham can't find his."

"I can help you with your quest, but it'll cost you another kiss."

"Oh no," Jordy deadpanned, "what a horrible price to pay."

He curled a hand carefully around the back of her neck, mindful of her hair, and gave her a toe-curling, foot-popping kiss that left her panting and more than a little damp between the legs.

"You know, there's condoms in the office," Annie said breathlessly, blinking up at him in a stupor. He chuckled, releasing her neck and putting his hands in his pockets to hide his own arousal. She ran her thumb across his bottom lip, amazed. "Wow. The makeup gal wasn't kidding. My lipstick didn't budge an inch."

"You look perfect. You did before I kissed you too." Jordy mimicked her spin gesture, so she indulged him by turning slowly. He let out a low whistle. "I am going to need pictures of this later."

"This dress looks this good thanks to shapewear and answered prayers," Annie warned him, running a hand over her stomach. "Suggesting a quickie in the office was overly ambitious."

"We've got time tonight," Jordy promised, stepping back to drink her in again. "Fuck, you're pretty."

"And we're both distracted," she said, handing him the envelope that said *Graham*. If she was wrong, they could exchange their papers during the ceremony. "I'll see you soon for pictures?"

Jordy nodded, tapping the envelope against his palm. "Want to make out in the elevator?"

Her pussy throbbed. "Absolutely I do."

It wasn't a long make-out. The groom's side was getting ready on the second floor, so it felt like the doors had barely short before they opened again. But the thirty-five seconds of extra kissing was glorious.

Annie wasn't even all the way in the door before Eloise anxiously pounced on her. "Did you find them?"

She held up the envelope triumphantly, and Eloise exhaled, probably for the first time since Annie had left.

"Thank you." She tore open the envelope, double-checked the contents, then folded up her vows and handed them to Sybil for safekeeping. "Where were they?"

"In the office, right where you said they'd be," Annie answered, checking her appearance in the mirror. Her lipstick was remarkably still in place.

"What took so long?" Eloise asked, and Annie couldn't stop the blush that rose from her neck up to her cheeks. Her cousin came up behind her, grinning at their reflections. "Did you get sidetracked by a certain groomsman?"

"It's possible that I ran into someone in the lobby," Annie admitted coyly.

"I like you two together," Eloise said, her grin softening to an approving smile. "He's such a sweetheart. What are you going to do when you're in Peru?"

"It's your wedding day. We shouldn't be talking about me and my problems." Annie turned and put her hands on Eloise's shoulders. "Today is all about you. And a little bit about Graham."

"But you'll tell me later?"

"Of course."

Once she figured it out for herself.

"IS it normal to be this nervous?" Graham asked his friends, adjusting his shirt cuffs for the millionth time. "I'm excited, but I feel like I'm going to puke."

They were sitting in the bar, waiting for someone to come get Graham so he could have his first look at Eloise in her wedding dress. Jordy didn't know how he was surviving waiting the whole day to marry the love of his life. The entire experience had convinced Jordy that he was going to marry Annie at nine a.m. on their wedding day, whether she was still in her pajamas or not, because there was no way he would make it to a four p.m. start time.

The way she looked walking through the lobby, like she had been pulled from an old black-and-white movie and dropped into a color-filled world, flashed through his mind. Green was rapidly becoming his new favorite color.

Better make it seven a.m.

"None of us are married," Sam said, making himself a seltzer water with lime.

"I think it's normal." Peter yawned. He was halfway through building a house with the square cardboard coasters that had been left on the bar. "It's a big life change."

"Not really." Graham sat down on a bar stool, only to pop back up when someone walked down the hall. When they didn't stop at the bar, he lowered himself onto the seat again. "We've been living together for a year and a half. She's been my wife in my head for...months, honestly."

"It's a little stage fright," Jordy reassured him, patting him soundly on the back. "Remember, left hand, this finger." He held up his hand and wiggled his ring finger. "Peter has your vows and the rings—" Jordy looked at Peter, who patted his breast pocket and nodded. "Peter has the rings."

No one would have been surprised if he left them in another room. He was half asleep and lost things when he was wide awake.

There was a soft knock on the open door, and Kiki stepped into the bar, hands folded demurely in front of her. Helen the wedding coordinator had roped her into helping with the wedding day logistics, and Kiki agreed because having her help run things made Eloise and Graham more relaxed. The dark red roses on her black velvet dress caught the light as she took a few steps forward.

"It's time, boss," she said, her smile becoming wobbly as Graham walked over to her.

"You look wonderful, Morticia."

"Not so bad yourself, Lucifer."

"Did you see her?" Graham asked, adjusting his shirt cuffs again.

Kiki nodded. "She's spectacular." She pulled a black handkerchief out of an invisible pocket. "You're going to need this."

Jordy moved to the stool Graham had vacated next to Peter. Things were still tense between him and Sam, like the first hard frost of an early winter, so he gravitated elsewhere.

"Are you okay? You're quiet," he said to Peter, who sighed and rubbed his face.

"I'm tired. Jet lag is terrible." He put his head down on the bar, the resulting thud tumbling his coaster castle. "What if I went to sleep right here? Is that an option?"

"Do you want pressure marks for pictures?"

There was a grumble, but Peter sat back up as the other parts of the wedding party filed into the bar. Bridesmaids, parents, siblings, Connor, and Chase and Cole, who were acting as ushers.

"We got banished," Chase pouted. "Apparently this is their 'private time.'"

Connor put his slim black leather portfolio on the bar top. "When you're a grown-up, you'll understand."

Annie stood in the doorway, talking to someone in the hallway. Connor noticed and went over to the door. From a quick headcount and a distinct lack of red hair in the room, it was Sybil. Jordy couldn't hear what they were saying, but his lipreading was good enough to see Connor say, "Come inside with everyone else."

The coaster castle Peter had started rebuilding fell down again. "Damn," he cursed, and turned his attention to the room.

Then he did something Jordy wasn't used to: he became very still.

"Jordy," Peter began, his voice whisper-thin like he was seeing a rare bird in the wild, "have you ever been so jet-lagged you started to hallucinate?"

"No" was the quick and easy answer.

"Then I'm going to need you to pinch me really hard— Ow!"

"You asked," Jordy reminded him, releasing his nipple from his pincer grasp. "What's wrong with you? You look like you've seen a ghost."

"That's another reasonable explanation." Peter rose in a trance, his gaze fixed and unblinking on the group at the door. Sybil had taken three steps inside the room. "There is a redhead next to Annie, correct?"

"Yeah." Jordy did a quick glance to ensure he was right. Sybil was still there, her arms folded tightly, with a look on her face that wasn't quite a glare, but was definitely kissing cousins with a scowl. "That's Sybil. She's your walking partner."

A weak laugh escaped him. "This isn't real life, is it?"

"That depends. Did you take the red pill or the blue pill?"

Peter rubbed his eyes, hollow little laughs shaking his shoulders.

"Are you okay?" Jordy asked, concern growing with every laugh. "Do you need to go lie down?"

"Yes—no. Maybe?"

Jordy looked to Annie for guidance, but she looked as confused as he did, her head bouncing between Peter and Sybil. At least he wasn't the only one who thought something was *off*. Finally, Sybil jerked her head toward the hallway, then turned on her heel and marched out of the room. Peter almost fell over his own feet scrambling to catch up to her.

"What the hell was that?" Jordy asked Annie when she reached him.

Annie looked over her shoulder at the door where Connor was still standing, watching the hallway. "I don't know. It was weird. Sybil kept saying she couldn't come inside. Do you think she's reaming Peter out for not making it to rehearsal?"

"I have no clue." He shook his head, baffled by what had happened. "Peter's jet-lagged as fuck, so I don't know how much a lecture is going to sink in."

Like he'd heard his cue, Peter shuffled back into the bar, his hands thrust deep into his pants pockets, and his head down. He reminded Jordy of a dog that had been smacked with a rolled-up newspaper.

"What was that about?" he asked Peter as he lowered himself onto his stool.

"Nothing," Peter muttered.

TWENTY-FOUR

KIKI HAD NOT BEEN EXAGGERATING when she said that Eloise looked spectacular. Jordy did a double take when he saw her, which made Eloise laugh.

Again, he couldn't help but imagine what his wedding with Annie might look like if he got lucky enough that she wanted him back. The ballroom was beautiful, adorned with flowers and the warm glow of fairy lights. It was perfect for Graham and Eloise. But if he had to guess, he would say that Annie would want to get married outside with the sounds of the birds and the sun on her face.

Annie squeezed his bicep as they waited for their turn to go down the aisle, the sound of the string quartet drifting into the hallway.

"This is Amanda and Christian's love theme from *Claymore Abbey*," Peter told Sybil, who had given him the cold shoulder ever since they talked in the hallway. She said nothing in return.

"Go," Helen hissed, waving her clipboard.

Right. There was a wedding happening.

Jordy counted their steps so he wouldn't rush to the end of the aisle. Connor and Graham were standing at the head, and

Graham looked so happy he was glowing. Everyone talked about brides being radiant on their wedding days, but maybe more people should be watching the grooms.

Annie squeezed Jordy's arm once more before they parted ways, and he missed her immediately, even though she was only on the other side of the makeshift altar.

Maybe he could commute from Peru for training camp and preseason play.

Sam and Maddy took their places, then Sybil and Peter. Connor lifted his palms to indicate that the assembled guests—some two hundred people—should rise. They did, and the music changed to a sweet, yearning melody. Eloise and her father Dave stepped into the doorway, and Eloise's smile outshone every light in the room.

Jordy stole a glance at Graham. His smile matched his bride's, though his eyes shimmered with unshed, happy tears. A lump formed in Jordy's throat that refused to be swallowed down, and tears stung his eyes.

Graham met Eloise at the end of the aisle. He shook Dave's hand, then offered Eloise his arm and they finished the walk to the front of the altar together. Eloise passed Sybil her bouquet, then joined hands with Graham. They mouthed "I love you" to each other at the same time, and the room chuckled.

"You may be seated," Connor said, his voice ringing through the room from his lapel mic. He took a deep, calming breath before opening up his leather folder. "Welcome, friends, family, and loved ones, to this special day. We have gathered to celebrate Graham and Eloise as they begin the next chapter of their lives together. This hotel has been the center of all the important moments in their relationship: where they met, where they fell in love, where they got engaged, and where they go to work together every day. It was this hotel that legally brought them together, so it feels fitting that this is where they make their relationship legally binding." Connor looked between them, his smile soft and approving. "Graham, Eloise, you have a partnership. Your love is not superficial. It does not waver when the days are long and hard. It is built on mutual admiration, adoration, and deep respect. When you have a problem, you seek each other. When there is a success, you celebrate each other. I have seen you both grow as people as you've grown as a couple, and it is my greatest joy and honor to marry you today." He glanced at his notes. "Graham won the pre-ceremony game of rock, paper, scissors so he will read his vows to Eloise first."

"I don't need to read them," Graham said, and cleared his throat. "Eloise, you are my very best friend. You are the first person I want to talk to in the morning, and the last person I want to talk to at night. Sometimes, you're the only person I want to talk to during the day. You have the most kind, gracious, and giving soul of any person I have ever met. Meeting you, loving you, and being loved by you has made me a better person. I promise that I will always try to do my best for you and our family, however and whenever it grows. I will be your protector and your safe place when things are hard. I will tell you every day how much I love you, even though words will never be enough." He brushed a tear off Eloise's cheek. "You've been my wife in my heart for a long time, and I hope I am always deserving of being your husband."

Jordy peeked at Peter, expecting to see tears streaming down his friend's face. But instead of watching the couple, he was staring at Sybil. Sybil was looking at Graham and Eloise, her eyes not moving at all.

"Eloise?" Connor prompted.

"How am I supposed to follow that?" she asked, and Graham took the handkerchief Kiki had given him from his pocket and handed it to her. She dabbed at her eyes. "Thank you." Eloise took a deep, shaky breath, and grasped Graham's hands in hers again. "If you're going off script, so am I."

Jordy glanced at Annie, who looked at him a heartbeat later, like she knew he was looking at her. The same eyes that had hypnotized him the night they met were filled with tears, and she mouthed "I'm a mess." The instinct to go to her, to wrap his arms around her and try to fix any hurts she had, was strong. It was only Eloise starting her vows that reminded him he needed to stay in place.

"Graham," she began, "I used to think you brought out the worst in me, but it turns out you bring out the best in me. My strength, my tenacity, my ferocity. You have always made it easy for me to be the best version of myself, and you have loved the pieces of myself that I thought were unlovable. You inspire me every day with your thoughtfulness, loyalty, and bravery. With you by my side, I feel like there's nothing we cannot accomplish. I promise to not walk away when things get hard, to communicate my needs and ask about yours. I promise to be your soft place to land, and your strength when yours is running low. I can't imagine doing this life with anyone else but you, and I am so excited and humbled that you're going to be my husband."

"May we have the rings?" Connor asked. Peter didn't so much as twitch. "Rings?"

Sam poked Peter in his lower back, and he jumped to attention. He dug into his inner breast pocket and produced the two rings.

"Rings," he confirmed, handing them to Graham, who then handed them to Connor.

"These rings are a symbol of your unending love for each other. May they always remind you of today and the vows you made to each other. I'm going to hand you each your rings, and you're going to place it on your almost-spouse's finger and say 'I give you this ring as a symbol of my love, devotion, and faithfulness.'" Connor handed Graham Eloise's wedding band.

Graham slid it onto her ring finger. "Eloise, I give you this ring as a symbol of my love, devotion, and faithfulness."

Connor handed Eloise Graham's ring, and she did the same. "Graham, I give you this ring as a symbol of my love, devotion, and faithfulness."

"By the power vested in me by the state of Oregon and the internet, I now pronounce you husband and wife. You may kiss your spouse."

Connor quickly stepped out of the photographer's shot as Graham and Eloise shared their first kiss as husband and wife. Music swelled, and guests cheered. Sybil handed Eloise back her bouquet, and the wedding party filed out in reverse order: Graham and Eloise, Sybil and Peter, Maddy and Sam, then finally Jordy got to touch Annie again. Even if it was just her arm looped through his.

The wedding party regrouped in the small conference room Jordy had used as a temporary office so Graham and Eloise could sign their marriage license.

"This makes it so real," Eloise said as she signed her name, her hand shaking as she did. The smile stretched across her face told Jordy it was pure adrenaline coursing through her system. Graham took the pen from her and swiftly signed his name too.

"It needs two witnesses," Connor said, looking at the assembled group. "Whose names am I writing down?"

There was an awkward silence as no one in the group wanted to speak up in case being on the license was very important to someone else. Finally, Sam did.

"Make it Peter and Sybil. They stood the closest."

Connor began to write. "Sybil Morgan and Peter G—"

Sybil grabbed his wrist. "It's Parker hyphen Green. Legally."

Connor looked up at her with an expression Jordy knew very well from his teachers. *Is there something here you'd like to explain?*

Sybil blushed and released his hand. "You were going to have to correct it. I was saving you a form."

Connor turned to Peter. "Is it Peter Parker *hyphen* Green?"

Peter nodded. "Peter Alan Parker-Green, if you need the full thing. A-l-a-n."

"Peter Parker *hyphen* Green is fine." Connor finished writing and tucked the license into a manila envelope bound for the county courthouse. "That's it. You're married."

ANNIE DECIDED wedding receptions were better when a blond hunk in a tux was in charge of her snacks and drinks. It was even better when the hot blond took her home at the end of the night.

Her feet hurt from dancing, her face hurt from smiling, and her stomach hurt from laughing too much. The evening had been a great distraction from the misery that awaited her in the morning. For the past two days, Annie had questioned her decision to go to Peru over and over again. Seattle to Los Angeles was long distance, but it was the same country, the same time zone, and the same hemisphere. There were about twenty-two daily, direct flights between the cities. She knew; she'd looked. Yes, the research trip was a dream, but so was Jordy. And whoever had said that your career would never leave you cold and lonely had obviously never lost their funding.

It had been on the tip of her tongue so many times that night to tell him that she loved him. To ask him to wait for her, to maybe give long, *long* distance a try. But she knew if she was going to go, she needed to do it without obligations back home.

She needed to be selfish and pick herself. That in the long run, this was what she needed to be sure.

A few months, and then she could figure out forever.

"Don't forget I want some pictures before you change," Jordy said as he removed his jacket from her shoulders. Annie shivered as she lost the warmth from the silk lining.

"You don't have enough of me in my sweats?" she joked, kicking off her high heels. Jordy liked to bring his camera out when she wasn't paying attention—or dressed for going out in public—and he had to have over a dozen candid photos of her around the lighthouse.

"No. I don't."

She flopped down on the couch with all the grace of a discarded rag doll. "Can you photograph me like this?"

He pretended to frame up some shots with his fingers. Or maybe he wasn't pretending. The camera Annie used the most was on her phone. What did she know?

"Yeah, I can do that. Hold still." Jordy jogged to his room and was back in moments with his camera. He took a test shot, adjusted some settings, then took another picture. "Say 'draw me like one of your French girls.'"

That made Annie laugh, and she heard the rapid click of the shutter.

"Jordy, I wasn't ready," she protested. "I'm trying to be sexy."

"You are sexy. Stop trying." He climbed onto the couch, one foot on the arm and the other on the coffee table and took a few shots from above.

"You're going to fall and get hurt."

"It takes more than a few feet to injure me."

"Okay, then you're going to fall and hurt me. You're heavy." Annie waited for Jordy to hop down before sitting up. "Can you unzip me?"

His face fell, but the recovery of his expression was remarkable. "Done already?"

She turned her back to him and moved her hair out of the way so he could access the zipper. "I think I've got a better idea. Ten minutes, tops. If you hear a thud followed by no swearing, come check on me."

His tux jacket was tossed over the back of one of the dining chairs, and Annie grabbed it on her way to her room. Despite Jordy asking her to be the girl in his camera, he hadn't pushed or suggested they take any risqué photos. It felt like the perfect night. Her hair was done, her makeup was done, and it was her last chance. All the ingredients to make potentially bad decisions.

The grunting and tugging to get her shapewear off was not sexy. Neither were the red indentations it left behind. But there wasn't time for them to fade, and the motivator Annie used for bravery was also her downfall.

"Good enough," she muttered as she adjusted her boobs in the cups of the embroidered green mesh bra she'd bought the day they went to the zoo. That day felt like a million years ago and moments earlier all at the same time. She picked up Jordy's jacket and slipped her arms through. It was big, but one perk to being a tall girl was that it didn't completely swallow her, and the effect was, in her opinion, spectacular.

Annie pulled open her door, put one arm above her head on the doorframe, and leaned. Jordy was in the kitchen, shirt sleeves rolled to his elbows, washing her Stardust coffee cup. A low whistle got his attention, and he fumbled her cup, juggling it from hand to hand before it clattered into the sink. He turned and slowly worked his eyes down Annie's body.

"Hi." The vowel was dragged out, and she hoped it was because his brain was buffering and not because she looked ridiculous.

"You like?"

"Do not move a muscle," he commanded, creeping forward to grab his camera from the coffee table like she would disappear if he moved too fast. His hand hovered over the camera. "Can I take your picture like this?"

"It's going to be a long summer. I wasn't going to leave you with nothing to look at."

The unspoken part, the part she couldn't bring herself to ask for, was that she hoped he wouldn't need anything other than a few pictures and his memories to get him through the summer. That she hoped he would wait for her and not explore things with other people. The hard part about being selfish was letting go of the expectation that he would be selfless.

"Push your tits out a little...that's it." Jordy took a photo, checked the result, then took a few more. "Left hip...yeah, like that. That's it."

He guided her through different poses, eventually moving her to the bed, praising her and her body as he went. How beautiful she was, how sexy, how perfect. He would tell her he needed to fix her positioning or adjust her lingerie, but that was an excuse to touch and fondle her.

"You're not being very professional, Mr. Photographer." Annie sighed as he stroked her clit through the embroidered mesh underwear. The scrape of the fabric sent a shiver of pleasure through her body.

"You want me to stop?" he asked, moving her hair off her neck with his other hand.

"No," she whined, pushing back against his hand. "That's the problem. I'm supposed to be an aloof model, and you're turning me into a needy mess."

"I didn't realize we were role-playing." Jordy trailed kisses down her neck, starting at the sensitive place behind her ear, and ending near her collarbone. "I like it when you're a needy mess for me. Begging for my cock." A sharp pull of flesh under his mouth was followed by a too-familiar warm sensation. A hickey to remember him by. "I like to pretend you're only like this for me."

"Only for you," she promised.

"Good, because you're killing me." He moved her panties aside and easily slipped two fingers inside. Pleasure radiated through her body like a pebble dropped into a puddle. Annie moaned and pushed herself back against his palm. The click of the shutter. "You going to fuck yourself on my hand?"

"I'd rather fuck myself on your cock," she gasped. "Please?"

The camera dropped onto the bed. Jordy undid his belt with one hand, then his pants. The zipper pull made her mouth water.

"Excited?" He worked his clothes off his hips, not relinquishing his place in her pussy. "I can feel you getting wetter."

"I want you to take me hard, okay? I want to feel you inside of me for days. Every time I move, I want to know you were there."

A bead of precum slipped out of the head of his cock.

"Whatever you want."

Annie pushed her underwear down her thighs as Jordy kicked off his pants and put the condom on. She arched her back, cocking her ass higher in the air as he lined himself up behind her.

"Remember, you asked me to do this," Jordy warned as he pushed inside of her in one long, torturously slow stroke. Fuck, he knew how she liked it. Annie pressed her face into the quilt and moaned.

The best and worst part about Jordy was that he always did exactly what she asked him to do. She'd thought the night on the hood of the car was the hardest he was capable of going. She'd been wrong. The bed rattled and shook beneath them, slamming against the wall in time with the slapping of his hips against her ass. Each stroke was punishing, and his grip on her hips was iron. But the edge of pain felt delicious because it pushed all the sadness from her mind. There was only room for this feeling.

She was thrown headfirst into her release, like being chucked into the deep end of a pool. Annie screamed into her pillow as orgasm gripped her body, making her muscles become rigid and then grasping, trying to wring every last ounce of pleasure from both of them. Another began to build immediately, but dissipated into a warm, fuzzy bliss as Jordy slowed, his sweaty forehead dropping onto her back.

"Fuck," he panted, shuddering as one of her aftershocks set off one of his. The last pulse of his cock emptying made her toes curl. He wrapped his arms around her stomach and squeezed. "Was that enough? Too much?"

"Perfect," she told him, rubbing his forearms with one hand. "You okay back there?"

"I think I saw God."

TWENTY-FIVE

"YOU HAVE YOUR TOOTHBRUSH? PHONE CHARGER?" Jordy asked, his hands on the lid of her trunk. "We didn't leave anything in the dryer?"

"I think we got it all," Annie said, running through her mental map of the lighthouse. She remembered grabbing her toothbrush and her phone charger. She had also stuffed a few of Jordy's T-shirts from the dryer into her bag as she picked out her clothes from the last load of laundry.

The smack of the trunk slamming shut cracked her chest open.

This was it. Their cars were packed. The keys were back under the mat. Jordy had to leave in twenty minutes or he was going to miss his flight. And that was assuming he didn't hit traffic. They'd put off goodbye as long as they possible could.

"One more thing," he said, holding up a finger like she was possibly going to leave a single second earlier than she needed to. He opened up the passenger side door of his rental car and unzipped his backpack. He pulled out the sketchpad she'd given him and tore out a sheet. "I've never done creature design, but I think I got it right."

Jordy handed her a picture, drawn with colored pencils, of a bird that looked like a prehistoric woodpecker. The design was heavily borrowed from a red-naped sapsucker, with fiery red plumage and a strong black-and-white-speckled body. The bill was large and had edges like a chainsaw.

"It's an iron-billed wooflespoof," he told her.

Her laugh became a sob almost as soon as it began. "I love...it."

Him. She loved him. She loved a man who drew her made-up birds and did her laundry so it was one less thing she needed to do before going on a trip that could ruin them.

Jordy wrapped his arms around her, and Annie hid her face in his neck. Her heart had shattered into a million, tiny, jagged pieces, and he was the only thing holding her together.

"I feel like I'm losing my best friend," she choked out, fighting the lump in her throat.

"You're not losing me," he soothed, rocking her back and forth, side to side. "You're not."

Sobs continued to shake her body. Tears and snot were gathering in the hollow of his collarbone, but fixing herself meant letting go, and she wasn't ready to do that. A few more seconds, another minute, she only needed a little bit more...and then a little bit more...

"Come to Los Angeles when you're done being brilliant," he pleaded, holding her tighter. She nodded, her vocal cords strangled by her sorrow. "You can come to a game, see my house...We can go to Disneyland and spin in the teacups until we puke."

That made her smile. "Can I get ears too?"

"All the ears you want, sweetheart."

Annie swiped at her eyes, failing miserably at stopping the tears flooding her face. "Peru for the summer. Los Angeles in the fall."

"Los Angeles in the fall."

TWENTY-SIX

IT WAS the longest summer of Jordy Taylor's life.

The only time he talked to Annie—really talked, where he could hear her voice and respond in real time to her words—was when she was pacing the terminal at LAX, waiting for her flight to Lima. He reminded her that she was doing the right thing, that this was the opportunity of a lifetime, instead of saying what he wanted to say, which was "You're in Los Angeles. Get a fucking cab and come to my house and never leave." Then they announced they were beginning boarding for her flight and her name was called for passport verification.

"Shit. I have to go." Annie's voice caught on the two little letters, and she sniffled. Before he could ask if she was okay or even say goodbye, she hung up.

She emailed him two days later to say she had made it to the research center. On her flight to Lima, she'd sat between a couple that had been together for forty-five years. She liked the window and he liked the aisle, and apparently that was their secret to a long, happy marriage. They were going to see Machu Picchu. Annie wanted to see Machu Picchu and hoped she would get a chance during her stay. Most of her time, she explained, would be spent in the field, but she was supposed to come back to town every few days and would have access to her email then.

It wasn't exactly radio silence after that, but the contact was sparse. Jordy resisted emailing her until she emailed him first, terrified he was either giving her too much or not enough space.

Jordy needed a project. May passed one minute at a time, each day taking a year as he waited to hear from Annie. He couldn't text Graham because he was on his honeymoon. Peter was filming and got back to him sporadically. And he hadn't spoken to Sam since their fight, and Jordy refused to cave this time. None of the people he wanted to talk to were available, and a guy could only work out so much before risking injury.

The perfect distraction arrived the second week of June in the form of Nelson Sims, his replacement and the future of the Los Angeles Phantoms. Camp Quarterback had been a stroke of genius. The ink was barely dry on the kid's communications degree when he lugged his two duffle bags and a hard-sided suitcase into Jordy's guest room. The suitcase, Jordy found out later when he was unpacking, was filled with shoes. The kid was a sneakerhead, which prompted the first of many life lessons Jordy gave that summer: Do Not Blow Your Paychecks On Stupid Shit.

Jordy sat Nelson on the couch, then sat on the coffee table in front of him, elbows on his knees, hands clasped in front of him. Most people eventually turned into their parents, and this move was classic Pat Taylor.

Jordy decided to stand instead, pacing as he talked.

"I know those Marty McFly whatevers are super tempting, but you can't blow forty grand on a pair of shoes you'll never wear because you're scared you'll crease them...." He pivoted and caught sight of Nelson's guilt-ridden face. "You already bought the shoes, didn't you?"

Nelson sank deeper into the couch. "Maybe?"

"Don't burn through your money on shit you can't use. Understand? You don't need a sports car yet. You don't need jewelry. You need an emergency fund, and by the end of the summer, a house."

Turned out that Nelson was a slow learner. The first time Nelson came home at four in the morning from the clubs, Jordy was waiting for him like a parent whose kid had missed curfew.

Another Pat Taylor classic.

"Going clubbing is only going to make you broke and sad. Let me guess. You dropped five grand tonight? Made out with an aspiring model or actress wearing a dress that was held together by dental floss? Maybe got your balls fondled under the table?"

Nelson swayed precariously, and Jordy helped him to bed, putting a garbage bag on the floor as a splash guard, then the trash can from the guest bathroom on the floor. When the kid grabbed the trash can, Jordy rubbed his back as he heaved. "You're not going to meet anyone you want in your life forever at a club, dude."

Jordy woke him up two hours later to go for a run.

"I'm only around for a year," he panted as they pushed up a hill that hurt on a normal day. "You're going to be ready to take the keys when I leave, okay? We're going to train and study like our fucking lives depend on it. Camp Quarterback!"

"I'm going to puke." Nelson veered into the bushes and lost what had to be the last of the alcohol in his system.

Jordy poured every hard lesson he had learned his first five years of professional football into Nelson in their month living together. He hosted a Fourth of July barbeque for all his retired teammates and let them pile on the wisdom, too. Darnell had a retirement account set up for Nelson before his kids were done eating ice cream, and Quinton told him how to make sure he didn't have any kids before he was ready for them. It was essentially what had happened to Jordy his rookie year, except they weren't in the locker room and no one was wearing only a towel.

Weeks went by without any communication from Annie. The gnawing pit in Jordy's stomach grew larger every day. He should have told her how he felt before she left. He shouldn't have been *quite* so supportive about her leaving for months. And he could have blamed it all on terrible service or lack of internet, except during one of his catch-up sessions with Graham, he heard Annie's voice in the background.

"Do I hear Annie?"

Graham moved further away from the competing sound. Jordy wanted to scream at him to go back, to get as close as possible so he could hear her voice.

"Yeah, sorry. She and Eloise are video-chatting. Again." A door shut and the background noise was gone. "Sometimes Annie calls, and they don't even talk. They just do data entry together."

Jordy went to sit on a pool chair and missed, crashing onto the concrete pool deck. Why didn't Annie ever call him? Or video-chat him? He would have watched her do data entry for hours. His tailbone throbbed from his hard landing, but it was nothing compared to how his heart hurt.

HOW NELSON MANAGED to pull off a surprise birthday party, Jordy never knew. He didn't even think the kid knew when his birthday was, so he hadn't been expecting a damn thing when Nelson invited him to brunch. In addition to football and life lessons, Jordy was trying to teach his protégé about the wonders of breakfast foods eaten midmorning, paired with champagne mixed with fruit juice.

The roar of "Surprise!" when he entered the restaurant

almost gave him a heart attack. The place was packed with current and former teammates, their significant others, and an assortment of people from his contacts list.

Nelson had a shit-eating grin on his face when they hugged.

"So, when you needed to use my phone to call yours last week...?"

"Gathering contact information." The kid wasn't going to be able to fit back through the door if his head got any bigger.

"What did I say about not spending your money on stupid shit?"

Nelson shrugged. "It's not stupid shit. It's your birthday, man. And everyone chipped in. Even your little Brunch Bros group chat. Do you really love waffles that much?"

Jordy rolled his eyes and shoved Nelson in the direction of the bar with an order to get him a massive mimosa. He took out his phone and opened his group chat.

BRUNCH BROS

> Jordy: You assholes almost gave me a heart attack. I'm too old to be surprised.

Sam's name appeared, followed by three dots, then disappeared. No message followed.

> Graham Cracker: Happy birthday! Sorry we can't be there.

> Peter Rabbit: Did you get my singing telegram?

> Jordy: No. Now I'm scared.

A featherlight touch whispered down his back, and the world around him froze for a split second while he was transported back to Graham and Eloise's engagement party and the last time someone had touched his back like that.

"Happy birthday, cowboy."

Reality crashed around him. It wasn't Annie. She hadn't flown up from Peru to surprise him for his birthday. Did she even know when his birthday was?

"Hey, Keri." Jordy tried to muster up some polite enthusiasm for his former fling, but he was scraping the bottom of the barrel.

"I haven't heard from you lately," she said, circling the middle button of his shirt with her finger. "I've missed you." Keri clocked the room quickly, then grinned at him, biting her bottom lip. "You know, since it's your birthday, I can forget that you've been ignoring me and we could slip into the bathroom and—"

Her offer had the opposite effect she'd intended. Instead of making him hard, it made Jordy miss Annie more. That was who he wanted to fuck in a restaurant bathroom: Annie.

"I can't, Keri." Jordy took a step back so she couldn't touch him anymore.

Her brown eyes grew wide, and she looked down at his crotch. "Oh. I'm so sorry. I didn't know you were having...trouble. Have you been to the doctor?"

"No, it's not that. That works fine."

"So what's the issue?" Keri crossed her arms, pushing her tits together as she did it. They were strong assets, and she knew it. Back in March, that probably would have worked. But then April had happened, and now he was ruined.

Jordy rubbed the back of his neck. "I'm...I'm in love?"

Keri gasped, then covered her mouth to muffle her squeal. "Seriously? Who? Is she here?"

Excitement was not what Jordy had been expecting, but it felt good. This was the reaction he had wanted from Sam.

"Her name is Annie. And she's in Peru on a research trip."

"Is she a travel influencer?"

"PhD. Ornithologist, actually."

"She has to study cancer in Peru?"

Jordy chuckled. Keri was exactly the kind of woman he should have been with on paper. Sweet but simple. Easy on the eyes, easy on the brain.

"Oncology is cancer. Ornithology is birds. She's a bird scientist."

Once Jordy started talking about Annie, he had a hard time stopping. He told Keri all about her, showed her pictures, bragged like Annie was his girlfriend, all while glossing over the fact that they were barely talking.

JORDY WAS ALREADY in bed for the night when an email pinged on his phone.

Annie.

He fumbled to open it.

The message was short. ***Happy birthday. I hope you have a great day.*** But there were two attachments. One video file and one audio file.

Jordy clicked on the video and Annie's face filled his phone screen. Her hair was piled into a hasty bun on top of her head, and the humidity had made it curly. She smiled, and waved both hands.

"Hey! I hope this works." She adjusted her tank top that slipped off her shoulder. "It's—oh gosh, what day is it? It's July twenty-fifth. Your birthday is in two days and I'm supposed to be back in town by then to send this, but if I'm not, I wanted you to know that I did not forget your birthday. I don't know how to get a timestamp on this thing...It's fine. It's fine. I didn't forget your birthday, Jordy. Um, as you can see, it's raining." She pointed to the window behind her. "But I wanted you to hear what I hear every day, because I think it's incredible. So I'm going to go record you an audio of it in a second, but I wanted you to know that I'm having an incredible time, and I'm really glad I came." Annie smiled, but it didn't quite reach her eyes, which were growing damp. "I miss talking to you, though. I miss hearing your voice and seeing your face. My cellphone is off because I'm really unsure what my international data plan is, and I don't want to go home to one of those sky-high bills that ends up in the news because no one can believe how huge it is—I'm rambling. I'm sorry." A self-deprecating grimace, and then her face brightened a fraction. "Oh, there's a bird here called the Andean cock-of-the-rock. I thought you'd think that was funny. Happy birthday, Jordy." Annie kissed her fingers and showed them to the camera before the recording clicked off.

Jordy opened the audio file.

The sound of hundreds of birds filled his bedroom. He closed his eyes and pretended he was in Peru with Annie.

DURING TRAINING CAMP, the media got wind of Nelson living with Jordy. The amount of clips from *Stepbrothers* that got played during sports talk shows was so ridiculous that Jordy and Nelson decided to film themselves doing karate in the garage. The video went viral after Nelson posted it on his social media pages.

"And you're positive that's an M for million and not for like...monkeys playing Monopoly?" Jordy asked when Nelson showed him how many people had viewed their silly video. He'd dabbled in posting videos, but they usually only got tens of thousands, maybe hundreds of thousands, of views. He had never broken the million mark before.

"People really like it," Nelson said, putting his phone back into his pocket. "If you want to do more, I've got some ideas. Trick shots. Reenacting other buddy movies."

"No dynamite, Butch," Jordy joked.

Nelson stared at him blankly. "Huh?"

"Have you never seen *Butch Cassidy and the Sundance Kid?* Fuck it, movie night this week is going to be an actual movie instead of game film."

AUGUST TOOK a full year and happened in a blink. Training camp turned into preseason, and Nelson looked good on the field. It was hard for Jordy to sit on the bench when he wanted to be playing, but the team wasn't risking injuring him before the season started, plus they wanted to see if their draft gamble was going to pay off. So many players never lived up to their draft potential for one reason or another, but Nelson Sims was not one of those players. Jordy felt like a proud dad watching him play.

A proud dad who was a little worried about losing his spot prematurely.

But when the media started hyping Nelson up as the next big thing, the kid choked. They lost their second preseason game abysmally to a team that they should have trounced.

"How did you deal with the pressure?" Nelson asked on the drive home, his hair still a little damp from his post-game shower. At Jordy's strong suggestion, the team had gotten him on and off the podium for the post-game press conference as quickly as they could.

"I didn't have the same kind of pressure you have. Everyone expected me to fail. I threw my first pass right into the ground." Jordy turned into a quiet shopping center and parked in front of an ice cream parlor.

Nelson leaned forward to peer at the signage. "What are we doing?"

"Getting ice cream to celebrate your first professional game with no interceptions."

"My completion percentage was shit."

"Yeah, but none of those completions ended up in the hands of an opposing player," Jordy pointed out cheerfully, turning off the car. "Look, I believe in you, kid. I really think you're going to do great things with your career, and I hope it's at least half as long as mine has been. At the end of this season, you're going to be ready to push me out the door so you can take over." Jordy grinned at him. "But not before. Don't think I don't see you gunning for my job."

HAVING Nelson around didn't quite distract Jordy from the fact that the woman he loved was in South America forgetting that he existed. It also didn't make him forget that Sam hadn't spoken to him since the wedding. Jordy hadn't reached out either, but he wasn't going to until Sam apologized for being an overreaching asshole. About a dozen times a day, Jordy picked up his phone to text Sam, only to see that their last messages were from the beginning of May. He got more contact from Peter, who had gone directly from the wedding to Hong Kong to work on a movie for four months.

Graham called Jordy around Labor Day. "Hey, so Eloise and I were planning on coming to LA for the Phantoms' first home game but since I don't have the corporate box anymore..."

"You want me to get you and Eloise tickets?" Jordy finished, highlighting the hummingbird head he was coloring in with a bright pink pencil to try and capture the iridescent feathers.

"And Annie. That's the same week she's coming back from Peru. She's flying into LAX."

Jordy put down his pencil. Annie hadn't told him when she was coming back. Hearing it from Graham felt like a late hit from behind: unexpected and painful as fuck. The silence between them had been hard but hadn't felt fatal. Annie was doing her thing. He was doing his. Why hadn't she told him when she was coming back?

"Jordy? Did I lose you?"

"I'll make some calls," he said, setting his sketchpad aside. "Three tickets."

"Four, if you can. So Sam can sit with us."

"Yeah, well, Sam and I aren't really talking right now, so you can see if he wants that."

"What? Since when?" Jordy heard the soft closing of a door on Graham's end. "What happened?"

Jordy sighed. "I told him I was in love with Annie at the rehearsal dinner, and he told me I was delusional and I said fuck you and—we haven't really spoken since."

"You were in love with Annie?" Graham didn't sound as surprised as Jordy expected.

"*Am* in love with Annie. Present tense. No clue where I stand there, but yeah." Jordy ran a hand through his hair. It had grown since May, but it was at the awkward stage where he wanted to live in headbands to keep it out of his face. "I wanted to tell you sooner, but it was your wedding and then she was leaving so it seemed a little pointless and—" The words rushed forward. Jordy hadn't realized how badly he wanted to talk about all of this until it was too late to *not* talk about it. "And she's barely talked to me all summer. I don't know what that means. Do I move on? Was her going to another country her way of letting me down slow and easy?"

"I mean, if it makes you feel any better, Eloise has known the date for months. She has copies of all of Annie's documents and itineraries in a binder." Graham sighed. "I don't know. I don't know what it all means. But if I'd known how you felt about her back when you were here, I would have been more supportive of your relationship. Maybe. I thought you were going to hurt her, and it never occurred to me that she might hurt you instead."

Jordy's eyes burned, and he pressed the heel of his hand against one. "I hate this. I really hate this. Why didn't you warn me that being in love really, really sucks when you don't know how the other person feels?"

"Me running around like an idiot two years ago didn't clue you in?" Graham chuckled sympathetically. "She's going to be home soon, okay? You can ask her yourself in two weeks."

"Two weeks," he repeated, his heart soaring like a bird with a broken wing.

He got an email from Annie later that night with a subject line of **TWO WEEKS!** and a copy of her flight itinerary inside. Had Graham emailed her asking why she hadn't told Jordy she was coming to town? There wasn't any other text in the body of the email, so Jordy went to sleep that night listening to the sound of the birds in Peru and wondering what would happen when she got back.

TWENTY-SEVEN

THERE WAS something magical about the first game of the season. A buzz in the air, a feeling that anything was possible.

And all of that was amplified when you crushed your opponent into the ground on their home turf.

The Los Angeles Phantoms headed into week two of the season with a win under their belts and their own home opener on the horizon. They'd beaten Detroit so soundly week one that Nelson got to play the last five minutes of the fourth quarter and scored his first regular season touchdown by exploiting a giant hole in the line and running for the endzone like he'd stolen the ball. When asked by the press at the post-game conference how he planned to celebrate, Nelson leaned down to the microphone and said with a wide grin, "I think Jordy is going to take me out for ice cream."

Jordy hadn't done badly himself. Four touchdowns, no interceptions, and the highest passer rating of the week. When they repeated Nelson's quote back to him, he'd laughed and said, "Uh, I think the rookie is supposed to buy. I'm trying to save my money for retirement."

There were more jokes about how Nelson had moved out so

how was he supposed to pay his mortgage, and who was supposed to explain to him what an influencer was, and would Nelson's views go down now that Jordy wouldn't be accidentally walking through the background of his videos with his shirt off.

Jordy smiled and laughed, but when he said his mind was already on the next week, he meant it. Annie was coming back to the States, and he was more anxious about that than any game he had ever played in, including championships. His stomach flipped and his heart did moves that had definitely been outlawed by whatever group governed gymnastics whenever he thought about it.

By Thursday he was so nervous he almost called out of practice sick. But he needed the distraction, or he would have torn his house down to the studs just for something to do with his hands. After practice, he was picking Graham up at his hotel, and the two of them were going to hang out at his house until Eloise picked Annie up from the airport. Then, the four of them were going to meet for a late dinner at a fantastic Italian restaurant by Jordy's house. Graham and Eloise were in town for a hotel conference, and Graham had scheduled a meeting that made it hard for Eloise to shuttle everyone around.

After being hot as the fifth circle of hell all week, Los Angeles was covered by a blanket of dreary grey clouds. It had rained on and off all day long, and a final torrential downpour caused the coaching staff to call practice off a little early. Jordy checked his phone after he got out of the showers and was surprised to find two messages.

GRAHAM CRACKER

Traffic is terrible. Eloise left for the airport early and my meeting was canceled, so I'm ready whenever you want to get me.

We just finished. Be there in 25 or so.

The next message almost knocked him on his ass.

SAM I AM

I heard Graham and Eloise were in town, so I invited myself to dinner. See you later.

Months of silence, and *that* was how he broke the stalemate? If Graham had arranged his, then he was on Jordy's shit list too. But Jordy didn't put it past Sam to invite himself to dinner and act like nothing had happened and he hadn't said the things he'd said.

"DID YOU INVITE SAM TO DINNER?" Jordy asked before Graham was even fully in the car.

"Hello to you, too, sunshine." Graham buckled his seatbelt. "I told him we were in town, and that we had dinner plans with you and Annie tonight. He kind of asked, kind of told me he was coming along."

Jordy growled as he pulled back onto the street and headed for his house.

"You two need to figure this out. *Talk* about it."

"Are you talking about me and Annie or me and Sam?" Jordy asked, scowling at a red light.

"Both."

Jordy asked a few benign questions about the conference and let Graham info dump to his heart's content. Jordy didn't care about the latest in anti-fog technology for bathroom mirrors, but it kept Graham talking about something that wasn't his personal life.

After he parked his car in his garage next to his motorcycle, Jordy's phone buzzed with a message.

HEAD BIRD NERD

LANDED! USA! USA!

Annie was back in the States. And she'd sent him a gif of Sam Eagle in front of an American flag.

HEAD BIRD NERD

Can't wait to see you! I've got BIG news.

"Annie landed," Jordy told Graham as he sent back a gif of Kermit flapping his arms back and forth with excitement.

"How do you feel? Are you excited?"

"Yes. And nervous as fuck." Jordy grabbed his bag from the backseat. "She said she's got big news. Any idea what that is?"

Graham shook his head. "No. You know what I know."

"Don't you and Eloise talk?"

"We're newlyweds," Graham joked. Jordy didn't laugh. "If Eloise knew something, she either purposely didn't say anything because Annie wants it to be a surprise, or thought she told me and didn't, or I wasn't listening."

"Slacking on those vows already?"

"Staying completely focused while she catches me up on small-town gossip was not in my vows. Check the video."

"Do you want a snack or something?" Jordy asked as they went inside, dropping his bag by the door. "I'm starving."

Despite claiming he zoned out during Eloise's recap of Crane Cove's gossip, Graham sure could regurgitate it. The way Graham told it, they needed to get a camera crew inside the Crane Hotel to make a reality show. After twenty minutes of getting names confused, Jordy finally handed him a takeout menu and a pen and asked him to draw a diagram of events from the Fourth of July celebration.

Jordy kept glancing at the clock on the microwave. Annie had landed an hour ago. Was she through customs yet? What did she need to tell him? "Can't wait to see you!" was comforting, but she could be just being nice.

Graham's story was interrupted by his wife. "Hey, babe. Did you get Annie yet? Oh good! How is she?...Jake? Seriously?...*Engaged?*"

Jordy's head snapped up.

"That's....yeah, I know it was ten years...That's—no, I agree, that's fast. How does Annie feel about it?...Mmm...Well, if she's happy, then we should be happy too."

His legs were going to give out, followed shortly by his heart. Annie couldn't be engaged, and she sure as shit couldn't be engaged to *Jake*. Had they reconnected over the summer? Was that why she had been so distant? Tingles like TV static spread over his body, pooling in his stomach.

"Anyone home?" Sam shouted from the entryway.

He couldn't do this. He couldn't do Annie being engaged and Sam's smug fucking face at the same time.

"You and Sam drive together. I'll meet you there," Jordy said to Graham, who was still on the phone. He frowned, but Jordy didn't stick around to answer questions. He walked quickly to the garage, grabbed his heavy motorcycle jacket and helmet, then punched the opener.

A ride would clear his mind. In twenty or thirty minutes, he could put a smile on his face and pretend to be happy for Annie until he could get home and fall the fuck apart. He wished Sam hadn't been such a dick, because if there was one person in his life who really understood what it was like to get their heart trampled on by the woman they loved, it was Sam.

The bike rumbled to life between his legs, and Jordy headed for the road.

It had been raining on and off all day, so Jordy wasn't going to go on the freeway. The road would be slick, and he wasn't in the right headspace to maneuver at those speeds, even though he craved the speed and freedom he got from going fast. It was as close as he'd ever gotten to flying. Surface streets would have to do.

Traffic was worse than normal, probably because of the weather. The rain had begun again, and everyone forgot how to drive. People stomped on their brakes for no reason and crawled down the road like thirty-five was a dangerous speed. Jordy didn't like riding in the rain because the people who weren't normally looking for him *really* weren't looking for him when they needed to use their windshield wipers. And then there were the impatient drivers who made it dangerous for everyone by weaving in and out of traffic.

A few cars ahead of him, a Lexus laid on his horn like it was going to move the long line of cars in front of him. Both lanes started moving and finally got enough speed that Jordy could stop contemplating walking his bike, and then the bus in the right lane stopped to let someone off.

It all happened so quickly Jordy barely had time to react. The bus stopped, and the Lexus, thinking there was an opening in the next line over, swerved right into Jordy. His front tire hit the Lexus's left front tire, and he became a projectile.

TWENTY-EIGHT

ANNIE HATED CUSTOMS. Not that anyone enjoyed the process, but she had places to go and a football player to tackle.

The line was taking forever. Her flight from Lima had landed early, and she was so excited to see Jordy sooner—then she entered the customs hall after the long, long, long walk from her airplane to find it stuffed to the gills. Someone ahead of her in the twisting line said that a bunch of international flights had all landed at the same time.

She rocked up onto the balls of her feet, trying to see how far away she was from the front of the line.

Too far.

Her summer in Peru had been amazing. Getting to spend time with other people who were as passionate as she was about birds was a gift. She didn't have to slow down or dumb herself down so they would understand her. But she had missed Jordy with a ferocity that shook her. Not just the way he touched her or how he looked at her, but the way he listened to her and asked her questions. How he made her feel like the most important person in the world. Bird people were great, but no one held a conversation like Jordy Taylor.

She had thought about asking him to video-chat at least a hundred times. She had done it with Eloise dozens of times over the summer. The connection wasn't great, but it was something. Peru wasn't any further behind Los Angeles timewise than Chicago or New York, depending on the time of year. But there was a nagging, gnawing sense in her chest that if she called him and saw his face, she would walk to the nearest airport with only the clothes on her back, get on the first plane bound for Los Angeles, and go straight to his house. She almost hadn't gotten on the plane to Lima because she realized she was in Los Angeles and it would have been so easy for her to get in a cab and go to him. If Jordy had asked her to stay, she would have. But he was wonderful and supportive, and she could have screamed.

The closest she got to a video call was recording a video message for his birthday, but that had been shorter than she'd planned because longing had strangled her vocal cords. So she talked about the weather and the cock-of-the-rock instead and avoided things like "I love you, I miss you, I wish I didn't feel like I needed to do this on my own, please don't forget about me."

After an entire summer apart, though, Annie could confidently say that she did love Jordy. He wasn't a vacation fling. If he still wanted her, she was his.

"Annie?"

Annie turned and jumped, her passport flinging out of her hand and hitting the person behind her in the back of the head. She spun around to grab it, apologizing profusely, and then tried to compose herself before standing back up.

"Jake? What are you doing here?"

Jake smiled at her. Once upon a time, Annie had thought he was handsome. And objectively he was, but the tropical print shirt he was wearing looked pathetic on him. Jordy needed to take out a copyright or a trademark or a patent on those kinds of shirts because no one else should be wearing them.

"Our flight from Mexico diverted because of a mechanical issue," he said. "So we have to clear customs here before we can go back to Seattle."

"We?" Annie frowned, then noticed some movement on his left side. A shorter woman with blonde hair and a nice smile was holding his hand. "Oh my god. I'm so sorry. I didn't see you there."

The other woman laughed. "It's fine. Are you *Annie* Annie? The one whose stuff is at his apartment?"

Annie nodded. "I am." She looked at Jake. "And I swear I'm getting it really soon. Like this month soon." She looked back at the other woman. "I'm sorry, I missed your name."

"I'm Jamie." She held up her left hand. A sparkling diamond ring was seated on her fourth finger. Jamie was so happy she was vibrating. "I'm his fiancée."

"Fiancée," Annie repeated like she'd never heard the word before. Jake had become very interested in the flags on the wall. "I didn't know he had a girlfriend."

"Really? We started dating in March. Well, we went on our first date in March."

March. Six months. Jake had met someone and gotten engaged in six months.

"I was going to tell you," Jake interjected, having the good sense to look a little ashamed of himself. "The timing was kind of weird, and then you went to Peru... This saves me a phone call, though. I didn't want you finding out through the grapevine."

"This is definitely not the grapevine," Annie said with a forced smile. "How did you two meet?"

"I'm a nurse," Jamie began, and looked up at Jake, "and he rounded on one of my patients."

"And when was that?" Annie asked.

Jamie thought. "December? Yes, because the dancing Santa kept scaring the crap out of me. It was December. But it took him until March to finally ask me out on a date." She bumped his shoulder with hers playfully.

Annie relaxed. They'd been broken up by December. Jake hadn't cheated on her. He'd just moved on quickly.

Jamie was a sweetheart who had almost no filter and talked a mile a minute. They talked the entire time they stood in line, trading Jake stories like kids traded baseball cards. Before Annie stepped forward to the CBP officer, Jamie gave her a tight hug and told her to watch for a wedding invitation. Jake nodded, though his face was unsure. Annie couldn't wait to see what his face looked like when she brought Jordy Taylor as her date.

As soon as she was through the sliding doors, she called Eloise.

"Hey, I'm almost out. Where are you?"

"Circling hell," Eloise answered. "I'm by Terminal Two, so it'll be a minute until I get to you."

"You are never going to believe who was standing behind me in customs."

"Madonna," Eloise tossed out.

"Jake."

"*No.*"

"*Yes.* And it gets better." Annie adjusted her overstuffed backpack. "He's engaged."

"How is that better?" Eloise screeched, and then laid on her horn. "Assholes. No one can drive in this city."

"I mean, it's interesting." Annie weaved through the clusters of people waiting for arrivals. "Her name is Jamie, she's a nurse, and they started dating in March."

"*Six months?* Seriously?!"

"Eloise, I think you're having a harder time with this than I am. I'm happy for him. I really am. She's a sweetheart. It's actually really comforting because it confirmed that I don't have any romantic feelings left for him. Once I found out he hadn't been cheating on me, the whole thing was great." Annie stepped outside to watch for Eloise.

"If you say so. I'm going to call Graham and give him an update on our ETA."

"And to tell him about Jake?" Annie ventured, grinning.

"Of course to tell him about Jake. You're not freaking out about this enough."

"And you think *Graham* is going to freak out?"

"He might. He never liked Jake. Okay, I'm going to call him. Watch for a black Volvo."

There were a lot of black cars circling LAX. And a strange number of them were Volvos. Should she have given Eloise a better description of where she was standing?

A black Volvo pulled up to the curb, and the passenger window rolled down.

"Dr. Price?" Eloise said from inside.

Annie loaded her luggage quickly, then dove inside, squeezing Eloise tightly around her neck.

"Can't. Breathe." Eloise tapped her shoulder.

"I'm sorry," Annie said, releasing her and settling back in her seat to buckle her seatbelt. "I missed you. A lot."

"I missed you too. I told Graham that we couldn't all come pick you up because I wanted you to myself for a little bit." She reached across the console and took Annie's hand, squeezing it tightly. "Tell me all about Peru!"

Annie glossed over the technical bits and hit the highlights, like the food and visiting Machu Picchu. Eloise turned on her windshield wipers as traffic slowed to a crawl.

"I know I shouldn't judge because no one in Oregon can merge, but it's just rain. We don't need to stop." She sighed and drummed her fingers on her steering wheel. The car stereo screen lit up with Graham's name. Eloise hit answer. "Hey, babe. Sorry. We're stuck in traffic. Maps says we're almost to the exit, though."

Graham's shuddering breath would haunt Annie's nightmares for months.

"Um," he began, his voice shaking, "we can't go to dinner. Sam and I are on the way to the hospital. Jordy was in an accident."

Annie's heart lost its regular rhythm, caught between stopping and racing. "What do you mean? What happened? Is he okay?"

"I—I don't know. A nurse called Sam and said that Jordy was struck by a car on his motorcycle. The ambulance just got there so they're still assessing his injuries."

"Which hospital?" Eloise asked. "We'll get there as soon as we can."

THE ONLY PARKING spot Eloise could find was wedged between two cars that had both parked on the line. Annie didn't care if she dented the car next to her as she wiggled out of the Volvo. She took off at a sprint for the building, vaguely hearing Eloise shout behind her. One shoe, and then the other, flew off her feet as she ran for the sliding doors.

Hospitals were strangely serene places from the lobby. Everything was cream, beige, and a primary color to promote a sense of calm.

Annie slapped her hands on the front desk, the momentum of her body nearly carrying her over the top.

"Jordy. Taylor."

"Is a football player," the secretary said. "Can I help you?"

"I need Jordy Taylor's room number please," Annie said, each word punctuated by a gasp as she caught her breath.

The secretary stared at her for a moment. "You think if Jordy Taylor was here, I would give you his room number? The woman who ran in here like a bat out of hell with no shoes on."

"Please. It's incredibly important," Annie begged, clasping her hands together.

"Are you on a deadline?"

"Annie!" Eloise shouted as she strolled through the automatic doors, Annie's shoes in one hand, her phone pressed to her ear with the other. "Graham was waiting for us down by Emergency. This is the wrong entrance." She handed Annie her shoes and smiled sweetly at the secretary. "I'm sorry. She's a bit panicked right now. Can you point us toward the Emergency Department, please?"

A security guard escorted them down a few hallways. It reminded Annie of lab rat experiments, except she was the rat and this was the maze. They turned the last corner, and there was Graham. His eyelashes were still damp, but Annie's heart rate calmed a little because he didn't looked scared.

"They said they could only take back two at a time." He opened his arms, and Eloise stepped into them, resting her head on his shoulder. "Annie, I thought you'd want to go back. Sam is already with him."

Annie nodded, fighting back tears. Graham vouched for her with the gatekeeper in the emergency department, and then the security guard walked her back to Jordy.

She was expecting him to look terrible, like they did on TV. But Jordy looked almost normal, except for the hospital gown, the monitors, and his left arm in a sling. He was even awake, but standing in the doorway listening to him chatter to Sam, she could tell he wasn't lucid.

"Issa...issa..." He tried to snap his fingers and was surprised by the oximeter. "What's that?"

"Don't touch it," Sam commanded, looking as drained as she felt. His eyes met hers. "He's trying to tell me about a bird."

Jordy turned—more like flopped—his head in her direction. His goofy smile melted some of her worries. "Hey, sweetheart."

"Hi." She floated to his bedside, barely tethered to her own body. "What about a bird?"

"The...the...that one...the picture..."

"Iron-billed wooflespoof," Annie answered, gingerly sitting on the edge of his bed. She looked at Sam. "Is he okay?"

"Considering he was a human cannonball? Yeah, he's great." Sam ran a hand down his face. "Uh, something some-thing, medical jargon, broken collarbone, a few busted ribs, some stitches in his thigh. Oh, and they pumped him full of the good drugs, but I think you've figured that one out for yourself."

"Hey. Hey." Jordy patted her leg a few times to get her atten-tion, then kept patting it even when she turned to look at him.

Annie brushed his hair back from his face. There was some bruising, presumably from the impact of his helmet hitting the pavement. "Yes, dear?"

"I love you."

She would have wholeheartedly believed him if his eyes had been in focus.

"Tell me again later," she said.

"No. I need to tell you now," he insisted. "You can't marry him. Marry me. Live with me. Pick me. I love you."

His pulse and blood pressure picked up. Annie cupped his cheek.

"Who are you talking about?"

"You. Jake. You can't marry him. He doesn't love you like I do."

"No, sweetie, he doesn't love me like you do," Annie agreed. "And I'm not going to marry him. Jamie is. She's very nice and invited us to the wedding."

"You're not getting married?" Jordy repeated in the lilting, sing-song voice of the drugged. Annie shook her head. "Live with me. Move into my house. You can have allll my clothes you want. All of 'em."

"Be careful what you say," Annie warned. "I have a witness. You promised me all of your clothes."

"So you're staying?" he said hopefully.

"We'll talk about this when you're not high as a fucking kite." She leaned forward and pressed a gentle kiss to his lips. Any residual terror drained out of her body as it recognized he was safe. Aware that Sam was still in the room, she whispered, "I love you too."

"Annie, can I talk to you in the hall?" Sam asked, rising from his chair next to the bed.

"I'll come back," she promised, kissing Jordy one more time. All she got in return was a dopey smile. Whatever they'd given him, it was doing its job.

In the hallway, Annie tugged her airplane sweater closer around her body. "What's up?"

"I—" Sam hesitated, pursing his lips and looking past her down the hallway. Annie checked over her shoulder. No one was there. "I don't think my therapist would be happy that I'm doing this, but I need to know: do you really love him, or were you saying that so he wouldn't get upset?"

She stared at him. "Of course I love him. Why would I say it if I don't mean it?"

"People say shit.... I've said some shit..." Sam stuffed his hands into his jacket pockets, rocking back and forth on his heels. "I just need you to tell me that you're going to take care of him and treat him the way he deserves to be treated. Because he's really special, Annie."

"I'm going to do my best," Annie promised. She squeezed his shoulder. "You're a good friend, Sam."

"No, I'm not." Sam pulled out a set of keys. "I can stay here with him while he's all doped up if you want. The nurse said they still need to run tests and it could be a while. You can take my car or get a ride with Graham and Eloise to his house, take a shower, get something to eat, sleep..."

Annie wanted to stay. After being apart from Jordy for months, leaving was the last thing she wanted to do. But as the adrenaline left her body, she was exhausted. She had been traveling all day. Her ex-boyfriend was engaged. The love of her life nearly died on her. A shower and a nap sounded like heaven.

"I'll get a ride," she said.

Sam removed a key from the ring. "This is my copy. I want it back after he makes you yours."

"If anything changes, you'll call me?"

"First person." Sam paused. "You wouldn't want to call his mom, would you?"

"That sounds more like a best friend thing. I'm just the girl he proposed to."

TWENTY-NINE

JORDY WOKE up with a dry mouth and a pounding skull. His left shoulder felt like shit, it hurt to breathe, and his thigh was throbbing.

He felt like he'd been hit by a car.

"Good morning, sleeping beauty," Sam said from the uncomfortable-looking chair next to his bed.

Jordy hoped his back hurt.

"What are you doing here?" Jordy groaned.

"Despite what I said about not showing up after the paramedics scraped you off the pavement, here I am." Sam sighed, tucking his phone into his pocket.

"You don't have to be here if you don't want to be here."

"Goddammit, Jordan." Sam hopped to his feet. "I'm here because I want to be here. I'm here because you are my best fucking friend and that was the worst phone call of my life and I swear to God if this ever happens again I will find the car that hit you and finish the job myself." Sam took a shaky breath, his eyes brimming with tears. "I thought I was going to lose you without ever getting to say I was sorry."

Staying mad at Sam was never something Jordy could do. It

was probably why they were still friends. He patted the narrow space next to his not-as-injured leg. Sam filled it before he could change his mind.

"I'm sorry." Sam wasted no time. "I was out of line in May. You were telling me something that you were excited about, and I found a way to make it about me and my feelings. I—" His voice caught and he paused, a sad smile forming. "I didn't want to lose you the way I lost Graham."

"You didn't lose Graham," Jordy reminded him. "He just lives somewhere else now. You built a cabin there."

Sam shook his head. "It's not the same. He has Eloise now, and she's his priority—she should be his priority. But our friendship changed." Sam laughed humorlessly. "I hate the idea of our friendship changing too. I like Annie. It's so easy to tell that you love each other. But I selfishly wanted to keep being your person." He twisted the rings on his fingers as he continued. "I realized a few days after the wedding that I had been the worst kind of asshole. That I've *been* an asshole since Graham left. So I've spent the whole summer in therapy trying not to be an asshole."

"Did it work?"

"I'm still an asshole. But I'm an asshole that's trying."

Jordy pulled Sam's hand away from his worrying hand and squeezed it. "I missed you all summer. You didn't have to isolate yourself like that."

"I didn't want to hurt anyone else."

"You *not* talking to me hurt. How the hell am I supposed to rub your face in your wrongness if you're not around? Hm?" Jordy rested his head back against the one thin pillow on his bed. "Not that there's a lot to be wrong about. Did you hear Annie's engaged?"

Sam's high-pitched "Ummm..." could have summoned dogs.

"What?"

"I think I'm going to let Annie tell you herself, but she might not be engaged to who you think she's engaged to."

"It's not Jake? She met someone in Peru?"

"No, not Peru. Definitely someone she met between Jake and Peru."

Jordy stared at him blankly. There wasn't anyone between Jake and Peru. The only person she had any kind of relationship with between Jake and Peru was...him.

"You know what's fun about you?" Sam said. "I can see the moment the lightbulb turns on."

"So Annie being here wasn't a dream?"

"No, no, that was real. Very, very real. Do you, uh, remember proposing? Several times. And begging her to pick you? Oh, and then you did bribe her to move in with you. With lots of 'I love you' sprinkled in for good measure."

"Do you still want to hit me with that car?"

"Did you not mean it?"

"No, I meant it." Jordy closed his eyes, trying to hide from the flood of embarrassment. "I didn't want the first time I said 'I love you' to be when I was high and not wearing pants."

"I know a lot of couples that started their relationships like that and were very happily married for a few months," Sam said, barely able to keep a grin off his face.

THE LIGHTS WERE on in his house when Sam pulled into Jordy's driveway that night.

The hospital discharged him with instructions to follow up about his broken collarbone. It was a good break, they said, but he might want to put a plate in to stabilize it for the rest of the season. Every doctor and nurse that had stopped by his room when he was at the hospital made sure to let Jordy know that he was a walking miracle and thanked him for wearing his protective gear. His helmet had saved his life, and his clothes had saved his skin.

"I shouldn't read into it that she didn't pick me up from the hospital, right?" Jordy asked Sam, clutching the plastic hospital bag of his belongings.

"Again, I told her to stay here." Sam was exasperated. Jordy had an entire summer's worth of relationship angst built up, and it had all poured out in the last twelve hours. "She didn't need to get a ride back to the hospital to then come straight back here."

Jordy nodded. "And she really did seem happy to see me?"

"Fuck, dude." Sam groaned. "Go see for yourself."

The smell of pasta, tomatoes, oregano, and basil filled his nostrils as soon as he stepped through the door.

"Annie?" he called tentatively. Her answer was the sound of her feet slapping against his wood floors as she ran from the kitchen to the entryway.

"Jordy!"

The impact put stars in his eyes and a cold sweat all over his body. Pain radiated through his bones. But Annie was hugging him and her hair smelled like his shampoo, so he would curl up in a ball and die another time.

"What's up, Doc?" he asked, laughing to mask the thread of pain in his voice.

"You're home," she said, releasing his body and cupping his face. "I am so, so mad at you and so happy to see you."

Fuck, she was pretty.

"How was your flight?"

Annie frowned. "That's what you want to talk about? My flight? You got hit by a car and you want to talk about my flight?"

"Well...yeah."

"It was fine. It was a flight. The plane went up, it sat at cruise forever, we landed. The end. Oh, and I had a ginger ale."

"That sounds nice," Jordy said, shifting all his weight to his better leg. "Anything else interesting happen?"

"Not really." Annie took his bag from him and set it on the ground. "I ran into Jake in the customs line. He's getting married. We're invited." She led him to the kitchen, like he needed to hold onto her to walk. He didn't, but it was nice to be touching her again. "Speaking of marriage, Sam said all of your proposals are null and void and wouldn't hold up in a court of law."

"I was hoping you'd forgotten about those." Jordy groaned as he lowered himself onto one of the dining room chairs.

"I don't know. It was nice. No one's ever begged me to marry them before." Annie smiled, but it didn't quite reach her eyes. "Did you mean any of it? Any of the things you said?"

"About loving you and wanting to marry you?"

She nodded.

Jordy sighed. "Of course I did, sweetheart. I didn't want to say it all when I was high, though."

"Is the offer to move in still on the table?" Annie asked, visibly bracing for a rejection.

"Were you planning on moving to LA?" Hope filled his chest like a kid trying to blow up a balloon.

"That was my big news," she told him. "I got a teaching position at a university nearby. I'm supposed to start in two weeks."

Pride mingled with fledgling hope. "And you need somewhere to live?"

"I do. Know anyone looking for a roommate?"

"Mine did move out a couple of weeks ago. It doesn't have to be permanent, if you don't want it to be. You can stay here while you look if it's too soon."

"Yesterday you proposed, and today you think moving in is too soon?" Annie gave an exaggerated, purposefully dramatic sigh and went to the stove. "I made spaghetti for dinner."

It was like hardly a day had passed since the lighthouse. He had been prepared for an awkward patch as they readjusted to each other, but it wasn't there. Annie looked like she had lived in his house for as long as he had. She fit. It all felt...natural.

"Hey, Annie."

She looked up from grating parmesan over their plates. "Yeah?"

"I love you."

She smiled. "I love you too."

THE FIRST WEEK of having Annie in his house was magic. They hung out all day, not doing much of anything except laying around the house, doing puzzles, and watching TV.

The second week brought a dose of reality as Annie prepared to teach her first classes.

"It's just basic biology," she explained to him as she tried on different combinations of the clothes she'd bought for work. "But I think it will be fun. And there's going to be room to move around later. Teach different classes." She held up different sweaters to the white shirt she had on. She'd picked it because it didn't contrast with her bird print skirt. "Will I need a sweater? Is it going to be too hot?"

"Layers are important," he reasoned from his spot on the bed.

"How was the appointment with the team doctors? Did they give you a timeline for when you're going to return to work?"

Jordy looked up at the ceiling. The doctors had been optimistic about his healing outcome, predicting he could be back in as little as eight weeks, ten on the outside. But as they discussed it, a heavy sense of dread sat on his shoulders and over his sternum. He was tired. His body was tired. And as much as he loved the game, after being hit by a car, he didn't want to get hit by a linebacker.

But watching Annie be excited about her job as a professor made him feel lost. Like he needed to be doing *something* with his life. Could he step away and hold his head high at the faculty holiday party?

"They did," he started cautiously. "They think eight to ten weeks. But, um, I'm not sure."

"You think it's going to be sooner?" Annie unbuttoned her blouse, and then frowned. "What's wrong? I thought you would be excited about going back to work."

"I...I don't know what I want." He sighed as Annie sat down on the bed next to him. "What am I doing if I'm not playing football? I don't have anything to fall back on."

"Jordan." She put her hand on his knee. "Whatever you want to do, I'm going to support you. If you want to go back to football, I will be there for you. If you want to retire, I will probably sleep better at night knowing that your job isn't going to send you back to the hospital."

"But what am I going to do?"

"Anything you want." Annie cozied up to his non-injured side. "You believe in me, right? You think I can do anything I put my mind to?"

"Of course I do." Jordy was a little offended she needed to ask.

"Good." She straddled his hips and took his face between her hands, staring deep into his eyes. "Because I believe in you the way you believe in me."

His heart dissolved into a pile of goo. "Will you still want to be with me if I never work another day in my life?"

"Jordy, I'm always going to want to be with you. No matter what you're doing, or not doing." Annie kissed him soundly to emphasize her point. "I love you. You don't have to earn that."

EPILOGUE

"WE ARE NEVER GOING to learn our lesson about April on the coast, are we?" Annie asked as Jordy lit a line of candles on the coffee table to combat the storm-induced darkness. "This is becoming a weird tradition."

"This is only the second time it's happened, sweetheart. I don't think that's enough to call it a tradition yet."

Annie pulled the quilt up higher on her lap and sipped her sangria. Outside, the wind and the rain whipped the sides of the lighthouse, battering the roof and windows, but the inside was cozy. Over the last year, Graham and Eloise had finished decorating and had finally gotten the HVAC installed. She was going to suggest a generator when they had dinner tomorrow.

"This is romantic," Jordy said, admiring his handiwork with the candles. "Nice, warm glow."

"It almost sounds like you *wanted* the power to go out," she teased, lifting half of the quilt so he could rejoin her on the couch.

"Maybe I'm trying to recreate the magic for our anniversary."

"Our anniversary is in September," she corrected. "We haven't been together long enough for you to forget."

Jordy shook his head. "Nah. It's April. About a year ago, you tried to kill me in the shower and I fell in love with you. And I've never looked back." He clinked his wine glass against hers. "Happy one-year anniversary, sweetheart."

Outwardly, Annie laughed, but inwardly, she melted. The spring break trip to Crane Cove had been Jordy's idea, and he'd planned the entire thing while she stressed about grading second-quarter finals and getting grades entered before the deadline. She didn't even have to pack her own suitcase. When they got to the lighthouse, she was surprised that there were even clothes in there because Jordy's idea of motivating her to finish her work was to talk about how much sex they could have in the "bed that started it all."

Living with Jordy was a dream come true. Every morning he brought her coffee in bed, and on days she had school, he had a second cup waiting for her on the counter to take to work. A private chef still came to the house once a week to prep their lunches for the week, but they made dinner together every night. Slowly but surely, Jordy was learning how to use his nice kitchen. He'd enrolled himself in a cooking class for retirees. He was the youngest member by at least twenty-five years.

Yes, Jordy was enjoying retirement. With the exception of a few lingering brand deals and sponsorships, he had a lot of free time. On Tuesdays and Thursdays, he drove her to school, dropped her off, and then took community center art classes. He had a few paintings hanging in a small coffee shop, exhibited under the name "J.M. Taylor". Two of them had sold—both birds— and Annie wondered if the owners had any idea they'd been painted by a former professional football player.

Sometimes he would audit her classes, sitting in the back of the lecture hall, trying and failing to be inconspicuous by wearing a baseball cap. When she'd asked why, he said he just really liked hearing her talk. Annie would have felt special if she didn't come home at least once a week to Jordy folding laundry while talking to her dad on the phone. Well, Hugh talked and Jordy listened.

Annie still hadn't done a single load of laundry since they'd been together.

"If it's our anniversary," Annie began, wiggling and scooting until she was on his side of the couch and snuggled against him, "what's your favorite moment from our first year together?"

"You moving yourself into my house," Jordy answered easily.

"You begged me to move in!"

"I was under the influence. It barely counts. Ask Sam. He's a witness."

She rolled her eyes, and he chuckled.

"My turn," he said, kissing her forehead. "What surprised you the most this year?"

She didn't have to think about her answer, but she hesitated. "I have something, but it's not about us."

"Is it that Sam got married?" Jordy guessed.

"It's that Sam got married!" Annie flung her head back. "I really thought you were lying when you told me! I was so mad at you, remember?"

"Oh, I remember." He kissed her, smiling against her mouth. "But they're good together, aren't they?"

"A nice balance," she agreed, stroking his cheek. "Just like us."

"Speaking of marriage—"

Annie's heart skittered like a baby deer sliding across ice.

"No, no, no. I'm not proposing," Jordy reassured her. Even though he'd asked her when he was high at the hospital, they'd agreed to wait to get officially engaged until after they'd dated for a little while. Annie had tacked on that he needed to wait until after Jake's wedding, out of respect for Jamie. "I mean, if I'd known the power was going to go out, I might have planned something but…"

"Then what about marriage?"

"Do you want a big wedding, or do you want to elope?"

"Something in between," Annie said after pretending to consider the question like she didn't browse wedding websites every day during office hours. "But as long as you're there, I don't care."

"I don't know how you feel about this, but I was thinking we could hyphenate our last names. Like Peter's. Dr. Roxanne Taylor-Price has a nice ring to it."

"Dr. and Mr. Taylor-Price. I like it."

ACKNOWLEDGMENTS

The acknowledgments are the hardest thing for me to write. I cry the entire time. It takes so much to bring a book into the world and in no way could I do this by myself. My first book, Keyed Up, was dedicated to my friends. In my heart, all of my work is dedicated to my friends, who love me, support me, and are mean to me when I need them to be. (I'm a procrastinator, okay?)

Eliza MacArthur, Nellie Wilson, Megan Cousins, Dani McLean, Jillian Meadows, Livy Hart, Hannah Bird, Erin Langston. Writers need other writers. No one else understands how wonderful and exhausting the creative process is (and how completely draining the rest of it all is) quite like you. Thank you for being there for me as I wrote this book. Thank you for being my sounding board and accountability partners.

Erin, Ada, and Kelsey. My magical, wonderful lovelies who keep my head above water and my Google Calendar updated and color coded. The team of my dreams. Without you I would still be crying every night because there aren't enough hours in the day. You're all so brilliant and kind. I don't deserve you but good luck getting me to give you up.

Dr. Izzy and Dr. Emma, my PhD advisors (I don't have a PhD. They do.) Thank you for lending your eyes and experiences to this book. You're both so incredible and I'm so proud to know you.

Tori, thank you for being my medical advisor. You deserve the world.

Esther, Kae, Danielle, Lara, Andi, Marni, Emily, Stacey, Tamara, Kate, Morgan, MC, Rita, Leelee, Michelle, thank you for being my early readers and constant cheerleaders. And anyone else who has slipped into my DMs to tell me how much you love the people that live in my head, I love you and appreciate you so much (but these acknowledgements have to be shorter than the book).

My editor Sarah and my cover designer Mia. Thank you for helping me bring Annie and Jordy to life.

And finally, my husband. All those football podcasts you made me listen to in the car finally paid off. On a serious note, I love you. You're a man written by a woman and the best thing that ever happened to me. Thank you for the love, support, and for always answering my questions before asking why I want to know.

ABOUT THE AUTHOR

Sarah is a Pacific Northwest based romance writer who would call herself "indoorsy". When she isn't traipsing around the country for work, Sarah enjoys buying more books than she can ever read, drinking an irresponsible amount of coffee, and not respecting her bedtime.

Find her on social media @remarkablysarah
www.sarahestep.com